From the Woods

What Reviewers Say About Charlotte Greene's Work

Legacy

"Greene does a good job of building suspense as the story unfolds. Strange things happen one by one in increasingly spooky fashion. Background information is revealed a little bit at a time and makes you want to try and solve the mystery. …I recommend this to those who like to read about hauntings, nature, history, DIY home maintenance, violent husbands, scary things in the woods, and water."—*Bookvark*

"The characters are well developed, and Greene hit just the right amount of tension between them. …I rarely like every character in a book, but I loved the whole group. The creepiness never let up, the tension built steadily, and…things escalated rapidly. The ending was very satisfying! Horror is definitely Greene's forte." —*Bookish Sort*

"This is a wonderfully scary paranormal novel. The setting is perfect and well described. The characters are well-drawn and likable. The romance between Jo and Andy is especially charming and fits perfectly into the tale. This is just a wonderful story, and I'm so glad I read it, even in the middle of the night. If you love a good scary story, I believe you will love it too."—*Rainbow Reflections*

"Greene likes to take her time to work up the suspense, starting with smaller and seemingly inconsequential things that build up a suitably creepy atmosphere. Placing the characters in an isolated setting ratchets things up. This isn't a gore-fest nor is it relying on jump-scares to set the atmosphere—instead it's a well paced ghost story with strongly developed characters…"—*C-Spot Reviews*

"Greene does a great job of establishing a creepy atmosphere by setting a rather slow (but not overly so) pace, taking the necessary time to describe the woods, the uncared-for cabin, the ominous well from the cover, the sounds, the smells, the weather and temperatures…"—*Jude in the Stars*

"Very fun horror story that just touches on the creep factor without going full blown scary. There's a lot of really good elements to the book, from the menacing spook, to the mystery, and even the relationship. …Great work!"—Colleen Corgel, Librarian, Queens Public Library

Gnarled Hollow

"Greene has done an outstanding job of weaving in all sorts of layers; mysterious patterns in the gardens, missing rooms, odd disappearances, blandly boring journals, unknown artwork, and each mystery is eventually revealed as part of the horrific whole. Combined with intensely emotional descriptions of the fear the characters experience as they are targeted by the tortured spirit and this book is genuinely a page turner…not only could I not sleep after reading it, I didn't want to put it down."—*Lesbian Reading Room*

"*Gnarled Hollow* by Charlotte Greene is an awesome supernatural thriller that will terrify and entertain you for hours on end."
—*The Lesbian Review*

"*Gnarled Hollow* is a creepy mystery story that had me gripped from the start. There was layer upon layer of mystery and plenty that I didn't see coming at all."—*Kitty Kat's Book Review Blog*

"Scared myself to death, but hauntingly beautiful! had my heart beating at rapid speeds, and my mind working overtime with this thought provoking story. Piecing together the mystery of Gnarled Hollow was both fascinating, and scary as hell. It takes talent to put that much suspense and thrill into words that build the picture so vividly, painting descriptions that you can imagine perfectly and see as you read."—*LESBIreviewed*

"I really enjoyed this. This is the fifth book I have read by Greene and by far my favorite. It had some good twists and kept me in suspense until the end. In fact, I was a little sad when it ended. This would be a perfect book to read around Halloween time. …I would absolutely recommend this to paranormal-crime/mystery fans. I really hope Greene takes the opportunity to write more books in similar genres. I would love to read them if she does. 5 stars."
—*Lez Review Books*

A Palette for Love

"The relationship really works between the main characters, and the sex is steamy but not over the top."—*Amanda's Reviews*

Pride and Porters

"Have you ever wondered how *Pride and Prejudice* would work if it were two women falling in love with a brewery as a backdrop? Well, wonder no more! …All in all, I would say this is up near the top on my list of favorite *Pride and Prejudice* adaptations."
—Amanda Brill, Librarian, Rowan Public Library (North Carolina)

"Greene's charming retelling of *Pride and Prejudice* transplants the Bennets into the world of Colorado craft beer. …The story beats are comfortingly familiar, with the unusual backdrop of brewing and beer competitions, modern setting, and twists on the characters providing enough divergence to keep the reader engaged. …Feminism, lesbianism, and class are all touched on in this refreshing update on a classic. (Starred review)"
—*Publishers Weekly*

By the Author

A Palette for Love

Love in Disaster

Canvas for Love

Pride and Porters

Gnarled Hollow

Legacy

On the Run

From the Woods

From the Woods

by

Charlotte Greene

2020

FROM THE WOODS

ISBN 13: 978-1-63555-793-0

This Trade Paperback Original Is Published By
Bold Strokes Books, Inc.
P.O. Box 249
Valley Falls, NY 12185

First Edition: December 2020

Credits
Editor: Shelley Thrasher
Production Design: Susan Ramundo
Cover Design By Tammy Seidick

Acknowledgments

This was my first time working with a writing group, and it was a great success. Thank you Kristin and Michelle for your kind and thoughtful responses to parts of this novel.

Thanks always to my dedicated, wonderful editor, Shelley Thrasher. You make everything so much better, and I sincerely appreciate your feedback and suggestions at every stage of the writing process.

Finally, to the Bone-Picking Monkey Man, who scared the heck out of me as a child.

Dedication

For my parents, who introduced me to the woods.

Chapter One

"How many times do I have to tell you? This is the chance of a lifetime."

"You say that every year."

"Well, this time I mean it. I'm serious. You can't get a permit for love or money."

"Why does everything you say sound like a sales pitch?"

Jill huffed and turned back to her beer, the high color in her cheeks suggesting strong feelings. Fiona felt a little guilty, but then she remembered the last trip they'd taken together. It had been a disaster in every sense of the word. She'd promised herself at the end of it that she'd never let Jill bully her into going somewhere again. Still, she didn't want to argue. They'd been friends for a long time, and she knew what Jill was like when she didn't get her way.

She put a hand on Jill's. "Look, I'm sorry. But why don't you let Carol plan it for once? Or Sarah? She's good at that kind of thing."

Jill rolled her eyes. "Sarah might be good at weddings, but she can't plan a vacation to save her life. Don't you remember Bali? We all agreed: never again."

Fiona grimaced. "Oh. Right." Bali had been even worse than Mexico. Fiona played with the condensation on her beer mug, letting the silence drag out. When Jill didn't say anything, she said, almost whispering, "So why not let me choose this time?"

Jill finally turned her way again, that color still bright in her cheeks. "I don't know how many times I have to say it—this is a chance of a lifetime. You were so excited about it before—don't you remember? And they only issue six permits a year. Doesn't that mean anything to you?"

Already, Fiona's resolve was slipping away. She fought against her weakness, desperately trying to hold on to the memories of their last several trips, but they were losing their power in the face of Jill's anger. After all, it wasn't as if all the crap in Mexico had been anyone's fault. Sure, Jill had suggested they eat the fruit from that street vendor in that mountain town, but other people on the tour had eaten it too, and they'd been fine. Everything else—the flat tires, the lost luggage, the stolen passports—had been bad luck. Most of her resentment had settled on Jill because she'd planned the trip, but it could have happened no matter who booked the tickets or where they went.

"I guess," she finally said.

Jill perked up, clearly sensing a win, eyes bright with excitement now. "Keep thinking about it for a few minutes before you decide. Sarah and Carol will be here any minute. I'm going to tell them all about it, give everyone some details, and then you can decide."

Fiona nodded, tuning out as Jill chatted with the new server behind the counter. She and Jill had been friends since early teen-hood, and despite widely varying experiences since, they'd managed to stay close. Know someone that long and you realize some things will never change. In their friendship, Jill was and always would be the leader and the decider, and Fiona had understood that the first time they'd met in AP Bio. Sometimes, like now, she resented their relationship, but most of the time she simply accepted it. Putting her foot down now would piss Jill off, and Fiona hated fighting with her more than anything. It would probably be pointless, anyway. Jill would eventually wear her down. Accepting Jill's plan would avoid all that. And anyway, they'd had good trips together before. Maybe next year she'd finally get to choose where they'd go.

Jill touched the back of her hand and gestured at the new server. "This is Gina. She just moved here from Denver."

Gina was very young—in her mid-twenties, maybe, with cute light strawberry-blond hair. Fiona could sense Jill's glee from the stool next to hers even without seeing her face.

Fiona forced herself to smile and extended a hand. "Nice to meet you. I'm Fiona."

Gina's hand was hot and a little sticky from the beer. "Nice to meet you, too." She held Fiona's hand slightly longer and tighter than necessary, making direct eye contact, and then she was called by another customer. Gina gave her a quick smile, almost seemed to wink, let go, and walked away.

Jill elbowed Fiona in the side, rough enough to spill her drink. "Huh, huh?"

"Yeah, she's cute." Fiona mopped at the beer with a cocktail napkin.

Jill slapped her forehead. "What? Are you kidding me? She's a knockout!"

She couldn't help but laugh. "I wouldn't go that far—like I said, she's cute, pretty even. But she's a baby."

Jill stared after Gina, frowning. "No, she's not! And anyway, who cares?"

"If you like her so much, why don't you ask her out yourself?"

Jill gave her a level stare. "You know what your problem is?"

"No. But I'm sure you're going to tell me."

"You're damn right I am. You're completely oblivious. Gina is totally into you, and you immediately find reasons to reject her. I'm not telling you to marry her or anything, but why not ask her out for drinks? Have some laughs?"

Fiona opened her mouth to reply, but Jill was suddenly turning and waving wildly behind them. Fiona spun her stool to spot Sarah and Carol coming through the door. It had been a few months since she'd seen them, and her stomach dropped. She'd thought she'd be okay with it by now, but she'd been fooling herself.

Jill launched herself off her stool and ran over to them, giving both a big hug, and Fiona followed, forcing a bright smile.

"You guys look great!" Jill said. "Don't they look fantastic, Fiona?"

She nodded, hardly able to meet their eyes.

"You been working out or something?" Jill asked them.

Sarah nodded. "CrossFit. We started right after the honeymoon. Carol's brother got us a year's membership."

Jill whistled. "Wow. Well, it shows. Come on—let's grab a table. Fiona? Can you get us some beer?"

"Sure. What do you guys want?"

Once they told her, Fiona went back to the bar, taking the opportunity to try to center herself again. The last time she'd seen them had been at their wedding, which had been one of the worst days of her life. Having to smile and pretend to be happy for an entire day had been difficult.

Long ago, in college, she'd nursed an unrequited, silent crush on Carol, but that hadn't been the root of the problem. In fact, a crush would have been easier, an actual motive for why she felt so terrible at their wedding. Instead, as she witnessed their vows, and then after, at the gorgeous reception, she'd felt an utter, empty solitude and crushing sense of doom. What had bothered her then and now wasn't the fact that an old flame was getting married; it was the realization that the wedding, the reception, all of it, would never happen to her. Throughout their whole wedding, she'd fought a very simple emotion, but one that filled her with shame: jealousy.

Instead of being happy for her friends, she'd been consumed with envious spite. She'd gotten too drunk, though luckily no one she was close with besides Jill actually noticed, and she'd thought it was funny. Still, she'd made a fool of herself. She'd avoided thinking about the wedding since, hoping she'd get past her reaction to it, but she clearly hadn't. That same jealous resentment was still there, still dark and ugly, festering in her heart.

Gina served her, and Fiona realized as she was paying that she'd been a little short with her when she ordered their drinks.

She tried to make up for her curtness with a wide, final smile, but Gina was no longer meeting her eyes, already looking behind her at the next person in line. No matter. She'd meant what she said to Jill earlier—she wasn't interested.

It took two trips to take the four pints to the table, and she slid into the empty seat next to Jill, unnoticed and un-thanked by any of them. All three were catching up, none of them attempting to bring her into the conversation, and Fiona took this extra time to arrange her face into something like casual friendliness.

She and Jill were sitting across from the others, so she had the chance to take the two of them in at her leisure. Jill was right—they were different. Their faces had slimmed, and their shoulders seemed broader, more defined somehow. Sarah had always been thin, but now her muscles leant her something like solidity rather than her previous, almost ethereal slightness. Her dark-umber skin, always gorgeous, was glowing with a kind of bronzed light, making the black curls of her hair a shimmering halo. Carol, already strong and fit, seemed almost dangerous, the muscles in her arms thick and corded, her previous pallor replaced with a healthy tan. She'd let her gray hair grow a little into a kind of rockabilly bouffant on top, and it suited her. It was like sitting with two centerfolds for a lesbian fitness magazine.

Fiona glanced at the mirrors on the walls and almost laughed at herself. There she was, all hundred and ten pounds of her, slunk in her chair like a sickly vulture over her beer. Her hair was a thin, messy pile of short, mousy brown wisps, her skin translucent and almost gray, nearly matching her pale eyes. Jill's long, blond hair was a radiant crown behind her, her all-American good looks and extroversion a draw for men and women alike. Seeing the others reflected around her was certainly a study in contrasts, and not a good one.

"Hey," Jill said, elbowing her. "Stop checking yourself out. I want to talk to you guys about what we're doing this summer on vacation."

Sarah and Carol groaned, comically and in unison.

"Jesus Christ, Jill," Carol said. "Not another of your bright ideas."

"Do you know how much weight I lost last time?" Sarah added. "I've never been that sick in my whole life. I still can't smell cantaloupe without heaving."

Jill made a dismissive gesture with her hand. "Forget all that." She paused, leaning forward and meeting everyone's eyes, clearly trying to build suspense. "Fiona already knows, but guys, I got the permit."

Sarah and Carol reacted as if they'd been slapped, jerking backward in surprise.

"What?" Sarah said.

"You did?" Carol added.

Jill's self-satisfied grin widened into a smile. "And I got the best one: the end of July."

Jill didn't have to explain what she meant. Three years ago, the four of them had independently read an article about a protected, isolated forest that stretched from Northern Colorado into Southern Wyoming. Fiona had read the article while waiting for her skis to be fixed at a local outdoors outfitter. Jill had a subscription to the magazine it was printed in, and Sarah and Carol had seen a link on their social-media feeds. All four of them had been interested but hadn't thought about it or mentioned it until they'd been at a barbecue at a mutual friend's house later that week. Fiona had brought up the article, and everyone had immediately started talking about how fascinating they'd found it. By the end of the evening, they'd talked themselves into figuring out a way to go.

The coincidence of reading the article on their own had seemed like a sign, and that superstitious omen leant even greater excitement to the idea of backpacking there. Three days later, Jill had gotten the farthest into researching the means to visit the forest and told them all, much to their dismay, that the permission was even harder to get than the article had suggested. Six two-week permits were issued every year, with hiking groups limited to parties of eight or fewer. At the time, that had seemed like the end of it, and they had gone on their disastrous trip to Bali together that summer. Fiona had forgotten about it since.

"But how?" Sarah asked. "I thought there was no way to get a permit."

"I didn't even know you were trying," Carol added.

Jill pointed at her. "Bingo. I wanted it to be a surprise. I put myself down when we were talking about it at the time, and I just got the news yesterday. We lucked out, actually, because another group backed out at the last minute. The woman who called me told me a bunch of other people were on the list, but they couldn't commit right away, and she needed an immediate response."

"Wait," Sarah said, holding up a hand. "You said yes before you talked to us about it?"

"I had to," Jill said, raising her voice, almost whining. "I'm going whether you want to come with me or not."

Sarah frowned. "Jeez, Jill. Chill. I didn't say I didn't want to go. It's just a surprise, that's all."

Sarah and Carol shared a glance, and Fiona saw Carol raise one shoulder and nod. Sarah smiled at Jill. "Okay—count us in."

Jill peered at Fiona, eyebrows up. "So, how about it, lady? You ready to cave yet?"

She was, but she needed to play it coy for a few more minutes to avoid looking like a doormat. "When do we go? How long?"

"We leave the morning of July 20, get back the afternoon of August 4. And don't tell me you can't get the time off, since those were the same weeks you took off last year."

This was, of course, true. Fiona had already submitted her vacation paperwork. The last week of July and the first of August was her usual long, annual leave. She'd taken a trip with Jill, Sarah, and Carol almost every year at the same time since college.

Fiona shrugged. "Okay. So how do we get there? I thought the road was closed to cars."

Jill glanced away, a little color creeping into her cheeks again. She played with her beer.

"The guides take us in on horseback," she finally said.

Fiona, Sarah, and Carol all spoke at once.

"What? Guides? You didn't say anything about—"

"That's totally different. I don't want to be around—"

"I like my privacy—"

Jill put her hands in the air. "Guys, guys, relax for a second. Jeez. Hear the details first, for God's sake."

Carol shook her head. "No way. I don't want some dude on my vacation, Jill. Doesn't interest me at all. It's one thing if you're in a country where you don't speak the language, but not out in the woods, alone."

Jill started counting off on her fingers. "First of all, you're being sexist. The main guide is a woman. She's the one who called me. Second, she and her assistants ride in with us from the parking lot for a few miles to the first campsite, where the wilderness begins. Third, the assistants take the horses back to the truck and meet us on the other end two weeks later."

"But the main guide stays with us the whole time?" Sarah asked.

Jill hesitated before nodding. "Yes. It's the only way you can visit. She leads us through the forest, making sure we stick to the trail and clean up after ourselves."

"But we do that already!" Sarah said.

Jill sighed. "You know that, and I know that, but we've all seen the kind of shit people leave in the woods, literal and not. This is one of the last protected, undeveloped forests in the lower forty-eight, and they want to keep it that way."

Fiona remembered their last backpacking trip together. Every backcountry campsite they'd stopped in had been full of litter and piles of poorly covered human feces. She'd never been as disgusted with humanity before or since. She could understand the idea of the conservationists wanting to avoid that, but having a stranger with them the entire trip was not a small concession.

"Have you met this woman?" Carol asked.

Jill shook her head. "But I'm going to, in May. You can all come with me if you still want to go."

Fiona noted the fact that Jill had already assumed that she was coming along, despite her earlier protests. She hadn't agreed to go yet, but Jill clearly didn't care or had forgotten. Even if Fiona objected again now, Jill would badger her until she agreed, so why bother? Still, she needed to voice at least one more objection to save her own self-worth.

"Two weeks is a really long time, Jill. We usually just do overnights or weekends. We've never been on a backpacking trip that long."

Carol nodded. "She's right. What was our longest—four, five days?"

"That's a lot of stuff to carry," Sarah added.

Jill laughed. "As if you two have to worry about it. Look in the mirror lately? You guys could carry a circus tent and not break a sweat." Jill slapped Fiona on the back. "It's the two of us that need some work, but we have time. July is what—three, four months from now? We can start going to the gym together."

Fiona opened her mouth, ready to object, but the three of them were already making plans. She wanted to remind Jill that she hated going to the gym more than almost anything in the world. Jill knew that, but she wouldn't care. Someday soon, she would be dragging Fiona to work out. Rather than pretend that she could do anything about it, she shut her mouth and tried to pretend she was as excited as everyone else.

Chapter Two

Fiona recoiled from the heat, almost slipping back inside the car. July in Colorado, especially on the Front Range, can rival parts of the South for its heat and humidity. While the rest of the summer was generally what is called a "dry" heat, the rain this time of year usually made up for the previous drought. This had been the hottest summer and month on record, and even here, in the shadow of the Rockies and long before noon, there was no escaping the awful power of the heat. Jill started pushing her from behind, and she finally made herself climb up and out of the backseat of the car into the harsh and unforgiving sunlight.

They were at a famous gas station, Ted's Place, at the turnoff into the mountains north of Fort Collins. While Poudre Canyon had built up over the last twenty years, with houses and other development stretching almost the whole length of the state to the west, Ted's was still considered the last pit stop of civilization before heading into the wild. It was also one of the last places they'd have reliable cell-phone service for the next two weeks, so a good place for meeting their guide. The guide and her assistants would pick them up here, drive them about thirty miles west and north, and then take them into the backcountry on horseback. Tomorrow morning, the assistants would take the horses back and leave them there in the woods with their guide.

It had been difficult to get all four of their backpacks and the five of them into the little Honda, but between the trunk and a large canvas rucksack tied to the roof, they'd managed. This morning, Jill's sister Ellen had picked them up to drive them to the drop-off spot for their trip so they could avoid leaving their cars. As the trip was about an hour from their respective places in Loveland and Longmont, the cramped quarters had been temporary, but Fiona was still happy to be out of the little car. She stretched from side to side, still a little stiff from Thursday's workout, but starting, finally, to catch the others' excitement.

Over the last four months, she'd gone back and forth from reluctant participant to eager enthusiast. She'd been bullied into this trip, but she could nevertheless recognize that what they were about to do was a privilege few people could enjoy. Further, she loved camping and hiking, and had never tried a backwoods trip this long. If she could shake off the last of her resentment, she might enjoy herself—that is, if she could deal with the physical rigors of the hiking.

She'd been working out and training with Jill fairly often since the day she'd heard about the trip, but she was still a long way from fit. She had some muscles again and had put on a little weight, but that didn't mean she was a superhero now. She and Jill had done a couple of long overnight backpacking trips and one three-day weekend to train earlier this summer with the weight she planned to carry, but two or three days was different than two weeks. Jill and the others had promised to help her as much as possible, but it would probably come down to whether she had the will to keep trying.

Jill and her sister Ellen were talking quietly together near the hood of Ellen's car. Fiona walked a little closer, and the two of them fell quiet. Ellen smiled at her.

"You're going to keep my sister safe, right? Don't let her get eaten by bears."

Fiona grinned. "You know I can't do anything to stop her if she really wants something."

Ellen laughed. "You're right. In that case, try not to get in the way."

"Hey!" Jill said, feigning indignation. "If they're going to eat anyone, it would be Sarah since she's so sweet."

"Who's eating what?" Sarah asked, walking closer with Carol.

The three of them laughed before Jill explained.

Ellen gave Jill a quick hug. "Be safe, lady, and call me when you're on your way back. Do you know what time I should be ready, more or less?"

Jill shrugged. "Some time in the afternoon or early evening on the Sunday the fourth—that's all I know. We'll be coming from Wyoming, so if you're out, you'll have some time to drive up here. Hopefully, I'll be able to call when we get back to the trucks."

A few minutes later, when they'd gotten all the packs out of the trunk and the canvas bag from on top of the Honda, two pickup trucks turned into the parking lot, both hauling horse trailers. The parking lot had long spaces for RVs and trailers, and this early in the morning they had no problem pulling into two subsequent spots. They kept the engines running.

Because of some work obligations, Fiona had yet to meet Rosalinda—Roz—Delmonico, their guide, but she'd heard all about her from the others when they'd met her this past May. Her three friends had gushed about how gorgeous and butch she was, Sarah going so far as to say she was no longer put off by the fact that they had to have her with them the whole trip. Fiona was curious to see if the woman lived up to the hype.

The driver's door to the truck on the right opened, and a young man jumped out, jogging over to them. He wore a bright-green bandana on his forehead, the color so glaring in the sunshine it was almost neon. Jill met him partway and shook his hand before leading him to the others.

"Jon, this is Fiona. You've met everyone else."

Jon extended a hand. "Hi, Fiona—sorry we didn't get to meet earlier. It's been a crazy summer." After they shook, he made a gesture at their bags. "Let me help you carry this stuff to the truck. You guys are riding with me. We're going to follow Roz and the others up to the trailhead."

It didn't take long for them to move the packs into the back, and then, after a final good-bye to Ellen, the four of them climbed into the extended cab of Jon's truck. Fiona tried to spy Roz, but her view was blocked by the other assistants, all of whom waved at them from inside the other truck. Like Jon, they too wore the green bandanas, and Fiona wondered if it was some type of uniform or if they'd chosen to wear them. At least they seemed friendly. Hopefully Roz would be, too. Female Adonis or not, the last thing Fiona wanted was to be around some sullen weirdo for the next two weeks.

The drive was uneventful. It was early enough that they'd avoided the traffic that would clog the canyon later in the day—tourists with RVs that were afraid to drive quickly and out-of-staters creeping along, looking for wildlife. Fiona had driven or had been driven up this road countless times since she was a kid, first with her parents, and then with her friends and girlfriends. Several nice campgrounds were located right here along the road, but she generally preferred to backpack at least a mile or so away from the sound of the traffic. Most of the campgrounds they passed were already full, normal for this time of year and this close to town. She spied the first sites she remembered staying in on her own—well off-season and virtually empty when she was there as a younger woman. All of this was familiar ground so far. They turned on the road toward Red Feather Lakes, and here, finally, something was different from her usual visits up here.

About five miles past the turnoff onto this secondary road, the truck in front of them slowed before turning onto a gravel road to the west, into the woods. The lead truck stopped about fifty feet in, and by craning her neck to the side and smashing her face against the window, Fiona could see someone getting out of the truck in front of them—one of the other assistants. A gated fence barred the way, and one of the men unlocked a padlock and took off a chain before pushing the gate open for the truck. Jon followed the other truck, and the assistant locked the gate behind them before running back to the truck in front of them.

"This is so much closer to the city than I expected," Jill said. She was sitting up front with Jon.

"Amazing, right? Sometimes the best things are hidden in plain sight. But don't worry. Once you're back in these woods, it'll seem like you're a million miles from anywhere. You guys will be really isolated in a couple of days. No one around for miles in any direction."

Fiona's stomach dropped at the thought. Of course she'd known this would be the case—isolation was the point of this whole trip, after all, the entire appeal. During one of the last trips they'd done together as a group, they'd had to share a camping space with other backpackers. That situation was becoming more and more common with the local population growth and increasing popularity of the Rockies. Still, now that they were almost in the protected forest, the reality of their situation filled her with something like dread. What happened if someone was hurt or wandered away from camp? They wouldn't have cell service back here. They would be on their own. Fiona's arms broke out in gooseflesh, but she chided herself for being so silly. After all, they'd have an experienced guide with them. She'd know what to do.

Branches of pines and aspens were swatting the side of the truck as they drove, the sunlight flashing inside the cab almost strobe-like. Every twenty feet or so, Fiona caught a sign warning off trespassers, the words harsh and red, with steep fines posted on the bottom for violators. If someone came this far without a permit and didn't heed the warnings, they clearly meant to break the law.

The trees suddenly broke in front of them, and Fiona saw that the growth had been cut back here a little for a small parking area. The lead truck pulled over to the left, and Jon turned easily to the right, the horse trailers now pointing toward each other. The trip from Ted's Place had taken less than an hour.

Everyone piled out of the trucks, and the area was a mass of bodies and activity for several minutes while Fiona and the others moved their gear out of the way. They waited near what was clearly the trailhead, another large warning sign propped nearby promising fines and jail time for trespassers. Two of the assistants were busy getting the horses out of the trailers, and by the time Fiona remembered to look for her, Roz was standing with her back to her, directing the others. She was too far away to hear clearly, but Fiona could see the assistants watching her and nodding at times as they were told their various tasks. From behind, the woman was tall, solid, her black, curly hair cut very close to her head on the sides, longer on top. She was wearing neutral tones, beiges and greens, and the muscles in her arms and shoulders were visible under the light cotton fabric. Unlike the men, she'd tied a dark-red bandana tied around her neck. Even from here, Fiona could see that it was wet, likely to keep her cool.

The operation was efficient, unhurried. The assistants' gear was set in a neat pile as the horses were lined up, attached to leads, and saddled. Roz inspected each horse, and Fiona finally saw her face when she moved to the horses on the far side of the line closer to her and her friends. Roz's expression was stern, hard, her brows low, her mouth and jaw set in a firm line. She was clearly concentrating, which explained her expression, but Fiona had the immediate impression of someone who knew what she was doing and suffered no fools. Her eyes and lashes were very dark, like her hair, her skin a warm, light-russet brown. Despite the hardness she saw there, Fiona couldn't look away.

Jill elbowed her. "What did I tell you?"

Fiona didn't reply, still staring at the woman. The sight of her was mesmerizing. Beyond seeming confident, sure of herself and what she was doing, Roz was clearly not a person to mess with. This woman could probably handle anything.

After Roz checked the last horse, she nodded slightly at her assistants before finally glancing their way. Her eyes rested briefly on Fiona's before moving on to the others. She lifted a hand and walked toward them. Fiona's heart leapt, and she forced her gaze away from the woman's face.

"Hey, guys. Nice to see some of you again. I don't think I've met you, yet, though. Fiona, right?"

Fiona made herself meet her eyes. Fiona was slightly shorter than average, and this woman had a good seven or eight inches on her. Their eyes met for a second, and Fiona's face heated. Realizing she was supposed to speak, she managed to sputter out a reply.

"Yes. That's me." She remembered to offer a hand at the last second. Roz's was warm and strong and strangely soft.

"Okay. Nice to meet you."

Roz gave her hand one more squeeze before letting it go, and Fiona had to force herself to put her own back at her side. Roz's gaze had already wandered away from hers, and Fiona made herself look away again. It was going to be hard not to stare at her this entire trip.

"I guess since we'll be spending some time together, I ought to let you all know now that I'm an early riser, and I'll expect the same from everyone this trip. I want to be on the trail no later than eight every morning."

"Sure, Roz, whatever you like," Jill said. Her face, Fiona noted, was slightly pink, and Jill wasn't hiding the fact that she was staring at Roz.

"Alrighty, then. I see you guys packed light, like I suggested, so that's good. After today, we have to carry it. Today we'll be on the horses for about five hours, with a nice long break halfway. We'll make an early camp this afternoon so you can adjust to the elevation. The guys leave with the horses tomorrow morning.

"Fiona, I don't know what the others told you, but after today, we'll do about sixteen to eighteen miles a day the first half of the trip, and twenty to twenty-two the second. If we keep to the schedule, we'll have one day about halfway for a break at the hot springs. We'll head northwest for the first three days, then basically due north after that. These guys," she gestured at the assistants, "will meet us in our final campsite with the horses on the third, and we'll ride out with them to the trucks on the fourth. That means almost two weeks of hard work. How's that sound?"

Fiona managed a quick nod. “Sounds good. I’m ready.”

Roz smiled at her. “Glad to hear it. Now let’s get these packs tied up to the horses, and we can be on our way.”

As Roz walked away out of earshot, Jill staggered a little, grabbing Fiona and Sarah’s arms as if to steady herself.

“Oh. My. God. That smile, guys. Jeez.”

Fiona laughed and pushed her away. “Get ahold of yourself, Romeo. She wouldn’t give any of us the time of day if she wasn’t being paid.”

Jill raised an eyebrow, frowning. “I don’t know about that. She was awfully friendly when we met her in May.”

“Yeah,” Fiona said, “’cause it’s her job, genius.”

“Maybe. But who knows what it’ll be like when we’re out in the woods by ourselves for a few days? Slim pickings might open doors.”

“Or tent flaps,” Carol said.

“Hey!” Sarah said. “I’m standing right here.”

Carol swatted her arm playfully. “A girl can dream.”

Roz gestured from the horses for them, and they lugged their packs over to her. There were two extra horses for the gear. They put two packs on one, three on the other, the assistants’ overnight bag fitting into a single pack on the first gear horse. Fiona’s was the lightest of their bags, and Roz was able to hold it up one-handed as she strapped it on. They’d been directed to avoid going over a quarter of their body weight, and as Fiona was the smallest of anyone, hers weighed five pounds less than the others’.

Almost all of her pack’s weight was food—a pound a day of calorie-dense meals and snacks. She also had a headlamp and extra batteries, a lightweight, extra-warm sleeping bag, a change of clothes and extra underwear and socks, long johns, a waterproof jacket, her inflatable sleeping pad, and a few toiletries. The others had cookware and water filters, so she didn’t need to carry any of that except her own plate, spork, and cup, and some matches. She was sharing a tent with Jill, but Jill had agreed to carry the entire thing to help her out. All in all, she could manage her load, but she was still looking forward to later in the trip when the food weight decreased.

Last week, she and Sarah had gone together for a quick tutorial on horseback riding at a local ranch, but now, as Fiona mounted her horse, she realized that it had probably been unnecessary. These were trail horses, calm and quiet, taught to follow the lead horse, ridden by Roz. Still, the lesson had made her a little less nervous about the whole thing, and the idea that the ride would last only part of today was comforting, too. Her horse's ears were soft and black, twitching slightly. She patted the side of its neck, and it turned toward her slightly, whinnying softly.

"Nice horsey," she whispered.

"All set?" Roz called from the front.

Fiona was three horses behind her, near the middle. Everyone called out in reply, and they started, Fiona's horse moving on its own. The horse was placid, the bobbing minimal, and once she'd gotten used to the feel of riding again, her stomach gave a quick flutter of excitement. This was really happening.

CHAPTER THREE

They made it to the spot for their lunch break with little effort. It was slightly after noon when they dismounted, and when Fiona checked her watch, Roz made an announcement.

"Uh, oh, I must have forgot to tell everyone else, so Fiona, don't take this personally, but no watches or any other technology besides your lights are allowed on this trip."

"Wait, what?" Jill asked. "Not even my GPS?"

Roz shook her head. "Especially not that."

Sarah frowned. "Is that some kind of rule here?"

Roz shook her head again. "It's a personal one. I promise you won't even miss them in a couple of days. Make a pile here, please," she pointed, "and the guys will keep everything safe for you until we see them again."

Fiona and the others looked at each other. They, like her, were all clearly trying to decide whether to argue. She saw Sarah and Carol share that silent exchange of theirs and Carol shrugged. They started taking off their watches, and Fiona followed suit. She set it in the pile and took her phone out of her back pocket, placing it near the others. She'd put it on airplane mode back at the gas station, knowing they'd lose service a few miles down the road, but useless or not, it was strange to let it go. Jill held back a little, obviously livid. Her face was red, her lips pinched, and she was clearly doing everything she could not to say anything. If Roz noticed this reaction, she didn't say anything, instead walking away to check in with her assistants and the horses. Jill let out a little breath of frustration when she was far enough away not to hear.

"The nerve!"

"Oh, give it a rest," Carol said. "What difference does it make? The watches don't matter, and it's not like our phones work back here. I'm kind of glad they'll be safe. I should have left them at home."

"Okay, but like, what about my GPS? I wanted it to track our progress and the trip for my blog post when we get back."

Carol stared at her levelly. "And? So you don't get to do that. Are you going to let it ruin the whole day?"

Fiona was surprised. Of their friend group, only Carol could get away with challenging Jill like this, and she didn't usually bother. Carol was fairly placid and even-keeled, rarely letting other people rile her. Even when she did challenge Jill, she almost never called her on her pettiness, as that usually meant that Jill would sulk even more.

"Fine," Jill said, ripping off her watch. She threw it onto the pile and dropped her phone next to Fiona's. She held her GPS, stared at it, and then set it down on the ground before storming off.

Carol sighed. "Goddamn it."

Sarah touched her arm. "She'll get over it."

They glanced over at Fiona, guilt in their eyes, and Fiona tried to keep her expression neutral. They knew she was Jill's best friend, but she didn't like Jill's moods any more than they did. She shrugged.

"Yeah—don't worry about it, Carol. Thanks for saying something. It has nothing to do with the stuff, anyway. Jill doesn't like being told what to do."

Carol nodded, one eyebrow up. "Ain't that the truth. And Roz's going to be calling the shots this whole time."

"I hope it won't be a problem," Sarah added, her tone subdued.

Fiona knew better, and she was pretty sure her friends did, too. In fact, some of her earlier reluctance at having a guide stemmed from the fact that Jill hated not to be in charge. Still, if anyone could make Jill listen to her, it might be Roz. Judging from her recent and quick exit, Roz already seemed to have an instinct for avoiding conflict with her, and Jill's crush might help a little, too.

Jon walked over to them then, smiling and holding a stuff sack. "Let's put all of that in here. I promise everything will be safe and sound when we see you again on the other side."

Fiona leaned down to help him, the two of them making quick progress. Their contact with the twenty-first century was cut off, and a quick, warm current of something like relief swept through her. It was comforting to be off the grid. She and Jon stood up together, and he smiled at her.

"And don't worry—you really don't need any of this stuff. Roz knows what she's doing. She's the best in the business and knows these woods better than anyone."

"I'm not worried."

He smiled again. "Good. Oh, and hey. You should take advantage of this rest stop. She won't be this easy on you guys after today."

He wandered off to join the other young men, all of whom were sitting on some rocks by the side of the river, eating their lunch. Including Jon, there were four of them altogether, all in their early twenties, all a similar outdoorsy type, lean and tan with scruffy hair and beards. She imagined this was a nice summer job for them between semesters at school, perhaps, or part of some kind of job training for something similar later on. Except for Jon, they hadn't introduced themselves, but she didn't think that was a slight on their part—just the usual divide between clients and providers. Two of them had pulled their green bandanas around their necks, and Fiona decided they wore them for visibility. It was easy to spot them from anywhere. The green was almost fluorescent, unnatural and obvious in this setting.

The river itself was calm here, a kind of low burble over stones that opened into a large pool about twenty feet away from where she was standing. She walked over there, stretching her butt muscles as much as she could and occasionally bending down to touch her toes. While they'd made a lot of progress riding the horses this far, she would be glad to be back on her own two feet tomorrow. She wasn't sure her butt or thighs could take more than a day of riding.

Roz was standing by the pool, staring at the water, her hands on her waist and elbows akimbo. The trees covered the sky entirely here, but it was still hot even here in the shade. The pool looked shallow, maybe two or three feet deep in the center, and the surface was buzzing with the activity of different insects—gnats, dragonflies, and water spiders dancing across the surface. A few puffs of cotton from the trees drifted through the air, lending the beautiful space a magical, ethereal feeling. Roz turned at her approach and smiled at her.

"Gorgeous, isn't it?"

Fiona couldn't reply with words, but she nodded, training her eyes on the water.

"Nothing back here has been named, not on any map anyway, but I always think of this as Serenity Pond."

"It fits," Fiona managed to say.

They were quiet for a long, awkward pause, for Fiona at least, and she fought to think of something to say.

"Have you been doing this long? Guiding people, I mean?"

Roz shrugged. "Depends on what you mean. I've led groups in this forest for only the last three years, but I've been doing similar work for about ten."

She didn't say anything more, and Fiona couldn't think of a way to ask for more details without seeming nosy. Instead, she let the peaceful quiet of the place wash over her, closing her eyes to listen to sound of the woods. The birds were squawking to each other, and somewhere nearby she could hear the chiding whir of a squirrel. Beyond this, nothing—no cars, no planes, nothing but the light laughter and talk of the others behind them to suggest that anyone on earth existed besides the two of them here by the pond.

When she opened her eyes, Roz was watching her, a slight grin pulling at the corner of her mouth, and Fiona flushed with heat.

"What?"

"You get it, don't you?" Roz asked, so quiet she was almost whispering.

"What do you mean?"

"This place. You get it. I can tell. Not everyone does, but you do, already."

Fiona was about to reply, but Jill was walking toward them, almost bouncing as she approached.

"Wow. Look at that!" she said, her voice echoing across the pond. "Man, that's pretty. And inviting! Do you think I have time to wade in for a minute?" She didn't wait for a reply, leaning down to untie her boots. "Come on, Fiona. Take off your boots." She turned her head around and shouted, "Carol! Sarah! Get over here! We're getting in the water!"

Fiona tried to throw Roz an apologetic look, but Roz had already wandered away, joining the men she worked with. Fiona hesitated and then knelt to unlace her boots, slipping them off with her wool socks. She and Jill clutched their forearms together and waded into the water, the cold so biting Fiona almost leapt out. This was snow run-off, and even pooled here, its chill was so bitter it made her feet ache. She tried to turn back to the shore.

"Oh, stop being a baby," Jill said, laughing and yanking her farther into the pond. "You'll wish you could have your feet in here after a few days of walking on them."

Fiona's feet were starting to go numb now, and she gritted her teeth to keep from complaining. Sarah and Carol were smart enough to stay on the shore, waving at them and pretending not to hear Jill's repeated invitations. Fiona finally managed to coax Jill out when Jill almost tripped on her own numb feet. They had just enough time to get their boots on and cram a quick meal before Roz told everyone to get ready to go.

Jill rolled her eyes. "Taskmistress."

She said this loud enough that Roz might have heard her, and Fiona flushed with embarrassment. Luckily Roz didn't seem to notice or chose to ignore her. Sarah and Carol shared that same silent, worried glance, and Fiona wondered then how long it would be before Jill decided to confront Roz. Judging from this morning, it would be soon.

As they all mounted up and got back on the trail, her worries about Jill and Roz deepened. She and Jill had been friends for over twenty years, but it had never been an easy friendship. When they'd met as teens, Jill had immediately taken charge. At the time, this had seemed natural. As a teenager, Fiona had been so anxious and depressed, she'd almost felt like she deserved to be bossed around. They'd supported each other as they came out, first to one another, having, perhaps, sensed it about each other from the beginning. Neither had ever had even the remotest kind of romantic feelings about the other, and Jill had been the only one to actually date while they were still in high school—an equally large number of boys and girls. By the time Fiona started having more confidence in herself, the habit of stepping aside when a pretty girl showed interest and going along with whatever Jill wanted was so deeply ingrained that she hardly dared to try to change things.

College had helped a little. They'd gone to different schools, and Fiona had made different friends, ones that let her make choices, pushed her to open up more and become her own person. Carol was one of them, and, unrequited crush or not, she'd had an enormous influence on Fiona's growth. She'd met Sarah later, too, and the three of them had become close, eventually sharing an apartment their senior year. Jill had visited once in a while, but she had always remained Fiona's friend first, theirs second. It was rare that the three of them hung out without Fiona. In fact, Fiona half-suspected they wouldn't see Jill at all if it weren't for her, but she never asked them about it.

After college, she and Jill had moved back to their hometown, and while things had certainly changed a little between them, their friendship still had an unequal power division. While Fiona was more aware and more ashamed of this dynamic post-college, she still did very little to challenge it beyond spending a little more time away from her. Limiting exposure to Jill was the only option to avoid being led around like a dog. Still, she usually saw her a couple of times a month, and they took a long, annual trip together. And in the end, despite all the generalized bossiness, she loved Jill like a sister—a bossy older sister, but a sister nonetheless. Jill could be incredibly supportive, and she always had her back. Her insistence on doing crazy, sometimes dangerous things could occasionally turn into a thrilling adventure. But Jill could also be tiring, like today, and like last March when she had pummeled her into this trip.

Still, Fiona reflected, things could be worse. These woods were incredible, like nothing she'd ever seen. They were thick, dark, far denser than most of the woods in Colorado. The pines were healthy, full, the aspens and narrow-leaf cottonwoods in full dress. She'd taken a few trips to the East Coast to backpack and hike, and this forest almost reminded her of those woods. The trail they were following was clearly delineated, but beyond the narrow path lay nothing but a snarl of growth and decay. The sun was blocked for most of the trail—a relief in this heat—but occasionally she yearned for it to break the shadows around her. Even in this long line of horses and people, they seemed already isolated, alone.

Her horse, as if sensing her apprehension, nickered a little and lifted its head back. She leaned forward and patted its neck, glad for its warm strength. She didn't know a thing about horses, but she liked this one. All it asked was for her to stay on its back, which she could do. Maybe when they were back in town, she could see about having more riding lessons.

After the deep woods, the trail narrowed considerably for about a mile, winding through a series of enormous boulders. Here the sun beat down on them in glaring power, the white light harsh and reflecting off the quartz in the stone. Her sunglasses did little to block the light, and she pulled the brim of her hat a bit lower, cursing her earlier anxiety about the shadowed trail. At least then she hadn't been baking.

They suddenly stopped, the giant rocks still hemming them in on all sides. Roz and her horse at the front were blocked from her view behind a boulder ahead, and Fiona craned to the side, trying to see or hear what was happening. Sarah, directly in front of her, made a quieting motion with both hands, and Fiona repeated it to Jon behind her.

Roz called from far away in the front, her voice echoing off the rocks in eerie reverberations. She sounded very distant, not mere yards away.

"Hang on back there, guys," she called. "I heard something."

Fiona's stomach gave a great lurch, and she closed her eyes, listening hard. She could hear only the light breeze whistling through this boulder canyon. Then she heard birds, another angry squirrel, and somewhere not far from here, running water, now sounding a bit more like a river. Then, suddenly, she heard something strange. She'd noticed it before, she realized then, but hadn't paid attention to it. It was a THUNK, following by a long pause. Then another THUNK.

She turned in her saddle, looking back at Jon, but he put a finger in front of his lips to shush her. His eyes were wide, startled. He mouthed something, and she shrugged, raising her hands, not understanding. He mimicked a swinging motion with both hands clutched together and mouthed the word again. Ah, she thought, suddenly understanding: ax. Someone was using an ax on a tree nearby. The boulders made sound travel in weird ways, but whoever it was must be close for the sound to be so loud and distinct.

Roz startled her by shouting again. "Let's get out of this canyon, everyone, and I can go see what's happening."

The boulders lasted another ten minutes, and by the time all the horses had cleared them, Fiona was certain the other sound had stopped. Roz led everyone a little farther into the trees, searching for a clearing large enough for all of them. She finally simply stopped when a smallish break in the trees appeared on the trail. She turned her horse around to face them.

"Jon, you and Mark stay here with the ladies. I'm going with Ben and Fred to check out what we heard. I think we might have scared them off, but we need to find out anyway. Ladies, you can dismount and stretch a little while we wait, but don't wander off too far, please. I want to make sure we make camp in the next hour."

Roz rode off with two of the men, all three of them moving much faster than they had as a large group. They disappeared back into the boulder field, their horses kicking up divots of earth in their wake.

Jill slid off her horse, followed by Carol and Sarah. Fiona had a slightly harder time of it, realizing as she tried how stiff she'd become. They'd been on the horses for an hour or so since lunch, but the morning's ride had apparently caught up with her. She saw her friends wincing, too, and she and Jill shared an amused smile as they both rubbed their butts and the insides of their thighs.

Jon and the other guy, Mark, dismounted, Mark taking the horses' leads and moving them as a group closer to a clump of ferny growth. It was nice to see the animals enjoying their snack, and she was amused at their happy grunting and the occasional sight of their long tongues flicking out to snag some of the greenery. Sarah, Carol, and Jill had walked over to a large, fallen tree and were sitting on it, joking and laughing. Fiona almost moved to join them, but in the end, she stayed where she was, watching the horses with Mark. They chatted, Mark explaining a little about their diet, but mostly they stayed there, simply watching the animals' antics.

After a few more minutes, she heard Jon approach. He'd stayed farther away, watching the trail for the others, and when she turned toward him, she saw that he was clearly upset—angry even. The deep frown was foreign and strange on his normally open face. He slid his bandana off his head, revealing a surprisingly bright head of red curls. He wet the bandana with his canteen and rinsed off his face before tying it around his neck.

"What do you think that sound was?" Fiona asked.

"Probably what it sounded like—some asshole chopping wood."

"Really? Way back here?"

He nodded, still glowering. "You wouldn't believe what people will do to save a buck."

"But how? Aren't we miles from the road at this point?"

He shrugged. "They might have driven in, for all we know. People do crazy stuff all the time. You'd be amazed what we've found back here before."

"Does someone keep an eye on the forest all year? I mean when groups like ours aren't here?"

He nodded. "Yes. Roz. She's the year-round groundskeeper as well as the lead guide in the summer."

Almost as if he'd summoned her, they heard the horses coming back through the canyon, the sound amplified by the stone. Roz appeared first and then the two men behind her, the three of them pulling up about ten feet away in a line abreast.

"That was quick," Jon said.

Roz nodded, appearing troubled. It took a moment for Fiona to read her expression. Her brows were low, her face grim, and Fiona detected something else, something unexpected: fear. A quick glance at the men on the horses confirmed this reaction. They were pale, their eyes stark and their lips tight. Whatever the three of them had seen, they didn't like it.

Roz threw a glance at the two men on either side of her and shook her head slightly at Jon before lifting her chin at Fiona's friends sitting far away. Fiona understood this charade at once: Roz had obviously found something but didn't want to talk about it in front of her or the others.

"That bad?" Jon said, almost under his breath.

Roz nodded at him. "Later."

Whether that meant she would talk to her, too, or only Jon, neither of them argued. Jon moved at once to lead the horses back to the trail. When her friends came over, Jill, Carol, and Sarah asked a couple of light questions about what Roz had found, and Roz when gave a general, almost casual response, they didn't push for more—clearly satisfied with what was obviously, to Fiona, a lie. The others mounted up, Roz moving to the front. Before Jon could do the same, Fiona grabbed his arm.

"What the hell?"

"I don't know, but it's obviously bad."

"You have to tell us, too."

He shook his head. "It's not up to me. Roz will tell you what you need to know, if anything."

She was about to object, but he removed her hand, gently, from his arm, and walked away to his horse. Realizing she had no recourse here, she climbed up on her own horse, and they were soon on their way. She would have to wait for an explanation, but she promised herself she would have it. Whatever Roz and the others had seen out there in the woods clearly concerned them all.

Chapter Four

Camp that afternoon was at the edge of an expansive, flower-filled meadow. A ring of aspens circled a natural clearing, and some facilities had been left here for the horses—the only man-made materials in this forest, according to Roz. A long, metal drinking trough had been nailed into the ground, and some tie rings had been drilled into different places around the meadow so the horses could be secured as they ate. The animals were given their fill of the water at a small pool on the far side of the meadow. The horses helped carry their own night water and the people's filtered water back to camp in large, plastic sacks tied to their backs. Someone had dragged logs into the clearing in various places for sitting or to use as surfaces, and a small stone fire pit had been dug into the ground.

"This is the one and only place we'll have a fire until the end, ladies," Roz said. "Enjoy it while you can."

Fiona couldn't help her disappointment. True, she normally didn't have a campfire when backpacking, but it was nice to have one when you could. It leant a kind of comfort to a dark night. Lots of summers in Colorado, fires were banned outright, both in the backwoods and at traditional campsites.

Apparently seeing something in Fiona's expression, Roz smiled. "Hey, at least we can have this one. Sometimes it's too dry, even here close to water."

Roz wandered away to help her assistants, and Fiona stared after her. Every word the woman said left her breathless, even when it was a mundane detail.

"What were you guys talking about?" Jill asked, so close to her ear that Fiona jumped and almost screamed.

"Jesus!" she said, putting a hand to her chest. "You almost scared me to death. What did you say?"

Jill, her grin self-satisfied, had clearly known she would scare her. "I asked what you guys were talking about."

Fiona raised an eyebrow. "We were deciding what time to start the orgy. She said six, but I argued to wait until dark. No one needs to see my pale skin in the daylight."

Jill threw her head back and laughed. "You perv. I knew you'd be into her."

"A corpse would be into her."

Jill rubbed her hands together. "And we get to look at her for two whole weeks."

They both stared after her then. She was helping with the horses. Each horse needed to be tied to one of the loops out in the meadow so it could eat. The animals would be given a bag of high-calorie food later, but until dark, they'd be free to munch whatever they could reach. Roz was walking next to one of the large yellow ones—a palomino, Fiona remembered—talking to it softly as they moved into the field. She appeared natural with the animal, assured, guiding it gently as they walked.

Jill swatted her. "Okay. We're being creeps. Help me set the tent up before you go all goosey on me."

This was easily done. Their tent, a small two-person affair, was designed to be compact and lightweight, with two poles. It snapped together a little like Legos and was up in a few minutes. Unsure about the weather overnight, they put the rain fly on before throwing their sleeping bags and pads inside. They'd be hanging all their food some hundred yards away in the bear canisters, so Fiona removed the food she'd stored in a stuff sack and brought it with her.

As they walked toward the others, Fiona touched Jill's arm. "Hang on a sec. I wanted to tell you something."

She recalled the exchange she'd witnessed between Roz and the others on the trail after they'd come back—their strange expressions and the tense fear.

Jill stared at her. "You think they're hiding something from us?"

Fiona nodded. "That's what it looked like."

"Well, screw that. Let's go talk to them." Jill started marching toward Roz, but Fiona managed to grab her arm to stop her.

"No! Hang on!"

Jill spun toward her, eyes blazing. "Let go of me!"

"Wait a second, Jill. I might be wrong. Maybe I can get something out of them later if I ask nicely. Just give me a chance, okay? There's no need to cause a scene."

"So why tell me about it? Isn't this what you wanted me to do?"

Fiona was stumped. Jill was right. She'd known that if she told her, Jill would do exactly this—storm in and demand answers. If she wanted subtlety, Jill was not the person to ask for help.

"Let me try, okay? If someone doesn't tell me anything, I'll ask for your help again."

Jill stared at her for a long time, frowning, and then, to Fiona's great relief, she sighed and seemed to let it go. "Fine. But they better spill it, or else."

After they'd dropped their food into the pile with the others', Jill wandered away to talk to Sarah about something, and Fiona was finally alone. She leaned on a tree, staring out at the horses in the meadow, letting the peaceful serenity and beauty of the scene quiet her nerves. Trees lined the edges of the meadow, and steep, snow-capped mountains loomed beyond them on the far side, but the grass and flowers rolled in the breeze like the ocean, in waves. She closed her eyes, inhaling the lightly fragrant air, the sun warm on her skin. Whatever had happened in the woods today, at least this place was safe.

"It's beautiful, isn't it?"

Fiona opened her eyes, not surprised to find Roz next to her. As she'd been back at the pond, she had a light, open expression and was clearly relaxed. Without camp or guide duties to attend to, she was approachable, friendly. And both times, she'd sought out Fiona to talk to. Fiona couldn't repress a slight shiver of warmth.

"It might be the most beautiful thing I've ever seen."

Roz's smile was breathtaking. To Fiona's shock, she took a step closer, almost touching her arm, and stared out at the meadow. Fiona couldn't look away from her profile. As if sensing this fixation, Roz glanced down at her, grinning.

"I thought you said it was the most beautiful thing you'd ever seen. So why are you staring at me?"

There was no mistaking her flirtatious tone, and Fiona let her mouth drop open with surprise. She sputtered, uselessly, unable to reply.

"Hey, Boss!" one of the men called. "Could you help a sec?"

Roz rolled her eyes and turned to go to him, and Fiona watched her leave, wanting, the whole while, to simply sink into the ground in self-hatred and resentment. She'd totally blown it.

Roz joined Mark and Ben, who had already begun to prepare their special meal for tonight—a fresh-food bonanza that would be their last until they reached the end of the trail. Mark was making a cheese, meat, and bread board, and Ben had put together a kind of crudité platter for them with veggies, fruit, and several kinds of dips and hummus. Roz helped them get the food arranged on paper plates and bowls. Fiona would miss this type of food in a day or two. For weight and to avoid spoilage, almost everything she carried in her backpack was freeze-dried, as was the food of everyone else she'd be hiking with. This was the one truism of backpacking—the food sucked.

Trying to get close to Roz again, Fiona offered to help, but the three of them were clearly capable of taking care of things. Roz, seeming to sense that she wanted something to distract her, asked her to direct her friends on firewood duty. She and the others spent the next half hour gathering whatever dry stuff they could find, Fiona kicking herself for her idiocy the whole time. Still, the work did help take her mind off that disastrous exchange. With a summer as wet as this, finding wood wasn't easy, and she had to hike far into the woods to find anything useable. Finally, she spotted a cache of pine branches under an overhanging willow and was pleased to find them entirely dry. She asked Sarah to help, and the two of them made a sizeable pile next to the fire pit after hauling it back to camp together.

Fiona sat down on a nearby log, exhausted, and Sarah dropped next to her soon after, sighing heavily.

"Man, I'm beat," she said.

Fiona nodded. "Me, too, and we barely did anything today."

"I guess we'll get used to it."

Fiona nodded, but her stomach was twisting with nerves. She'd been afraid she would feel like this, too weak to contribute much to the effort, but she'd hoped it wouldn't happen the first few nights. She could easily climb into her sleeping bag and go to sleep right now.

"Say, do you know where the little girls' room is?" Sarah asked.

Fiona nodded and pointed. "Actually, I have to go, too. I can show you."

Sarah hesitated and then nodded, and the two of them stood up. That slight hesitation was natural. It wasn't as if either one of them intended to watch the other go. It was about being there for support. Peeing in the woods was always a little creepy, as it put women, especially, in such a vulnerable position. Still, Fiona usually went alone. Being with anyone was platonically intimate in some strange way. Some women, like Jill, for instance, wouldn't have thought twice about it, but she and Sarah were perhaps a little more prudish or maybe modest.

They grabbed their toiletries before heading down toward the latrine area. A faint trail led them there, away from the water and camp.

"We have to pack out the TP?" Sarah asked as they walked.

Fiona grimaced and nodded. This was another thing she hadn't looked forward to, but, having done it before, she could do it again. How she'd feel several days in with all that waste in her backpack was another story, but for now it was nothing new. Toilet paper could biodegrade in a year or two in wet conditions but had a harder time doing so at altitude. In very high elevations, like they'd be in soon, it could last years, which meant that in general, in many places in the mountains, you were either encouraged or required to pack it out. Plus, of course, they were in a protected forest, so regardless of whether it could break down here at 7,000 feet, they had to take it with them. She was carrying the TP and her double-ziplocked bag in her pockets, along with a little baking powder in the bag for odor.

The actual latrine area was protected by a thick copse of bushes and trees, and Fiona waited on the trail for Sarah to go first, her back to the bushes to give her friend more privacy.

Sarah had been gone for mere seconds before she called out. "Uh, Fiona, could you come back here for a second?"

Hearing the fright in her voice, Fiona went at once, edging around bushes into a small, dark clearing. It took some time for her eyes to adjust to the relative dark, and her breath caught when she saw where Sarah was pointing.

About ten feet up from the ground, on several trees on the far side of the small clearing, strange, geometric symbols were cut into the bark. The soft, lighter insides of the trees made the symbols stand out in sharp contrast to the rest of the tree. The smell of pine was sharp and clear—pungent for having been exposed from the inside this way. The marks themselves were careful, precise, and overlapped in clear bands around the trees. Fiona was reminded of Celtic braids, or something similar—the ancient knotwork she'd seen on antique armor and vases. It had been expertly done here—no mistakes she could see. Whoever had done this had practice working with wood. Altogether the bands were perhaps two or three feet tall, marking three trees total. This was not the work of a bird or an animal. A person had done this.

As she moved her gaze from tree to tree, she could detect slight differences in each of the band's patterns, but judging from how fresh the scent was and how newly crisp the cuts were, this had happened very recently.

"Someone must have done this in the last couple of days," Fiona said, almost to herself.

"Yes, but how?" Sarah asked. "Did they bring a damn ladder out here?"

Fiona walked a little closer, staring up at the cuts from the ground, but they were harder to see from directly underneath. She peered down at the ground, seeing wood chips, and leaned down to pick one of them up. The bark was thick and slightly wet, about the size of the blade of a small kitchen knife, blunted on all sides. She backed up, examining the marks more clearly from a few feet away, and sensed Sarah siding up closer beside her.

"They seem to be made with a thick knife, or maybe a chisel and hammer," Fiona said, still staring up at them.

"Yeah. I think you're right."

They stared at each other in the gloomy light, and Fiona saw her own fear reflected in Sarah's eyes.

"Do you think this has anything to do with what we heard earlier, on the trail?" Sarah asked.

Fiona nodded without hesitation. "Yes. Roz and the other guys were really creeped out when they came back." She gave a quick summary of how they'd behaved. "Seeing something like this would explain how they were acting. Maybe they'll admit what they saw if we show them this."

Sarah rubbed her arms despite the heat. "Agreed. Now let's get the hell out of here. I don't have to pee that bad."

They almost ran back to camp. Once there, it took them a few minutes to find and gather everyone, as they were all either working on something or had drifted off to explore. Something in her expression must have alerted Roz, however, as she gathered everyone into the center of camp when Fiona asked her to.

Once the group was assembled, Roz asked, "Okay—so what's the problem?"

Sarah explained, and Fiona could hear the fear in her voice. Roz's face hardened as she listened, her eyes narrowing with fury.

After Sarah finished, Roz said, "Okay. Me and Ben are going to go check it out. Everyone else stay here and don't wander away."

Roz and Ben left, and the moment they were out of sight, everyone around Fiona started talking at the same time, seeming nervous and scared. Fiona's ears were ringing slightly, and her head felt strangely light and disconnected. Her vision blurred then, and her legs started to buckle. She managed to make her way to a nearby stump of wood, sitting down on it before her legs gave way entirely. Her hands were tingling, and the buzzing in her head increased, darkness now almost entirely obscuring her vision. Her heart felt high and heavy in her chest, pounding in her ears, and her breath was so loud she could hear nothing else. She clasped her shaking hands between her knees and bent forward as far as she could, trying to get the blood into her head. She was vaguely aware of the others falling silent, and then, dimly, she realized Jill was next to her, kneeling on the ground by her side.

"Just breathe," Jill whispered. "You're okay. Take deep breaths, okay? In through your nose, out through your mouth, in through your nose, out through your mouth…"

Fiona did as suggested, and the ringing gradually faded. She tried to sit up, but Jill kept a hand on her back.

"Stay down for another minute, okay? You almost passed out. Keep breathing. I'll get a cool rag for your neck."

Jill disappeared from her peripheral vision, and Fiona closed her eyes, concentrating on her breathing. Time seemed to flicker slightly, as Jill was suddenly next to her again, the damp cloth on the back of her neck heavenly cool.

When Jill finally let her sit up again, the others had all retreated to a distant part of the camp. They were talking quietly. Roz and Ben were back, Roz in the middle seemingly answering questions. Every person had their arms crossed or their hands stuffed into pockets, appearing tense, expectant.

"What happened?" Fiona asked Jill.

"You almost fainted. All of the sudden, you were stumbling around. You almost went down, but you managed to sit on this stump here. Scared the hell out of me."

Fiona was confused. She could remember most of this, but she also seemed removed from it somehow.

"Weird," she said. "I've never fainted before."

Jill looked scared, eyes wide, face pale. "And you better not do it again."

"What did Roz say when she came back?"

Jill glanced that way and shook her head. "I don't know. I was too busy taking care of you."

As if they'd called to her, Roz started walking toward them, and Fiona managed to sit up a little straighter, the damp rag sliding off her neck and falling to the ground behind her. Her head was pounding, but that strange weightless weakness was gone.

"Are you okay?" Roz asked. She seemed worried, almost frightened.

She nodded, suddenly embarrassed. The last thing she wanted this woman to see was her frailty. "Yes. I don't know why that happened. I've never fainted before."

"I'm just glad you didn't hurt yourself."

"Did you guys see the trees?" Jill asked.

Roz met Fiona's eyes, raising an eyebrow, and Fiona waved a hand dismissively. "I'm not going to pass out again. I want to know what's going on."

Roz stared at her a beat longer before focusing on Jill. "Yes, we did. It was like Fiona and Sarah said, and just like what me and the guys saw earlier when we went to check out the noises on the trail. Earlier, three trees about a hundred yards past the boulder field had marks and symbols like that on them."

"Why didn't you say something about it then?" Jill asked. Fiona could hear a hint of anger in her voice.

Roz sighed. "I don't know. I guess we didn't want to scare you. I was going to have the guys report it when they got back to town. Now I'm not so sure we should wait that long. Obviously whoever is doing this is still out here—we heard them, after all."

"Can you tell how long ago they were here at the camp?" Fiona asked.

Roz shrugged. "Not long—last few days, or maybe as soon as this morning. The trees haven't started healing yet, so within the last week, anyway."

"Jesus," Jill muttered.

"Exactly. I don't think it's safe to wait to report it. I want the forest service to know what's happening as soon as possible."

"Do you think we're safe?" Fiona asked.

Roz didn't answer right away, and Fiona's stomach dropped with dread. Roz had her hands bunched into fists on her waist, staring off into the meadow.

"I don't know," she finally said.

"What? How can you not know?" Jill said.

Roz frowned at her. "I don't know, because I don't know what this person or people's intentions are any more than you do. It could be kids, trying to mess with us."

"Or it could be a maniac," Jill said.

Roz shrugged. "Unlikely, but I guess so."

Jill laughed. "Are you serious?"

"How could I know?"

Fiona could see that Jill wanted to debate Roz, and she touched the back of Jill's hand to cut her off. Of course Roz couldn't know. All of this was new to her, too. Jill was reacting to her fear with anger.

Jill looked down at Fiona and frowned, but the anger disappeared from her expression, and she sighed.

"I'm sorry," she said. "Of course you don't know."

Roz's expression cleared as well. "It's okay. We're all in the dark here."

They were quiet so long, Fiona couldn't take the suspense. She needed to ask what they were likely all thinking.

"Should we go back to the trucks?"

Roz sighed. "Part of me thinks we should, but it'll be dark before we get back there, even if we hurry. It's too dangerous for the horses. I could send one of the guys to alert the forest service, and the rest of us could wait to leave until we hear from him again. One person on his own could get back well before sunset if he leaves soon and travels light."

"Goddamn it," Jill said. She turned abruptly and strode away, toward the meadow. She was nearly stamping, her arms swinging wildly as she walked. Jill was obviously upset at the idea of an interruption to their trip, but of course they had very few options. Even Jill had to know that. At best, a rampaging vandal was stalking these woods, cutting up protected woods. At worst, a nutcase was on the loose with a hammer and chisel at his disposal. Either way, things couldn't go on as scheduled until they figured this out. The police, or whoever, needed to be involved and put a stop to this. If that meant cancelling the trip, so be it.

Roz raised an eyebrow at her, and Fiona shrugged as an apology. Roz might not know Jill very well, but she clearly understood not to try to follow her. Instead, she turned back to the others and gestured them over to her. By the time they'd walked across the camp, Jill had also come back, though Fiona could see that she was still upset.

"Okay. I've made a decision. Fred, I want you to ride back to the trucks and call the forest service. I don't want to wait until tomorrow morning. The rest of us will stay here until we hear from you, or thirty-six hours, whichever is first."

"What happens then?" Carol asked.

Roz frowned and shook her head. "We'll have to decide—either to go back or keep going. We can make up one day on the trail with a few extra miles here and there, but not more than that, so we'll wait until Monday morning if we don't hear from you, Fred."

Roz waited for objections and more questions, but no one said anything, everyone simply looking around at each other, worried and upset. Jill was still fuming, but even she had to recognize a compromise when she heard it. With no voiced objections after several seconds, Roz nodded with what seemed like dismissal and turned to Fred. She and Fred made their way across camp toward one of the horses, talking quietly, and Fiona and her friends were soon left behind as the other men moved apart to talk to each other.

"Well, this sucks," Jill finally said.

"It sure does." Sarah nodded.

"Sure, but what are you gonna do?" Carol asked. "At least we're not going back now. The last thing I want to do is ride a horse any time soon. And who knows—maybe everything will be okay. Maybe we'll get to keep going after all."

"I sure as shit don't want to go back the day after tomorrow," Jill said.

"But we'll have to, if Roz decides that's best," Sarah said.

"Why?" Jill said in almost a whine. "It's just some asshole cutting up trees. It shouldn't ruin our vacation."

Fiona knew Jill would say something like this eventually, but she was still momentarily stunned. She could see that Sarah was startled as well. Jill must have seen identical expressions staring at her, as she threw her hands up in the air and walked away in a huff. Carol and Sarah shared another of their silent exchanges, and Fiona closed her eyes, suddenly exhausted. At this point, she would have paid any amount of money simply to be at home, away from all this, and in her own bed.

Fred suddenly rode by at a brisk trot, and the three of them waved to him as he passed. He touched his fingers to his baseball cap in a mock salute and quickly disappeared down the trail, toward the trucks. His green bandana was still visible long after he'd gone, the color flashing through the trees before it disappeared.

She glanced at her wrist before she remembered that she no longer had her watch. Judging by the sun, however, it was perhaps four or five. Unencumbered and moving that quickly, he could probably make it to the trucks in three hours. He would be cutting it close but should be there before full dark.

"Come on, guys," Carol said. "Let's get something to eat."

She and Sarah walked away toward the food, and Fiona waited for Jill to turn around and join them. She didn't. She continued to stand about ten feet away, her back a solid wall of indignation, and Fiona finally decided to let her pout on her own. She couldn't be bothered to talk her out of her snit, no matter how much Jill clearly wanted her to try.

After dinner, everyone sat around the fire in almost complete silence, the light, excited mood from this afternoon a distant memory. Hardly anyone spoke, though almost everyone made a half-hearted attempt to play cards for an hour before people seemed to wander away by themselves or in small groups. Fiona tried two or three times to work up the courage to talk to Roz, but the longer she waited, the more she dreaded trying.

By the time Fiona finally headed for bed, just as the first stars appeared in the sky, she was so emotionally and physically spent, she fell asleep almost the moment she was in her sleeping bag. When Jill joined her in the tent and roused her, it was full dark, and Fiona said nothing to her, pretending to sleep through it.

CHAPTER FIVE

Fiona was startled awake by a commotion outside her tent. She was surprised to find it already light outside. She usually slept poorly the first night or two in the woods, waking up on and off and getting up at first light. Judging by the sunshine inside her tent, she'd managed to sleep well past dawn. She fought her way out of her sleeping bag, slipped off the fleece skull cap she wore when she slept, and unzipped the tent flap, struggling to get out of her tent and into her boots without touching the ground with her socks.

The commotion was coming from the far end of camp. Roz and the others were standing close together, and she could hear Jill's tone from here, though not her words. Her voice was raised, angry, and Roz stood in front of her, a foot or two away, hands on her hips—defensive and angry herself. Carol and Sarah were standing nearby, so close to each other their arms were flush on one side. Fiona leaned down to tie her laces and then hurried over to them, rubbing the sleep out of her eyes.

"What do you mean you don't know?" Jill said. Her face was mottled red, her body tense.

"I mean I have no fucking clue what happened," Roz said. Unlike Jill, the anger in her tone was quiet, cold.

"What the hell does that mean?"

"Exactly what I just said. I have no idea where they are."

"How is that even possible? Didn't you hear them?"

"Did you?"

Fiona touched Sarah's arm. "What happened? What are they arguing about?"

Sarah's eyes were dark and scared. "They're gone. All of the guys are gone, and so are the horses."

"What?"

Sarah pointed at the spots where the men's tents had been, and at the area where they'd tied the horses last night. Both were empty.

"But—"

"Shhhh!" Sarah said, holding a finger to her lips. "I want to hear this."

"So let me get this straight," Jill was saying. "All your employees managed to pack up camp and disappear with ten horses, and you didn't notice?"

Roz threw her hands in the air. "None of us noticed! I don't know about you all, but I didn't hear a fucking thing!"

"How is that possible? Explain it to me—I'm all ears." To emphasize this point, Jill cupped a hand over one of them.

Roz let out a restrained groan. "How can I explain it? I don't know what the hell happened any more than you do."

Jill took a step toward her, fists clenching. "Some leader you are! What fucking use are you?"

Carol stepped between them and held out a palm to each. "Guys, hold on a second. Yelling and swearing at each other is getting us exactly nowhere."

"She's incompetent!" Jill screamed.

"Jill, cut it out." Sarah's voice was dark, furious but quiet. Jill opened her mouth to object, and Sarah held up a single finger. "I mean it, Jill—shut the hell up."

Everyone stood still, Jill and Roz breathing heavily. Fiona's heart was double-timing, anxiety squeezing her chest and throat, vise-like.

Roz and Jill had calmed a little, so Carol let her hands drop and backed up so the five of them were standing in a loose circle.

"Okay then," Sarah said. "Let's approach this situation logically and take it a step at a time. Just to clarify, Roz, you didn't ask the guys to leave—they left on their own?"

"That's what I've been saying!"

Sarah touched her fingers to her forehead. "I'm clarifying for everyone, okay? No need to jump down my throat."

"Fine. Sorry. No. I didn't ask them to leave."

"Okay. So the guys left on their own for some reason. Can anyone think why they might have done that? Or why they took all the horses?"

Fiona read equal amounts of fear and confusion on everyone's face. All of them were quiet before everyone shook their head or muttered no.

"So again," Sarah said, "to be crystal clear, no one heard them talking last night? None of them said anything about leaving early?"

More negative responses.

"Who was up the latest last night?"

Again, they glanced at each other before Jill raised her hand.

"Me, I think. Roz—you went to bed right before I did, right?"

"Yes."

"What were you doing, Jill?" Sarah asked.

"One of the guys—Mark—had some whiskey. We all had a little before turning in. Barely anything, really—a mouthful or two."

"Did they stay up after you left?"

Jill shook her head and then shrugged. "Not exactly. I mean, technically yes. They were still up when I got in the tent, but they were all putting out the fire, that kind of thing, getting ready. I'm pretty sure I remember one of them going into his tent about the same time I did, but I can't be sure. I guess it's possible he was pretending for some reason, but I don't know."

Everyone was quiet again as they digested this information. Fiona's heart was doing that funny skip again, her chest still tight and hot.

Sarah sighed. "So I guess we can all agree that sometime in the night they packed up camp, tied up the horses, and left, and they did it entirely on their own for unknown reasons. Now think back to yesterday. Even if they didn't mention leaving, exactly, did anyone hear them talking about anything else? Something they wanted to do when they got back to town, maybe? Something they were worried or excited about, maybe?"

More silence before Carol said, "Jon mentioned missing his girlfriend."

"Mark said something about a river-rafting trip he was going on later this week," Jill offered.

"I think I heard Ben say he has a sick grandma," Roz added.

All of this seemed inadequate, and Fiona assumed the others were thinking the same thing. Even a dying grandmother wouldn't merit abandoning them like this, especially without saying something to one of them first. Anyway, no one had any way to receive this news, this morning or otherwise.

"I don't get it," Fiona said.

Sarah nodded. "Exactly. It doesn't make any sense."

After a long pause, Roz spoke again. "And even if we knew why they left, that would solve only part of the puzzle."

"What do you mean?" Fiona asked.

"None of us heard anything."

"No shit," Jill said. "I can't imagine how that's even possible."

The five of them were quiet and, like Fiona, probably hoping someone would offer an explanation. None would be coming, but she hoped for it anyway. A light sleeper even in the best of circumstances, she couldn't even imagine how she'd slept through all the noise they would have made. Ten huge animals and three men packing up camp would never have been a quiet affair. Even if they'd done everything in their power to move quietly, they could never have kept the horses silent. Yet they had.

"It's just not possible," Roz said.

"But it is," Jill said, her voice low and angry again. "They did it, so it's possible."

Roz barked out a bitter laugh. "But how? Explain to me how the five of us slept through a three-ring circus out here without hearing a damn thing. Explain to me how I managed to sleep three hours later than I have for most of my adult life."

Fiona glanced up at the sky, suddenly recognizing that it was long past dawn, well into mid-morning. She'd never once slept this late camping, let alone the first night.

"What time is it now?" she asked.

Roz stared up at the sky for a long time. "At least eight or nine—maybe closer to ten."

"You don't know?" Jill asked.

Roz shrugged. "No watches, remember?"

"Jesus," Jill said, suddenly speaking in a quiet voice. Although Fiona hadn't liked her anger earlier, she liked her fear even less.

"Do you guys think…" Carol shook her head.

"What?" Sarah asked. "What were you going to say?"

Carol hesitated again, staring at her wife, her lips twisted in a kind of grimace. "Do you think we were drugged?"

"Oh, come on," Jill said, letting out a false laugh. "That's ridiculous."

"Is it?"

"Of course it is! How would we have been drugged without noticing it?"

"The water?" Fiona suggested.

Jill shook her head. "The guys were drinking it, too."

"Maybe they had some kind of antidote."

Jill laughed again. "Do you hear yourselves? This isn't a spy novel, for Christ's sake."

"Anyway," Roz said, "I don't feel like I was drugged. I feel good. Rested, alert—no hangover."

"So we're back to square one," Sarah said. "No one knows anything, and no one heard anything."

"Exactly," Jill said. "Maybe we need to let it go for now and move on to the next thing: what to do about it."

Everyone seemed to relax. Even Roz, who had been bunched up like a fist, unwound a little, her posture now more natural and less threatening. It was true, after all—they had a problem to solve that involved them, first and foremost. The other mysteries could wait.

Roz spoke first. "Okay. Let's check the supplies. Jill, Fiona, make sure the food is still hung in the trees and bring it back here. Carol, Sarah, check the rest of the gear while I get the maps and scout out the trail a little, too, see if I can find anything."

No one argued, each of them setting off at once. Fiona was relieved to have a task—anything to take her mind off what had happened. The men had hung the food about a hundred yards from camp, hidden by the trees around it. As she and Jill walked together, neither spoke. Jill was visibly upset, chewing her lip, her brows knit, and Fiona didn't prompt further discussion. One thing at a time, she told herself.

Four bear canisters hung in the trees, and she and Jill shared a long, relieved glance before they moved to grab the tall, hooked pole someone had propped up on a nearby tree. The canisters had served as counterweights to each other to avoid a trailing line to the ground. Three of the containers held only food, and the fourth had a little food, their lotions, sunscreen, soap, and toothpaste, and the rest of the cooking utensils—anything with an attractive smell for bears.

Jill, a couple of inches taller, managed to snag one canister with the hook. She dragged it down, pulling its counterweight over the branch it hung on. She did the same with the others, and each of them grabbed two to carry back to camp.

In camp, Carol and Sarah had made a small pile of the other gear in the middle of the clearing near the fire pit. Jill and Fiona set the food next to it, and Roz walked over a few minutes later, holding an open map. She reviewed the pile and nodded, clearly relieved.

"Okay—so that's something. They didn't take any food, at least. Things aren't quite so dire if we have the food and the rest of the supplies. Everyone still have their backpacks?"

Fiona had noticed her backpack in the vestibule when getting out of her tent, and she and the others nodded.

Roz let out a long, whistling sigh, closing her eyes. "Okay. So that's something. Things aren't quite as fucked as I thought."

Jill let out a little huff, and Fiona threw her a warning glance.

Roz continued as if she hadn't heard. "I checked out the trail going back toward home a little and found some fresh horse manure—warm, not hot. It was pretty cold overnight, or at least it was getting that way before I turned in, so they must have left sometime in the last three or four hours, or it would be colder. Some of the horse tracks lead that way too, so I think we can safely assume they used the trail to leave, probably right after dawn. With three of them, especially with all the horses, they'll beat us back to the trucks no matter what we do."

She paused and set the map down on top of the pile of supplies, then motioned for them to gather around her to look at it. "We're going to have to get back and find some help. I'm assuming the trucks will be gone, so that means hiking back to the main road and flagging someone down. There should be plenty of traffic on the weekend, even late in the day, so it shouldn't take long to get someone's attention." Fiona leaned down closer to the map as Roz traced her finger along the route.

"How long will that take?" Sarah asked.

Roz considered. "Longer than it took to get here, anyway. We might make it by six, seven tonight if we really book it. I don't like to leave anything here, but we could lighten our loads a little for speed—leave most of the food, maybe. That could cut it down to maybe five or six o'clock."

Fiona and her friends shared a silent exchange. Faced with the obvious choice, Fiona could tell that none of them were happy about it. Beyond the fact that they would be cutting their trip short, the idea that they would probably end up spending the night talking to the police or some other officials was entirely unappealing. Still, what choice did they have?

"There has to be another option," Carol said, clearly frustrated. "Couldn't we just keep going?"

"Yeah," Jill said, nodding vigorously. "Fuck them. We've got our gear. I'm with you, Carol. Let's move forward, not back."

"What?" Fiona said. "That's crazy. What about—"

"Those guys abandoned us!" Sarah said. "It's not like they'll be waiting for us at the end of the trail like nothing happened, ready to take us home. We'd be in the same situation we are now, but two weeks from now and with fewer supplies."

"Anyway, someone needs to tell the police, or whoever, what happened," Fiona said. "They left us here. Someone should do something about it."

"Fiona's right," Roz said. "I'm sorry, guys, but we have to go back. Something's seriously screwed up here."

Jill waved a hand at her as if dismissing this point, turning to face them. "Think of it this way: why let them ruin our vacation?"

"Exactly," Carol said, nodding.

Sarah stared at her, clearly shocked. "Are you kidding me?"

Carol shook her head. "Nope. I want to keep going. Fuck those horse-thieving bastards."

Everyone laughed, though it took Sarah a few seconds to join in. She relaxed a little, Fiona saw, but she was shaking her head.

"What about the marks on the trees? Isn't Fred supposed to come back here by tomorrow?"

Like her, Fiona guessed from their expressions that her friends had forgotten all about the marks on the trees in the turmoil of the morning.

"We have to assume the guys are all in it together," Jill said. "Hell, maybe they even made those marks themselves, had a partner or something yesterday to throw us off."

"How can you possibly assume that?" Sarah was almost shouting.

"Sarah's right," Roz said. "That doesn't sound like them. I know these guys—I trust them." Fiona could hear the dark anger in her voice again.

Jill shrugged, either ignoring or dismissing her tone. "Just a hunch. Anyway, even if they didn't make those marks, we don't know whether Fred was part of this other plan to leave us out here for whatever reason."

"What the hell do you mean?" Roz said, raising her voice.

"None of this matters, Jill," Sarah said. "Even if what you're saying was true, are you seriously saying you're going to let them leave us here? You must be crazy!" She turned to her wife. "How on earth could you be on her side? Back me up here."

"It's not about sides, hon. It's about dealing with the situation. Those guys tried to screw us, but we don't have to let them. We have food, supplies. We can move on."

Sarah was visibly stunned. "I can't believe you. Can you hear yourselves?

"Look," Jill said, holding up her hands. "Maybe this isn't a big deal. Maybe I was too drunk last night to remember what they said. They probably just decided to roll out a little early—no biggie."

"They wouldn't do that," Roz said again.

"What are you even saying?" Fiona asked. "Five seconds ago you were claiming it was some kind of big conspiracy—now you want to pretend it's all some big misunderstanding. And you weren't drunk."

"How would you know?" Jill asked.

"It sounds to me like you'll say anything to get what you want," Sarah said.

"It's not happening, Jill," Roz said, still clearly struggling to contain her anger. "We're heading back. Now. Get packed so we can beat the dark."

She turned as if to do that, but Jill grabbed her arm, clenching it with her fingers. Fiona was sure Roz would swing around and hit her, rage flashing in her eyes so black and hot Jill immediately let go and backed up a step, holding up her hands.

"Jeez, chill. We're not done discussing this, Roz."

"Like hell we're not!" Roz said, finally shouting. She jabbed a finger into Jill's chest, pushing her back slightly. "You don't get to make the decisions here. I do. That's why you hired me."

"Exactly," Jill almost screamed. "We hired *you.* That means you work for *us*."

"What the hell are you saying?"

"Ladies, ladies," Carol said, stepping forward and forcing them apart. "Let's keep our cool here. Calm down."

"She pushed me!" Jill said.

"Walk away, Jill. Take five, would you, Roz? We need to talk, just the four of us."

Roz stared at Jill, still breathing heavily, and Fiona was certain she'd go after her again. She finally stormed off, pounding the ground as she walked away, her posture so rigid she was almost hunched over. Fiona had to fight not to chase her, wanting desperately to explain away Jill's stupidity. But there was nothing to say.

"She can't stop us," Jill said.

"What the hell does that mean?" Sarah asked.

"Exactly what I said. We can go on without her."

Sarah laughed. "And get lost in like a day."

"Sarah's right, Jill," Carol said. "We need her."

"It's impossible without her," Fiona said, feeling desperate now.

"Not if we get the map."

"Can you hear yourself, Jill? Honestly." Sarah shook her head. "And you," she turned to her wife, "what on earth are you thinking? We have to go back."

"But do we? I mean, really, what's the harm? This is supposed to be the chance of a lifetime. We've been excited about this for years now, hon. We have to keep going."

Sarah stared at her for a long, quiet pause. She and Carol were facing each other, almost squared off, like two gunslingers in a shootout. Carol's eyes were open, almost pleading, and Fiona recognized the second Sarah's resolve slipped away.

Sarah sighed. "Fine. But just so you know, I'm still not excited about it. I'll do it only if Roz agrees to come with us."

"What?" Fiona said, incredulous. "You're on their side now?"

Sarah lifted her shoulders. "Not really. But I'm not leaving my wife. Let's all agree, now, guys. I'm sick of fighting. If we can get Roz to agree, yes. If not, then we go home."

Jill opened her mouth as if to argue, but Carol held up a warning hand. "No, Jill. Sarah's right. It's the only way. Roz has to be with us."

Jill finally nodded. "Okay. But who's going to convince her?"

The three of them turned to Fiona, like she'd expected them to, and once again, she was reminded of the afternoon at the brewery four months ago when she'd been bulldozed into all of this. After a while, no one had even asked her if she wanted to go, least of all Jill. They all assumed that, decision made, she'd go along with everyone else. Then, like now, no one cared what she thought.

"So will you?" Carol finally asked. "Go talk to her?"

Fiona had a wild image of herself finally putting her foot down, of telling them all to go to hell. Forcing them, somehow, to listen to her for once in her life. As if that was something she could ever, would ever do.

"Okay. I'll try."

"Try hard!" Jill called after her. Fiona didn't respond.

After a few minutes of searching for Roz, she finally found her. She'd wandered a good distance away from the main camp into the meadow, but Fiona caught a glimpse of her black hair against the rolling green grass. It took her a few minutes to walk over to her, not masking her footsteps so the other woman would hear her coming.

"Hey," she said when she was finally close to her.

Roz was sitting on a log, her back to Fiona. "Hey."

"Look, I'm sorry about Jill earlier. She can be a real—"

"Pain in the ass."

"I was going to say bitch, but you're right, too."

Roz turned around, eyes narrowed. "And let me guess. You're here to do her bidding."

"Everyone's, actually. They all want to keep going now."

Roz sighed and broke eye contact. "Well, that's not going to happen."

"How would you stop them?"

Roz jerked around again and stared at her, clearly incredulous. "How can you say that?"

Fiona held up her hands. "I'm not trying to argue with you. I'm asking you, honestly. I should have asked how *we* could stop them. I mean, if they start walking, what are we going to do? Tie them down?"

"It would be a start," Roz said, a smile tugging at the corner of her lips. "Especially your friend Jill."

Fiona laughed. "She might enjoy it too much."

Roz grinned then, getting to her feet. She walked closer, hands on her hips. "So what do you suggest? What can I say to convince them how stupid they're being?"

Fiona had no response. As a matter of fact, she hadn't thought much beyond coming over here to fill Roz in. She tried to come up with something to say, her mouth opening almost of its own accord, and she blurted the first thing that came to mind.

"Isn't there some kind of compromise?"

Roz huffed. "Like what?"

Fiona spun her hand in the air. "I don't know—maybe like hiking somewhere closer? I mean, instead of going the whole way, maybe going for a week? A few days, even? That might work."

Roz stared at her in silence for a long beat. Some of the anger in her eyes died away. She looked tired, beaten. Finally, she shook her head.

"Why do you let her do this to you?"

"What? Who?"

Roz sighed and grabbed Fiona's shoulders, squeezing them gently. Their eyes met, and Fiona couldn't ignore the flush of heat that swept through her. When Roz finally spoke, her words were quiet, almost a whisper.

"Why do you let her bully you like this?"

She didn't have to ask who she meant. It was Jill. It was always Jill.

"She's my friend. She's my best friend."

"Is she, though? Would a good friend treat you like this? Make you do something you don't want to?" Her tone was still gentle, not accusatory, her eyes deep pools of concern. "You deserve better than her, Fiona. You really do."

Fiona said nothing, unable to meet her eyes anymore. She stared at her shoulder, her emotions suddenly choking her. Roz stepped a little closer and tilted Fiona's chin up to meet her eyes again.

"Do you really want to keep going? Even for a few days?"

Fiona shook her head, her eyes suddenly filling with tears. Now, finally honest with herself, she realized that what she wanted more than anything in the world was to follow this woman anywhere she wanted to go. They were close enough to kiss, and for a wild, hysterical second Fiona almost expected it to happen.

But Roz dropped her hands, stepping back. "That's what I thought. But you still want me to offer it? A compromise?"

Fiona sniffed and nodded. She would never be able to explain why, but Roz seemed to understand. Roz closed her eyes, breathing deeply for a minute before letting her breath out in a long sigh. When she opened her eyes again, she shook her head slightly as if disappointed—whether in Fiona or not, it didn't matter. Fiona's stomach twisted with shame and self-loathing.

"Fine," Roz said. "Give me a few minutes to check out the map. Go tell the others."

Fiona was still disappointed in herself and wanted to make it better, but Roz was no longer paying attention to her. Instead, she was staring up at the mountains, grim and pale.

Realizing she had no way to fix this right now, she walked back to her friends, moving slowly to give herself enough time to compose herself. She wiped her eyes, grateful for the sunglasses in her pocket that would hide her emotion. The others were where she'd left them, sitting on various logs in a loose bunch around the pile of food and supplies. Jill had arranged her expression into something like casual interest, but Carol and Sarah looked anxious.

"She agreed to a compromise."

"What?" Jill said, leaping to her feet. "We never discussed—"

"Jill, quiet," Carol said. "Let's hear it, Fiona."

Jill huffed in anger, crossing her arms across her chest. "Fine. So what's this compromise?"

"A couple of days or so instead of—"

"Nope," Jill said. "Not happening."

"Would you can it, Jill?" Carol asked. "Jesus. Let her finish, for God's sake."

Fiona waited to see if Jill would fight back, and when she didn't, she continued. "That's it, really. That's all I could manage. A few days—no more."

"Well, it's not good enough," Jill said, shaking her head. "Nowhere near good enough."

"No—I think it's a good idea," Sarah said. "It's better than nothing. We'll still get to see some of these woods, and everyone gets something they want."

"Didn't you hear me earlier?" Jill said. "She can't stop us! We can keep going without her."

Carol laughed. "Yes, and like we said—we'll get lost. You know that as well as I do, Jill, especially if she doesn't give us her map."

"Why would she?" Sarah added.

"Exactly."

"So that's it?" Jill asked. "You guys are giving up? Carol—what happened to the chance of a lifetime?"

"Give me a break, here," Carol said.

"And stop making everything so dramatic, Jill," Sarah said. "You know as well as the rest of us that this is better. And really, I was only half-convinced it was a good idea to keep going at all. If it weren't for Carol, I'd probably be heading back right now—on my own, if necessary."

"But—" Jill said.

Everyone turned at the sound Roz's approach, Fiona's stomach fluttering with pleasure at the sight of her. Roz seemed calm, sure of herself again, her earlier anger gone now, or hidden. She was holding the map loosely folded in her hands. She opened it in front of the four of them, pointing down at it.

"About three days from here, there's a side trail we could take out of the forest, toward Old Roach."

"Old Roach? What's that?" Carol asked, bending close to the map.

"It's a ghost town, but it gets a lot of traffic this time of year—four-wheelers, off-roaders, mountain-bikers, that kind of thing. We probably wouldn't have to wait long to ask someone for help. There will probably be people there already." She looked up from the map and stared at Jill. "This is literally the only option. Everything else is too far away. Either we head there, or we go back right now."

Everyone watched Jill to see how she'd take it. She was frowning, her face slightly mottled, but she kept her lips pinched tight. Fiona could see her visibly shaking with her effort to hold back. Finally, she nodded, clearly unable to speak without fighting.

Everyone seemed to sag with relief, and after a few brief words, they moved away to start packing.

Fiona held back and approached Roz, who was bent over the map again, studying it closely. She touched her shoulder gently.

"Thanks. And I'm sorry about them." She meant Jill in particular, but that was implied.

Roz nodded and lifted her shoulders. "Like you said earlier—what can we do? At least this way we'll get back to civilization sooner. It's a shit compromise, but it's all we have. Thanks for helping me, even if it's not the best choice."

"Will you get in trouble—with the forest service or whatever? If we wait, I mean? Don't you have to report crimes right away?"

Roz tilted her head back and forth. "Yes and no. It would be the responsible thing to do in one way, but on the other, I'm obligated to guide the four of you in these woods. Technically, if I leave you alone, I would also be in trouble."

Fiona smiled. "That seems like a reach, even to me. So why do it? You could just leave us here with the map. Why back down now?"

Roz took a step closer, meeting her eyes. "Because you asked me to," Roz said, almost whispering. "No other reason."

Fiona's mouth went dry. Roz's presence was forceful, almost overpowering, and it was all Fiona could do not to take a step closer to her and wrap her in her arms. She caught a faint whiff of sandalwood coming from the woman—warm and natural in this setting.

Fiona swallowed and then nodded. "Okay. I'm with you—wherever we go."

Roz's answering smile was broad and genuine, pleased for the first time since this started. Fiona was suddenly breathless. They were barely more than a foot apart at this point. All she would have to do is lean forward—

"Hey!" Jill called from behind her. "This tent won't take itself down. Get over here and help, you lazy bum."

Fiona couldn't help a little groan of frustration. She turned toward her and yelled, "Just a sec!"

By the time she turned back, Roz was already walking away, and Fiona's stomach dropped with disappointment. She didn't think she was fooling herself, but she'd never been very good at knowing whether someone liked her. Still, she guessed Roz liked her more than anyone else at this point, and that was a start.

Chapter Six

After everyone had broken down their tents and packed their bags, they had a quick, cold breakfast of energy bars and jerky before heading out. Roz had explained that it would likely be about three days to the trail that led to Old Roach. The first and second day would be the same route they would have taken if they were going the whole length. The third, they'd be going off course, on a lesser-developed path. Altogether, it was slightly shy of sixty miles to the ghost town. If they did twenty today, closer to thirty tomorrow, and the rest the next day, they would make Old Roach long before nightfall of the third.

The woods beyond the meadow were thick and dark, much like yesterday before the boulder canyon. Already, the trees were changing slightly, with fewer cottonwoods the higher they climbed. Aspens were still plentiful, but for the most part the trees were different varieties of pine. Despite the gradual lack of leafy foliage, the pine here was dense and tall, and at ground level very little sunlight made its way down to them. So much of the Rockies in other parts of the state had been thinned out by the pine beetle, and Fiona found it strange to walk in a forest that hadn't been affected by it. Her childhood hikes had been like this. She could vaguely remember seeing trees this old and thick here in Colorado maybe twenty or thirty years ago, ancient and grand.

Most of the ascent was gradual, with a few switchbacks up some steeper parts, the rest a gentle upward slope. Their campsite last night had been at near seven thousand feet, and Roz had told them the next camp would be closer to nine. Fiona was used to these kinds of elevations, but that didn't necessarily make it much easier on her. With the weight of her pack and the constant upward slant, she was struggling within the first hour. Luckily, the trail followed the same river they'd walked along yesterday, which meant she didn't have to carry as much water as usual. Every couple of hours, the five of them could stop and filter more into canteens, leaving their larger water bladders empty.

While the trail was generally easy to see and follow, Fiona could tell that, unlike more traditional, established trails, the one they were following hadn't been fully developed or dug out. Fiona had volunteered for several trail-breaking and maintenance crews in the past, and the labor of creating or maintaining any kind of trail was intense but long-lasting. Maintenance or building anew meant digging, cutting, and basically plowing a path through the woods, generally entirely with hand tools. What they walked on today was likely something natural—an old game trail, perhaps. Some work had been done here and there to cut the fallen trees and branches back, but the earth hadn't been turned up and plowed.

For the most part their path was usually easy to see and follow, but occasionally the five of them had to stop as Roz got her bearings. She would pause, stare into the woods, sometimes glance at her compass, and then start walking. When this happened, it was rare that Fiona had guessed the right direction to continue—all directions were the same to the naked eye. Then, as they started walking again, she could occasionally see the subtle signs that this was, in fact, the trail. Whatever minimal work had been done to cut this path for them, it was subtle on purpose. The farther they went, the more certain she was that having a guide was an absolute necessity back here. Had they been on their own, they would have been totally lost. They could follow the river back to the road if it actually came to it, but that gave her little comfort out here in these dark woods.

Few talked in what remained of the morning and early afternoon. Roz maintained some distance, some twenty or thirty feet ahead, and Fiona suspected Jill knew she needed to keep quiet for now. Once or twice, Fiona caught her and Carol sharing a satisfied grin, almost seeming to gloat, but they were careful to do this when Roz's back was turned.

In fact, the only time anyone spoke much before their late lunch was when they hit the bottom of a long, steep rock scramble. Approaching it, Fiona assumed they would start moving in a different direction, parallel to it, until they reached an easier ascent, but when Roz stopped and dropped her bag at the base of a tall boulder, she realized she was wrong.

"We're going up that?" Sarah asked.

Roz nodded, grinning slightly.

"How?" Fiona couldn't help but ask.

Roz laughed. "Very carefully. Actually, it's easier than it looks. Everyone will be roped together, and we'll go slow. I know a little shortcut."

Fiona and her friends shared a dubious glance, and Roz laughed again. "Don't worry, ladies. I've done it a hundred times. Get something to eat and rest for a few minutes before we head up. We'll take another longer break at the top, so be quick about it now—a snack and some water."

She wandered away, disappearing around the edge of another boulder. Fiona suspected that she would continue to keep her distance, from Jill, if no one else, until this was all over. The thought made shame and guilt swell in her chest, her throat constricting with tears. She took a couple of deep breaths and blinked, grateful again for her sunglasses.

"Is she serious?" Sarah asked, still staring up the scramble.

Jill clapped her on the back. "Don't worry about it. The expert will tell us what to do."

Fiona could detect sarcasm in her voice, and she was very glad Roz wasn't here to hear her. She was going to have to tell Jill to shut it, and soon, or they might finally have a real fight. At some point Roz was going to lose it, and however confident Jill might be, she would lose.

The four of them sat down in the shade of the boulder, and it was blissfully cool in the thin mountain air. There had been little to no vegetation on the approach to the scramble, and the sun was scorching and fierce. Fiona was so relieved to release her pack that she had to stifle a moan. She could barely muster the energy to get a snack out of her bag, and her energy bar tasted like dust. She leaned onto her pack, closing her eyes, and started to drift almost at once.

"This is great, isn't it?" Jill asked, startling her awake.

"Hmmmm?" She made herself sit up, rubbing her face.

"Out here, far away from everything and everyone. Isn't it awesome?"

"Sure, Jill. Whatever you say."

Jill frowned. "What the hell does that mean? Aren't you glad to be here?"

Fiona sighed. She didn't want to get into this with her now, so she shrugged.

"What are you guys talking about?" Carol asked. She and Sarah sat a few feet away.

"Nothing," Jill said. "Fiona is being an asshole."

"For God's sake," Fiona said, standing up. "What do you want from me? You want me to be excited about a bad idea? Cause I'm not. This is stupid. We should have gone back."

"You're the one who asked Roz to do this! I thought you wanted to keep going."

"No, Jill. You did. And you bullied everyone into going along with you."

"You didn't say anything like this before."

"Of course I did! You just didn't listen. As usual."

"But why—"

Roz appeared then, a coil of climbing rope hanging off one of her arms. She paused when she hit the shade, taking in the scene unfolding between them.

"Everything okay?" she asked.

"It's fine," Jill said, standing up. "Fine and fucking dandy. Can we get this done already?"

Jill knocked Fiona with her shoulder as she walked by, and for a wild, tantalizing moment, Fiona almost pushed her back. She fought with her anger for the next ten minutes as the five of them roped up together, a loose loop around everyone's waist. Fiona tied in fifth since she would be last in line behind Carol. Her blood was pounding in her ears, and she was even hotter than she'd been walking in the noontime sun. When they finally approached the scramble in earnest, her hands were still shaking with suppressed rage. She didn't have time to be afraid of what was coming.

Nothing had prepared her for this kind of climb. Almost immediately, she realized she was out of her depth. Neither her months at the gym nor her training on the rock wall in town had equipped her for anything this strenuous or difficult. While the ascent wasn't vertical, it was near enough that everyone was forced to nearly crawl on their hands and knees as they moved up the hill. Her boots slipped several times, and the drop onto her knees was worse each time. A little trickle of blood started running down her calf after her third of fourth slip, and her pack was threatening to pull her back and down the hill. The rocks here had pieces of quartz that scratched and cut her palms, skinning them, and she snagged a fingernail on one so hard and so painfully at one point that she called out.

"Okay back there?" Roz called from the front.

Fiona was biting her lip so hard she could only nod, but Roz, not hearing anything different, started moving again. Eventually the slack rope cinched her waist, and she was forced to start inching her way forward again. She lost count of how many times she slammed onto her knees, the weight of her pack throwing extra force into the pain. On top of all this, the sun shone on them as if it were trying to fry them on the rocks. Sweat was streaming into her eyes, stinging and hot, and she could do nothing to stop it, still busy trying to stop herself from falling backward into oblivion.

Tears ran down her cheeks freely, almost of their own will, her mind focused, razor sharp, on moving onward, upward, for what felt like eternity.

When Carol stood upright in front of her, she realized it was finally over. Standing up herself, on solid ground at last, she immediately burst into tears. She was dimly aware of the others removing the rope around her waist and of someone finally steering her away from the cliff, gently pushing her into the shade of the nearby trees.

"Holy shit, look at her hands," Carol said.

Fiona took a deep, rattling breath and finally opened her eyes. The others were clustered around her, clearly concerned, and she managed to shake her head.

"I'm okay. I'm fine."

"Why don't you sit down for a second. Take that pack off and let me see," Roz said, moving forward.

"I'm fine," she repeated.

Roz didn't listen, gently removing Fiona's pack. She pulled Fiona's arm, leading her to a thick trunk that had fallen near the tree line. Fiona sat down on it with numb legs, watching, detached, as Roz dug through her own pack for the first-aid kit.

The others were standing in a cluster some ten feet away, Jill looking distinctly guilty, Sarah and Carol concerned, almost scared. Jill was staring down at the ground, and Fiona's throat constricted again, her shame back, wanting all this to be over.

"Let me see," Roz said, grabbing her hand.

Fiona hissed at the pain but didn't pull away. Her hands were bloody shreds, and the nail she'd pulled hung on her middle finger on a thread of bloody gore, the back of that hand dark with dried blood.

"Jesus, Fiona. Why didn't you stop me?"

Fiona shook her head, unable to come up with a single reply. There was, after all, nothing to say. Even in the midst of perhaps the worst pain she'd ever experienced, she hadn't once thought of asking for help.

Roz spent the next few minutes cleaning and bandaging Fiona's hands. She started by simply washing off the crusted blood with clean water, causing the pain to sing through her, then wiped at them with several little alcohol pads, each of which was dyed a deep red by the time Roz discarded it. When she was done, the tip of Fiona's finger was firmly bandaged, and her hands had been wrapped in gauze, almost gloved.

"That should do for now," Roz said, sitting back on her heels. "We'll need to change the dressing on your finger later since it's bleeding so much."

"Thanks," Fiona said.

Roz touched her knee. "You don't have to feel bad, Fiona. Anyone can get hurt. I just wish you'd said something earlier. You have to ask for help if you need it."

"I wanted…" Fiona shook her head. "I didn't want to slow anyone down."

"You'll slow us down more if you can't keep going. No one will be mad at you if you need help."

When Fiona didn't reply, Roz put her fingers on Fiona's knees, the sensation causing gooseflesh to rise all over her.

"I'm worried about you, you know," Roz said.

"I wish you weren't."

"These guys forced you into this—I know that, but I really wish you'd gone back, even alone."

"I can take it, Roz. I promise."

Roz smiled at her. "I know you can. You're one tough cookie. If I'd lost a fingernail, I'd be crying right now."

Fiona laughed, knowing she was being flattered, but loving it anyway. "You're damn right I'm tough."

Roz smiled more broadly and squeezed her knees again before standing up. "You okay by yourself for a bit? I need to get something to eat."

"Go ahead. I'll be fine."

Roz squeezed her shoulder before walking away. The others were seated far across the little clearing they were in, and, almost as if she'd been waiting for her turn, Jill came toward her.

"Hey."

"Hey."

Jill sat down next to her, both quiet for a long time.

"I'm sorry about earlier," Jill said.

Fiona was surprised and must have shown it, as Jill smiled back. "I know. You're not used to me admitting when I'm being an asshole."

"I didn't say—"

"It's okay, Fiona. I know you're thinking it. And I'm sorry if you think I bullied you into all this. I really thought you'd come around. I honestly didn't know you still wanted to go back."

Fiona stared at her, realizing that she meant it. Jill was so oblivious to anyone but herself, she hadn't read Fiona's actions as anything but consent. Not that this was new. Jill had acted this way throughout their friendship.

Once again, there was nothing to say, and Fiona nodded. Jill brightened at once, clearly understanding her response as acceptance, and shot to her feet.

"Let me have your pack for a few minutes. I'm going to take a little more of the weight."

"You don't have to—"

"I know. I insist. You're hurt. Let me help you out for the rest of the day, at least. I want to, okay?"

"Okay, Jill. Thanks."

Jill smiled at her, looping Fiona's backpack off her shoulder, and Fiona's spirits rose a little at the sight. Maybe, despite everything, things would be okay after all. Jill was trying to make amends, and despite her injuries, the long rest had done Fiona some good. She'd embarrassed herself in front of Roz again, but that was nothing new. The woman was obviously just being nice yesterday and today—she was fooling herself to believe there was any other motive. If she could let go of her crush, maybe she wouldn't have to feel so bad about how she acted in front of her. She could just be herself.

Fiona took a long pull from her water bottle, dumped some on her face, and scrubbed briefly at the sweat and crusted tears with her fingertips. The warm water was still cooler than the hot, almost sultry air.

When she opened her eyes, Roz had approached again, so silently she was almost startled. Roz grinned at her.

"Better?"

Fiona smiled back and nodded. "Much."

"You okay to keep going soon? In fifteen minutes or so?"

Coming from anyone else, she might have found the question a little patronizing. After all, what choice did she have? They couldn't stay here forever. But when Roz asked her, it didn't come off that way.

"I'll be ready."

"Good," Roz said, flashing that gorgeous smile. "Give me your bottle, and I'll fill it for you. Eat something solid, too. We have a long way to go before camp."

She walked away, Fiona's heart lifting even further at the sight of her lithe, almost mesmerizing gait. The last hour had been a disaster, but it hadn't broken her, and it hadn't broken the group. No one was angry with her for the delay, and with the scramble behind them, things could only get better.

Chapter Seven

Roz pushed them hard—almost harder than Fiona could take. Her knees, battered from the scramble, seemed to complain the entire time. They were hiking at a disadvantage today, as they had to go farther, faster than usual to make camp on time. Normally they'd have been on the trail several hours before they started, and with the delay at the scramble, they had to hustle to make up for lost time. Roz had a contingency plan in case they couldn't reach the campsite before dark, but she wanted them to try to make the original destination before implementing the backup option. This meant very infrequent and very short breaks, but with all the recent drama, not talking to each other for any length was probably a good thing.

The sun had started to fade into early evening almost exactly when Fiona was about to call it quits. For what felt like hours now, she'd been battling the urge to simply sit down and stop, and her legs and knees felt like they were beginning to shut down. Already, she was starting to trip more often, losing coordination, and she'd fallen behind the others. She could still see them ahead in the woods, but they were getting farther and farther away. She watched her feet, concentrating on putting one in front of the other without stumbling over them, and when she glanced up again, the others had stopped. At first she thought they were waiting for her, but when she finally hustled up behind them, they were all staring into the woods in front of them. Fiona was panting, and it took her a second to get enough air for words.

"What…" She had to pause and take a shaky gasp, "are we looking at?"

"Shhh!" Jill said.

"I heard something," Roz said quietly.

Fiona could hear nothing over the pounding blood in her ears and her own whistling breath, and both Jill and Carol made quieting motions. She put a hand over her mouth to stifle the sound and tried to listen as she bent at the waist, her other hand on her knee. She heard nothing but the usual sounds of the woods, and when she stood up again, the others were looking around at each other, confused.

Roz shrugged. "I guess I imagined it. Come on. Let's get going."

She started to move, and Fiona almost began to cry. "Wait, wait. I need a minute. Please. I can't keep going like this without a longer break."

Roz turned toward her, looking almost annoyed, but the others were nodding agreement, already taking off their packs. Fiona saw now that their faces were strained, everyone smudged with sweat and dirt. Even Roz seemed a little peaked, her eyes ringed with fatigue. She stared into the woods again and sighed before turning back to them.

"Okay. Ten minutes."

Everyone talked at once.

"What?"

"That's not enough—"

"I'm about to fall over—"

Roz held up a hand. "Guys, I know today has been rough, but we're almost there."

"How close is almost?" Jill asked.

Roz glanced into the woods in front of them again and shrugged. "Half an hour, maybe forty-five minutes from here. Definitely not more than an hour."

Jill sighed and rolled her shoulders and neck. "Okay. Fine. But give us fifteen, okay? I'm about ready to fall down right here." She turned to Fiona. "How are you doing? You okay? Your hands all right?"

With her pack off her back, Fiona felt much better, and she managed a weak smile. "I'm okay. I can go a little farther."

Jill squeezed her shoulder. "I'm proud of you. You're holding up better than the rest of us."

In her near-exhaustion, Fiona found this remark touching rather than patronizing, and tears prickled at the corners of her eyes.

"Thanks."

Jill grinned and winked. "Since you're in such good shape, you owe me a massage when we get to camp. I feel like knives are jabbing me in the shoulders."

Fiona winked back. "I'll do you if you do me."

"Who's doing whom?" Carol asked.

"You can do better than this tramp, Fiona," Sarah said, nudging her.

"She wishes," Jill said, rolling her eyes.

The four of them sat down on the ground next to each other, and Roz wandered ahead a little, ostensibly to check the trail. She was clearly still keeping some distance from them. While they had trekked most of the afternoon in near silence, the atmosphere had been stressful from the moment they woke up. The strain had to be particularly hard on Roz. She had to keep the four of them going, adjust the speed to make up for the lost morning, and deal with whatever emotional turmoil she had to be in after the guys' abandonment and the argument with Jill. Fiona was tempted to walk up to her and offer her recognition and gratitude for all she'd done and gone through today, but she looked peaceful over there on her own.

Jill nudged her in the ribs. "She likes you."

Fiona rolled her eyes. "She does not."

"More than me, anyway. She thinks I'm a pain in the ass."

"You are a pain in the ass."

Jill touched the back of her hand. "I'm serious, Fiona. I think you have a real shot with her. I've seen her watching you a few times and the two of you talking together. Every time she gets a little moony. I'm not kidding you here. She's really into you. You should go for it."

Fiona was about to retort, but Jill was pulled into a conversation about dinner with Carol and Sarah, and she was left to her own thoughts. The idea that Roz might find her attractive was flattering, but she also didn't quite believe it, certainly not with the three of her friends here, too. She was the runt of the litter compared to them. Still, she couldn't help but watch as Roz continued to examine the trail and the woods, her solitude clearly chosen, part of who she was. What would it be like to be part of that quiet peace?

As if she'd sensed Fiona's gaze, Roz turned back toward them, walking softly and surely through the woods, almost silent. She seemed as much a part of these woods as the trees and animals around her, her neutral-colored clothing nearly camouflage.

"That's fifteen," she said.

The four of them groaned in unison, then laughed. Fiona felt suddenly jubilant, excited, even. The fact that they were going to make it to camp felt like a dream. Even an hour ago, she honestly thought she wouldn't be able to do it. Now, as she struggled into her pack again, the aches and pains of the day immediately back and barking for attention, she knew she could do anything. Between the speed, distance, and elevation gain, today had been the hardest day they would have this entire trip, and she'd done it. She could be as proud of herself as she pleased.

"I like the smiles, guys," Roz said, cinching her pack. "I thought you all would hate me by now."

"Oh, we do," Jill said, smiling. "But we're too hungry to care right now."

Roz smiled a little, obviously recognizing the attempt at a joke. "Okay. Let's get you to camp then, and you can eat as much as you want. Maybe you won't hate me so much when your stomach is full."

The trail here had evened out, and, perhaps because of the break, or perhaps because they were almost finished, the final leg didn't feel as arduous as before. Fiona even felt a little spring in her step, as if her pack had magically lightened. The woods were a little thinner, too, the sunlight breaking through a little more often than before. Fiona could tell by the angle of the light that it was late in the day, but they probably had at least another hour to go before they began to lose the light. Even then, there would likely be another hour of dim sunset before it was difficult to see without a headlamp. If camp was as close as Roz thought, they should have everything set up before that happened.

The sound of the water gradually faded, and Fiona remembered that Roz had mentioned that the river diverted from the trail in a few places. She didn't like the idea that they would have to trek farther for the water they would need, nor did she like the thought that they were well and fully lost back here if something happened to Roz. Perhaps because of the lack of water here, the trail was even harder to detect through the woods. Everything was carpeted with dried pine needles, with very little broken undergrowth to point the way. Roz, however, was walking surely, carefully, following some path she could clearly see. Watching her from behind, her strong legs eating up the miles, was the single pleasure of the day.

Right as Fiona's second wind died, and just when her shoulders started to scream again in protest, Roz suddenly slowed to a stop. She turned back to them and pointed.

"We made it."

There, ahead in the woods, was a wide clearing, the end of the day's sunlight streaming down on it like a little oasis. Everyone around her sighed with relief, and the four of them nearly staggered the final yards. Fiona tripped her last few steps, but she managed to snag the side of a tree before going down entirely. She unclipped her chest and waist belts and let the pack drop off her back, the relief so overwhelming she groaned.

"All right," Roz said. "One person should start dinner, one should get water, and someone should set up the tents. I also want to hang half the food so we're not doing all that in the dark, and I'll need a hand. We can do the second half after we eat."

"I'll help you," Fiona said, surprising herself.

Roz gave her a strained smile. "Thanks. Okay. Let's get started."

They divided the food bags into two piles while Sarah started on the tents, Carol set off on the faint trail toward the water, and Jill started dinner. Between the five of them, each person had carried a different part of tonight's meal. Roz had sent them a very detailed list of what to buy and what to divide for every night of the trip. Doing this meant that they could have slightly more elaborate meals at the end of the day, as one-person cooking was slow and generally monotonous.

Fiona and Roz loaded two of the bear canisters, and then Roz led the way through the woods some hundred yards away. Like last night, the canisters were hung as counterweights on a high branch. Bears had learned long ago that they could simply chew or claw through any trailing rope that attached to the ground, so the trick was hanging food in a tree far enough off that ground that they couldn't climb up to it. Obviously, Roz had chosen a specific tree for this long ago, as the one they walked to was ideal—no low branches to climb, the nearest one to the ground far too high to reach. Roz needed her to hold the ropes to keep them from tangling and to keep them taut. She used the hanging branch as a kind of lever to haul the food up with the second rope.

The process was usually slow and tedious, something Fiona had struggled to do well in the past, but this was anything but. Fiona enjoyed watching Roz work. As with everything, she was efficient and sure, none of her movements wasted or rushed. Fiona stood far enough back to be out of the way, which gave her an excellent view of the woman. She didn't even have to worry about staring at her, as she needed to watch her to help effectively.

Roz twitched the second rope, and the other end dropped to the ground. The food hung perfectly above the ground. She gave Fiona a warm smile.

"Thanks for your help."

"Sure," Fiona said, a little breathless. That smile undid her every time.

"You can leave the second rope here since we'll need to do this again after we eat."

"Of course." Fiona dropped it in a heap.

"We should help Carol get the water."

"Mmm hmmm," Fiona said, starting to lose her ability to make coherent speech. Her cheeks were burning, but she couldn't break eye contact with the woman. Roz was staring at her, one eyebrow crooked up in a question, and the expression was so endearing, so adorable, Fiona almost said something about it.

"So we should go," Roz said, clearly waiting for her now.

"Yes."

Roz laughed and shook her head, then walked toward her, in the direction of camp, passing close enough that Fiona felt the heat from her body. The edge of Roz's shirt brushed against the exposed skin on her forearm, and Fiona shivered, closing her eyes. It was all she could do not to grab Roz's arm and…there the fantasy broke down, and Fiona's eyes snapped open. She wasn't brave enough to imagine what came next.

"Are you coming?" Roz asked, already several feet away.

"Yes," Fiona said, and started following her.

They hadn't walked more than a few feet before the screaming started. Both froze for a second, and then Roz took off, running so hard and fast Fiona couldn't keep up with her. She disappeared around a particularly thick clump of bushes, and Fiona almost called out to her to slow down, but someone screamed again, closer, and she made herself keep going. Once she could see Roz again, some hundred feet away back in camp, Fiona pushed herself to speed up. The screams were louder now, and she saw Roz pause, listen, and then race toward the sound.

Fiona was vaguely aware as she dashed through camp that the others weren't there, and the dread she'd been fighting washed through her, closing off clear thought. Who was hurt? Who was screaming? What had happened?

Roz was far ahead now, but her light-colored pants were visible as a flash of brightness in the woods. Fiona made herself go faster, bending slightly at the waist where a stitch had begun, working hard to avoid hitting trees as she ran. Branches were slashing at her face, and she was dimly aware of a sharp, stinging pain across her cheek, but she ignored it, her focus entirely on her moving legs.

She ran into a clearing and almost collided with Jill before she was able to stop herself. She took in the scene in a sweep of terror before she could make sense of what she was seeing.

Carol had been swallowed by the earth, only the top of her head visible. Her face was pinched in pain, and she let out another ear-piercing scream. She'd fallen into some kind of hole. It was some six feet deep, judging by how much of her could be seen, but Fiona couldn't understand what had happened. The ground around Carol seemed to have caved in, but Fiona could see branches sticking up out of the hole around her, too. Almost as if—

Jill said it before she could think of the words. "It's a pit trap. Like for wild boar."

These were, of course, exactly the words she'd been trying to think of. Someone had dug a hole here and covered it with earth and branches. But why? Who?

Sarah was crouched some five feet to the left of the hole, face ashen with horror. Roz sprawled on the ground, flat on her stomach, her hands stretched out in front of her like a swimmer.

"Carol," Roz said, her voice loud, but clear and calm. "Grab my hands. I can't get any closer to you without falling in."

Carol tried, jumping a little inside the pit, but her reach fell far short of Roz's. Roz inched forward a little farther, but the branches underneath her started to snap and crack. She scooted backward quickly and then sat back on her heels. Her expression was frantic, nearly panicked, and Fiona realized then that Roz, for once, needed help.

Fiona checked behind her on the ground and spotted what she needed in seconds. A large branch, almost as thick as the trunk of a small tree, had fallen on the ground nearby. It had been buried on one end by mud and other debris, but it pulled out of the ground with a solid yank.

Seeing her struggle with it, Roz leapt to her feet and moved to help, and the two of them knelt, far from the edge of the pit, and started sliding the branch toward Carol. Carol didn't need to be told what to do. She waited until it was nearly in her face and then grabbed two smaller branches sticking out of the sides. Roz moved slightly in front of Fiona to grip their end of the branch, and the two of them moved backward together, hauling Carol out of the hole and back onto solid ground.

Fiona collapsed backward, a startling, piercing pain shooting through her lower back and tailbone, and watched as Sarah pulled Carol into a close hug. She and Roz stayed where they were, panting, Jill hovering a few feet away.

"Are you okay? Are you okay?" Sarah kept repeating, kissing Carol all over.

Carol was crying, still clinging to her wife, but she managed to shake her head.

"What's wrong?"

"My ankle," Carol said, sobbing. "I think it's broken. I landed on some rocks and branches down in the pit."

She was also scraped up, bloody scratches on her arms and face mixing with the dirt and pine needles on her skin and in her hair.

"Let me see," Roz said, pushing Sarah, not too gently, to the side. She picked up the ankle Carol indicated, and Carol cried out, throwing her head back.

"Sorry. I need to get this boot off to see better." Roz looked back at Fiona and Sarah, and Fiona moved forward, grabbing Carol's shoulder. She lifted her chin at Sarah to suggest she do the same on her side. Sarah paled considerably, but she nodded, putting her hand on Carol's right arm. Carol's instinct would be to try to stop Roz, and they needed to hold her back.

Using her utility knife, Roz cut the laces off Carol's left boot and then spread the edges of the boot as far as she could. Finally, she slipped the boot off. As predicted, Carol tried to sit forward to stop her, but Fiona and Sarah managed to hold her back. Carol shrieked again and then collapsed backward, but Fiona managed to stop her from hitting her head. She'd passed out.

"Maybe that's a good thing," Roz said. She pulled Carol's sock off, and Fiona had to look away, gagging. Sarah's ankle was twisted, misshapen, the skin purple and torn. Even with no experience of any kind of medicine, Fiona could tell it was broken.

"Oh, Jesus," Sarah said, sounding nearly breathless. "Oh, my good God."

"How did that even happen?" Jill asked. "The hole's not that deep."

"She said something about rocks down inside there," Fiona said.

Jill inched closer to the hole, peering inside it as best as she could from a safe distance. "There's something down there, all right. Big, loose stones and thick branches. She must have landed hard when she fell in and twisted her foot or something. Couldn't be more than six or seven feet deep."

"Quiet," Roz said. "Let me think for a second."

"Who would do something like this?" Sarah asked. "Who would dig that pit out here, right on the trail?"

"Shhhh!" Roz said, her patience clearly breaking. "I need to think, but first I need to splint this ankle. I have some first-aid stuff in my pack, but nothing for something like this." She looked at Fiona. "Go find some sticks—six of them, about this long and this thick." She indicated the size with her hands. "If you can't find anything like that in five minutes, make something with a pocketknife. Jill, come with me to the backpacks. Sarah, stay here with Carol, and don't let her move. If she wakes up, try to keep her calm. We'll all be back as soon as we can."

The three of them scattered, Fiona racing into the woods almost as fast as she'd run here. She needed to find the sticks before Roz returned. They had to stabilize that ankle, or Carol would be in excruciating pain. Even stabilized, it was going to hurt terribly. Fiona expected they would get used to her screaming long before they got her out of these woods.

She was bent close to ground, her eyes glued to the dirt, searching for the wood they needed for the splint. She'd found several pieces thick and long enough but needed at least three more. She started moving some of the leaves and brush aside as she walked, and if she hadn't been doing that, she would have walked right into the bear trap. It was buried slightly, with leaves and pine needles, but she saw the jagged metal teeth mere seconds before she stepped on it. She froze, her foot still in the air, and managed to take a wary step backward. She jerked around, visually sweeping the area behind her. More traps were here—three or four she could see, which meant likely more she couldn't. Each had a pressure plate in the center which, when depressed, would make the trap snap onto whatever had triggered it, clamping those jagged teeth into an ankle. While they'd been placed slightly to left of the trail, it would have been easy to stumble into them if you were, like she was, searching for something in the woods.

A scream started rising to her lips, but her terror was deep enough that it stuck in her throat. A high-pitched, whistling moan escaped her lips. She stopped herself from running away, knowing suddenly, instinctively, that if she did, she would run into something else. She froze, peering around wildly before choosing her path backward, moving with mincing steps as she scooted around the traps. Once clear, she walked back toward camp, starting to shake and tremble when she was safe. She almost tripped again but caught herself, grabbing another tree and hugging it fiercely to keep herself from going down.

"What are you doing?" Roz asked, making her jump.

She pointed a shaky finger. "Traps. Bear traps. I almost stepped on them."

Roz's eyes opened wide, and she walked over to them. Fiona almost called out a warning, terrified she would miss one and step on it, but Roz stopped long before she reached the traps, peering down at them from a safe distance. She turned and walked back and held out a hand.

"Come on. We all need to get back to Carol as quickly as possible. We don't know what else is out here, and we can't deal with it now."

Fiona took her hand without thinking, letting the taller woman lead her back to Sarah and Carol, both still down on the ground. Sarah had put Carol's head in her lap. Carol was awake again, her pale face pinched and tear-stained. Jill returned with three first-aid kits, which she opened in front of Roz. She pulled out all the Ace bandages from kits and ripped open a little astringent cloth.

"Did you find the sticks we need?" Roz asked her, kneeling next to Carol's ankle.

Fiona had managed to cling to them despite her earlier terror and held them out. "Only four."

"I need two more. Here, take this," she pulled her Leatherman out of her pocket and tossed it, "and make a couple more from that branch we used to pull her out of the hole."

Fiona set to her task, using the little saw on the Leatherman to cut off two of the secondary branches from the bigger one. She handed them to Roz and watched as Roz prepared the splint. Roz motioned Jill forward, and Jill scooted next to her, her face pale and lips quivering.

"Carol," Roz said, voice low and calm, "I'm not going to lie to you. This is going to hurt like hell. But we need to do this so we can move you back to camp. Also, it will hurt less once it's stable."

Carol nodded, tears still leaking from her eyes, and Sarah squeezed one of her hands. Roz made eye contact with Sarah and Fiona, and Fiona knelt to help hold Carol down again.

"Jill, I need you to help hand me things. We're going to wipe the skin with the astringent, just in case the flesh is broken. Then we'll wrap it once and wrap it a second time with the splint wood to hold it in place."

Jill swallowed and nodded.

"Everyone—try to stay calm. I'll do this as quickly and carefully as I can, but Carol, you yell all you need to, okay?"

"Okay."

Carol bucked backward the second Roz touched her, and it was all Fiona and Sarah could do to hold her in place. Jill grabbed the second foot to keep her from kicking out at Roz, and Carol screamed again in a loud, peeling shriek. The next thirty seconds stretched into eternity, Fiona using all her strength to help. When Carol collapsed into unconsciousness again, she almost collapsed on top of her. Everyone was panting, but Roz worked with her usual efficiency, wrapping the entire ankle once to protect the skin, then walking through the next step with Jill, who positioned the sticks—two on each side, one on front and back—as Roz wrapped them into the next layer. A final layer of bandage was tied on, and the splint looked solid, stable.

Everyone sat back, breathing heavily. As Fiona looked around, she could see equal levels of exhaustion in the way everyone held themselves. Shoulders drooped, faces were tight and pinched, everyone filthy and drenched in sweat and dirt.

"Here," Jill said, handing her an alcohol wipe from the first-aid kit. "Use that on your face."

"What? Why?" Fiona asked. She touched her cheek, and her fingers came away sticky with slightly congealed blood.

"You must have cut yourself when we were running," Roz explained. "Here, let me help you."

Roz scooted closer, resting on the balls of her feet, and took the little towelette out of the package. She leaned closer, her breath warm on Fiona's face, and then touched her face with the cloth. Fiona gasped, reeling back, and then bit her tongue and let Roz work on her, leaning onto her bandaged hands to give her leverage. The towelette was soon entirely red, and Roz had to use two little butterfly bandages to pull the two sides of her cut together.

"You're going to have a gnarly scar there, I think," Roz said, smiling as she sat back.

"That's okay. Scars are cool."

"And badass," Jill added.

She stood, and she and Roz helped Fiona to her feet.

"You'll want to put some Neosporin on it later," Roz said.

"We'll do no such thing," Sarah said, leaping to her feet. Her voice was dark and low. "We're getting the fuck out of here this second."

Everyone stared at her, surprised.

"What the hell are you talking about?" Jill asked. "I don't know about you, Sarah, but I'm dead on my feet here. No way I can hike out of here tonight."

"Of course you would say that," Sarah said, stepping toward Jill, fists clenched. "You're the one that got us into this mess in the first place."

"How is this my fault?" Jill asked. "I didn't booby-trap the damn camp, for Christ's sake."

"We wouldn't be here if it weren't for you. We should have turned around this morning."

"Carol wanted to keep going, too, you know."

"Don't you bring her into this!" Sarah said, taking another step forward.

"Ladies, please calm down," Roz said, moving forward. She held a hand toward each of them, and Fiona was reminded of Carol doing the same thing this morning with Roz and Jill.

"Fuck, no, I won't calm down!" Sarah shrieked. "This is all your fault, Jill!"

"You can't seriously believe that," Jill said. Her anger had deflated, her expression soft with disbelief.

"You're damn right, I do!"

Jill reacted as if slapped, taking a step backward and away. Her eyes darted from Fiona, to Roz, to Sarah, and down to Carol on the ground.

"You all believe her?" Jill asked, her voice trembling.

When no one spoke up, Jill burst into tears, turning away from them and sobbing into her hands. Fiona was initially shocked. She'd seen her friend cry perhaps five times in all their long friendship—twice over breakups, the others for deaths. Her surprise lasted long enough that she hesitated too long to comfort her. Jill stopped sobbing almost as quickly as she started. She spun around, clearly furious with hurt and pain.

"How dare you put this on me, Sarah? How dare any of you? This isn't my fault, goddamn it!"

"Jill," Fiona said.

"Can it!" Jill said. "You've been on me all day! I don't need to hear any more from you."

With that, she stormed away, leaving the three of them standing there, staring at each other.

Fiona moved to follow her, but Roz grabbed her arm, shaking her head.

"Don't. Give her a few minutes. We need to take Carol back to camp, anyway. That should give Jill a few minutes to calm down. And anyway, I think she needs the time to accept the facts."

"I'm not staying here a second longer," Sarah said. "Someone is trying to kill us, or had the two of you forgotten?"

Sarah pointed up into the trees. She and Roz looked up, and an overwhelming horror swept through her. There, up on three trees around the pit, were the same symbols they'd seen carved into yesterday's campsite.

Chapter Eight

As the light began to die out of the day, Sarah finally accepted that, despite everything, they would be spending another night here in the woods. Fiona and Roz hadn't even needed to convince her. In the end, Carol had done most of the work, and not by arguing. She was clearly exhausted, and her exhaustion seemed to make Sarah recognize her own.

She, Roz, and Fiona managed to carry Carol back to camp, using a crude litter made from a tarp. Carol promptly fell asleep, and Sarah and Roz had searched the camp carefully for traps. They discovered another patch of bear traps, this one on the path to the latrine, but the camp itself, as far as they could tell, was completely clear.

While they'd searched, Fiona had talked Jill into helping her set up the tents. Jill wasn't speaking at all at that point, but she hadn't hesitated to help, moving on to getting the dinner things ready once the tents were up.

Everyone ended up eating another cold meal, all of them too exhausted to whip up the energy for anything else, everyone silent except for Carol's occasional groans of pain. Jill wouldn't look at anyone, her eyes downcast, face pale. Fiona wanted to offer her something, some absolution or forgiveness, but she was so tired she couldn't think of anything to say. Time would help, but maybe Roz was right. Maybe she needed to feel this way.

Finally, long before full dark, everyone helped Carol into her sleeping bag before they all went to their own tents and collapsed.

Fiona and Jill were woken several times by screaming in the night. Carol would pass out or fall asleep for an hour or two, only to wake everyone again with her cries. Fiona could hear Sarah soothing her from twenty feet away, her voice low and unintelligible, and Carol's whimpers would gradually quiet and then cease again. Fiona would be tense for a long time after that, finally drifting off into an exhausted sleep before, almost as soon as she closed her eyes, it would start all over again.

Startled awake by screams for the fifth or sixth time, Fiona finally gave up and started getting out of her sleeping bag. A dim light filtered through the tent walls, which meant that dawn was finally here.

"Where are you going?" Jill asked, blinking sleepily.

Fiona met her eyes and frowned. "I can't take it anymore. If I don't get out of here and walk around a little, I'm going to lose my mind. I barely slept."

Jill snatched her wrist, squeezing it painfully. "Don't leave me. Not until I go back to sleep. Please, Fiona. I can't stay in here alone."

Fiona's stomach dropped with dread. Besides Carol's injuries, Jill's fear and shame were possibly the worst part of all this. Always brave, always confrontational and brusque, the very definition of confidence, this diminished, frightened version of her friend was more terrifying than Fiona would ever have believed.

She relaxed a little and patted Jill's shoulder through her sleeping bag. "Okay, Jill. I'll stay for a little while. Close your eyes. Carol will quiet down again soon."

Almost as if she'd willed it to happen, Fiona could hear Sarah again, soothing her wife, and Carol's whimpers and groans once again subsided.

Jill's grip gradually relaxed a few minutes later, and her face lost some of its tightness as she drifted off. Still, even sleeping, she appeared troubled, upset. They'd all been too tired to do much of anything last night, and Jill's face was filthy with dirt and sweat.

Fiona brushed a lock of sweaty blond hair off her face and rubbed her shoulder again, lightly. A deep and powerful tenderness swept through her, and tears prickled at the corners of her eyes. Her own exhaustion was making her sentimental and overly emotional, but she suddenly felt closer to Jill than she had in a long time. A fierce, almost angry protectiveness clenched at her heart, and remarkably, for a few minutes, she was no longer afraid. She would do everything to protect her friends. They were going to make it through this.

By the time she finally crawled out of the tent, leaving a sleeping Jill behind, the sunrise had already turned to a weak daylight, and the camp seemed almost bright in the early morning sunshine. She zipped up the tent as quietly as she could behind her and bent to lace her boots. Her body was screaming with aches and pains, and she limped stiffly toward Roz, who was already up and fully dressed. One look at her face, and Fiona could tell she'd either skipped sleep altogether, or had gotten very little. That confident strength seemed dim, weakened somehow, her tanned face drawn and pale.

"I hope I didn't wake you," Roz said, gesturing at the two little camp stoves she'd set up. "I was trying to be quiet, hoping everyone could sleep in a little to give you some extra energy."

"What about you? Don't you need sleep, too?"

Roz gave her a wan smile. "I'm okay. I'll be okay. I couldn't really sleep."

Fiona glanced toward Carol and Sarah's tent and nodded. "Me either. Not deeply, anyway."

"This is such a fucking disaster," Roz said. They'd been talking in near whispers, but she said this almost normally. Fiona made a quieting gesture, and Roz nodded and lowered her voice again. "Sorry. I'm just upset. I'm angry with myself."

"What? Why? You didn't do anything."

"Exactly. That's exactly right. I didn't do a goddamn thing. We should have gone back yesterday. I don't know what the hell I was thinking to agree to this."

Fiona took a step closer to her, tempted to touch her arm. She didn't like seeing this woman, previously unshaken, so down. Her hand rose slightly at her side, and she forced it back down. Now wasn't the time.

"You agreed to a compromise. None of us thought things would get this bad," Fiona said.

Roz sighed and shook her head. "Yes, and now here we are, up shit creek, and all of this could have been avoided. I'm a goddamn idiot."

"Hey," Fiona said, louder this time. "Stop saying that. You helped plenty yesterday. None of us knew how to help Carol—only you. And you got us here."

Roz laughed, the sound bitter and dark. "Yes, Fiona, and where are we? In the middle of fucking nowhere, surrounded by traps and God knows who or what the cause is, or why they're doing this shit to the trees."

"So what are we going to do?"

Roz stared at her, clearly surprised. "We? What do you mean? I'm the one that has to get us out of this."

Fiona didn't argue, biting back a hurt retort. "Fine. What are *you* going to do?"

Roz shrugged, sighing again. "The one thing I can do. I'm going to go get some help. If I leave after breakfast, I should be able make it to the road by dark if I run part of the way. I'll travel light—some snacks and my water filter. I've done thirty miles in a day before, no problem."

Fiona stared at her, horrified. "You mean you're going to leave us here?"

"Of course. That's all I can do."

"Are you kidding me?"

"Hey!" Sarah called from her tent. "Can the two of you keep it down out there? We're still trying to sleep."

"No, it's okay," Carol said, loud enough for them to hear. "I'm done pretending. What are you guys talking about out there?"

Sarah opened their tent flap, and she and Carol were revealed, both on their stomachs and propped up on their elbows, their faces small and strained inside their tent. Fiona was about to share what Roz had said, but she turned at the sound of another zipper. Soon Jill had climbed out of their tent, fumbling with the flap and the laces on her boots. She made eye contact with them and looked away, that shame and fear still clear on her face. Finally, she, Jill, and Roz walked closer to Carol and Sarah's tent and sat on the ground so that they all faced each other.

Roz rubbed her mouth. "I was telling Fiona that I'm going back. It's faster going back than going forward—thirty miles instead of a little over forty. I should be able to make the road if I run some of it—there's a couple of stretches where I can do that safely. I'll get Search and Rescue here as soon as I can—tonight maybe, or tomorrow morning."

"I'll come with you," Jill said, moving as if to stand up.

Roz grabbed her arm and pulled her back to the ground. "Hell, no. You're staying right here. I can move faster on my own."

"And leave us here?"

Roz nodded. "Yes. If I go right now, by myself, I might make it by four or five this afternoon. I could get people here quickly, maybe before midnight if they use vehicles."

"Can they do that?" Fiona asked. These woods were incredibly dense. With no roads in these woods, she couldn't imagine how they would bring a car or truck here.

Roz shrugged. "They use a helicopter sometimes, and horses. If they come on foot, it would be tomorrow sometime, and that might be too late."

"What do you mean?" Sarah asked, her voice rising with fear.

Roz leaned over and touched her arm. "I don't mean anything, Sarah. I'm just worried about Carol's ankle. It could set funny if a doctor doesn't see it soon, and she's obviously in a lot of pain. She needs sleep and rest, and she can't get it out here like this. But I don't really know how serious her ankle is. I only have a little first-aid training. Anyway, I don't want to risk it."

"Look," Jill said, frowning at the ground. She finally made eye contact with Roz. "I know this is all my fault." Her voice broke, and Fiona surged toward her, putting an arm around her shoulders. No one said anything as she cried, and some of the anger drained from Roz's eyes.

Finally, Jill wiped her eyes with her arm and continued. "I'm sorry. You were right, everyone. I was a dumbass. We should have gone home yesterday. I admit it now. And I know you're pissed at me. I'm pissed at myself, too. But I need you to hear me right now. Especially you, Roz."

Roz chewed on her lip before nodding. "Okay. Say it."

"You're forgetting something."

Roz frowned. "What?"

"Someone in these woods is trying to kill us. They've trapped us here on purpose."

"There's no—"

"Do you honestly think we're safe here? What about the traps and the shit in trees, for God's sake? And what if something happens to you? We'd be totally screwed. You're telling us you might not come back until tomorrow. What happens if you don't come back at all?"

Roz opened her mouth to retort but didn't say anything. If she'd thought of this possibility earlier, she clearly didn't have an answer for it. Maybe she'd hoped no one would bring it up. It was true. Things would be even worse if they waited another day and she never came back, and Roz had either ignored this fact or had suppressed it. Fiona had remembered thinking yesterday that following the river would eventually lead them back to the road, but how long would that take? Days? Longer? And what about Carol? Would she and Jill leave her here with Sarah if Roz didn't come back?

"So what's your suggestion?" Roz finally asked.

Jill flinched in surprise—clearly expecting more debate. She licked her lips. "Like I said—I'll go with you. I'm fast. That way, we can watch out for each other, and, if need be, the second person can go on alone and get help."

"I'm faster," Fiona said, the words out of her mouth almost the second she thought them.

Jill laughed. "Bullshit."

"I am, too. Remember that last time trial we did? I beat you by thirty seconds."

Jill shook her head. "Yeah, but I was still getting over that cold—"

"You were not, and you know it. I beat you fair and square."

"What is this, kindergarten?" Carol asked. "Jesus Christ, who cares who's faster? Just decide already and go."

Fiona stared at Jill, her anxiety a desperate burning in her throat. She knew why she wanted to go with Roz, and it had nothing to do with how attractive she was. No, her motivations were pure cowardice. She didn't know if she could stay here and remain sane. Jill was motivated by her shame but, at the same time, her pride. Her fear this morning in the tent was gone now that she had a task. She wanted to be the hero.

"Okay. I won't argue with either of you anymore," Roz said, standing up. "I'm going to start getting some supplies ready. Whichever one of you comes with me, be ready in half an hour."

After she'd walked away, Jill put a hand on Fiona's shoulder. "Look—I know you want to help, but you also know I'm right. I'm faster and I'm stronger. I can see you're on your last leg. And you're injured."

"It's a scratch—"

Jill shook her head. "No, honey, it's not. If you could see yourself in a mirror, you'd know it's not just a scratch. You look terrible. And there's no way you could make it thirty miles today."

"Why can't we both go?" Fiona could hear the whine in her voice and flushed with embarrassed shame. Jill was right. They both knew that.

"Because I can't do this without you," Sarah said, squeezing her hand. "I need help with Carol until they come back. And, if worse comes to worse, I would need help getting her out of here. I can't do that on my own."

Maybe it was the terror of yesterday, or maybe it was her emotional and physical exhaustion, but Fiona's eyes filled with tears. Hurrying to avoid embarrassing herself, she launched herself to her feet, hands clenched at her sides. She was being childish, petulant, but she couldn't help it.

"Fine. Just leave, Jill. You got us into this, so you can sure as shit get us out. Go. Be the fucking hero."

"What are you talking about? Fiona, come on—don't be this way."

But Fiona was already walking away, seconds away from a full-on tantrum. She could hear the others calling her, but the blood pounding in her ears drowned out all sense from their words. She walked quickly, almost jogging away, heading in the direction of the hanging food. Still, when she hit the end of that trail, where most of the food was still hanging from the tree above, she kept going. The trees here were a little sparser, so she could find her way back, no problem. She needed to get away from her friends for a few minutes. If she didn't, she would end up saying or doing something rash, something she'd regret. And surely Roz and Jill wouldn't leave without saying good-bye.

Almost as if obliging her sulk, she spotted a large fallen tree some fifty feet beyond the food. She found a kind of seat in the center of the tree trunk, almost as if nature had carved it for her. She threw a quick glance behind her as she approached, relieved to see that she could spot her path backward quite easily. The plastic bear canisters were obvious in the morning light. Despite her earlier confidence, the last thing she wanted was become lost back here.

The tree seat was at the edge of a small clearing ringed with pine and a few hardy-looking, twisted aspen. Her seat was shaded, and her legs dangled forward, toward the clearing. She closed her eyes, taking a deep breath of the clean, warm mountain air, catching a whiff of baking pine needles. The birds were well into their morning song now, loud and cackling in the trees, and the air was nearly dead-still and breathless. Even here at nearly 9,000 feet, it would be a warm day.

She opened her eyes, feeling some of her earlier tension already draining away. After all, she told herself, Jill was the better athlete, and that's all that mattered. She needed to go back and apologize, wish her and Roz success, then see what she could do to help Carol and Sarah. Maybe a hearty breakfast would make everyone feel better about all this. Her stomach growled at the thought, and she smiled in weary relief, feeling almost normal for the first time all morning.

With that, she launched herself up and onto her feet, her muscles groaning in protest. She'd pushed herself too hard yesterday, she knew that, and so did everyone else, apparently. It was true. She'd never make it thirty miles today, even without a heavy backpack.

She turned to return to camp, but something caught the corner of her eye. She spun back toward the clearing, puzzled, thinking that she'd sensed movement—an animal perhaps—but there was nothing. Her gaze darted around the trees, and she squinted, wondering what she'd seen. She shaded her eyes with a hand, peering into the trees. Frowning, once again turning to go, she finally saw it—a flash of bright green just beyond the trees across the clearing. It was a little patch of some plant, she told herself, but even before she moved closer, she knew better. That green was recognizable, very specific.

She walked toward it carefully, almost tiptoeing, as if afraid to startle or scare something wild hiding there in the woods. She wasn't even halfway across the clearing before her suspicions proved right.

There, knotted around one of the mottled trunks of a young aspen, was a bright-green bandana.

CHAPTER NINE

Fiona walked toward camp, her legs and body stiff and wooden. She walked as if expecting a blow from behind, but she was too terrified to run. She could hear the others' voices long before she saw them, and some dim part of her was aware of laughter and something like excitement in their tone. When the camp finally came into view, somehow Carol had been moved from her tent to a makeshift seat, a large log, her ankle propped up on a rock. Jill, Sarah, and Roz had also dragged over pieces of wood to sit on, and everyone was smiling at something. Jill spotted her first.

"Ah, there she is." She didn't sound happy.

"Back there," Fiona managed, pointing vaguely behind her.

Jill must have seen something in her face, as she rushed forward, just in time to catch Fiona as her knees weakened and buckled.

"Jesus!" Jill said, grabbing her under her armpits.

Roz and Sarah joined them, and all three helped Fiona across the camp, lowering her gently onto a second log. Jill knelt next to her, meeting her eyes.

She put her hand on Fiona's forehead and told the others, "She's cold as ice." She grabbed Fiona's shoulders. "What's wrong? What happened?"

Fiona was shivering now, but she managed to raise a shaky hand and point back the way she'd come. Her teeth were chattering as she said, "Back there. On a tree in the clearing."

All four of them looked that way and then at her.

"What? What is it?" Jill asked again.

Fiona shook her head, unable to say anything.

"Someone get her something hot to drink," Roz said, pointing at the little stove. "There's some coffee."

Sarah came back with a steaming plastic mug. She knelt and placed it in Fiona's hands, wrapping her fingers around it.

"Take a drink, honey," Sarah said.

Fiona tried, but her trembling hand made some of the liquid slosh out. Sarah steadied her and helped her raise the cup to her lips. The warmth coursed through her at once, and Fiona closed her eyes, the pleasure intense despite the bitter flavor. Almost at once, she felt steadier, stronger, and when she opened her eyes, Sarah seemed relieved.

"Thank God. You were as white as a sheet."

"I'm okay now," Fiona said, her voice stronger than before. Her fear, so overwhelming less than a minute ago, felt tamped down, but she could sense it there, waiting to pounce.

Sarah took a deep breath, motioning for Fiona to do the same. She did, and on the second breath, the air was no longer hitching in her chest. They did this together a few times, the fear finally ebbing away again.

"Tell us what you saw," Roz finally said.

Fiona pointed again. "Back there, in the clearing past the food, I saw a green bandana tied around the trunk of a tree."

Everyone reacted as if slapped. Roz actually took a step backward, her eyebrows shooting up.

"What? Are you sure?"

Fiona nodded. "I'm sure. I got close enough to see it. It's exactly like the ones the guys were wearing."

Roz rubbed her mouth, staring down the trail. Her eyes were troubled, dark, and Fiona knew then that she was as scared as any of them. Her control and courage, which she'd managed to draw on all day yesterday, were slipping.

"I need to see it," Roz finally said.

Fiona climbed to her feet, the world swaying, and Jill leapt forward, grabbing her arm. Fiona brushed her hands away, frowning. "I'm okay. I can walk."

"You almost fainted—"

"I'm fine now. It'll be faster if I show her."

"Okay, but I'm coming, too."

"No," Roz said, surprising them both. "No more risks. We don't know what's back there. The fewer that go, the safer you'll be. Jill, stay here with Sarah and Carol. We'll be back soon."

With a task to accomplish, Fiona felt more of her fear subside. She handed the mug of coffee to Jill and gestured for Roz to follow her. "Come on—let's go."

Everyone shared a look, and Jill gave Roz a quick nod of agreement. "Okay. But be careful." Whether she meant Fiona or Roz, they both nodded.

Fiona walked back toward the clearing, her mind sharper than it had been since yesterday morning. Her previous terror—so overwhelming, so tremendous—had turned from a fear-choked fog into something else, something precise and clarifying. It seemed, as she walked, as if she could see and hear more distinctly now. Even her muscles and injuries, which had ached and groaned last night and this morning in a way she'd never felt before, seemed to have loosened. She felt agile now, almost quick, the sharp awareness in her head and body something like readiness.

They hit the edge of the clearing, and Fiona stepped over her previous seat on the fallen tree. Although it had been mere minutes since she sat there, smiling to herself, that version of herself seemed remote, removed, almost as if she'd never existed. She could hear Roz behind her, but she hadn't waited or watched for her a single time since she'd started leading her this way. Part of her knew that if she allowed herself to stop or hesitate, this sharper, clearer fear inside her would turn into something like panic.

She paused a few feet from the tree with the bandana, and Roz walked up next to her, stopping to stare.

"Oh my God," Roz whispered.

Roz was rubbing her mouth again, hard. Fiona touched her arm, and she jumped, her hand dropping back to her side.

"Sorry," Fiona said.

"It's okay. Just jumpy."

Roz stepped forward and examined the bandana closely, her face pinched with confusion.

"There's more than one," she finally said.

"What?"

"There's more than one bandana here. They're tied together, like a rope."

"Should we take them?"

Roz's eyes flashed at her for a second, and then she nodded. She started working at the knot with her fingers but soon stopped to pull out her Leatherman. She flicked out a knife and cut at the fabric.

"Too tight."

The bandanas loosened into her hands, one of them falling to the ground. She leant down to pick it up, holding both up for Fiona to see. They were quiet for several long seconds.

"Why are they doing this?" Fiona finally asked.

Roz frowned. "What do you mean?"

"Why are they trying to scare us like this? Why did they put those traps in the camp?"

Roz continued to frown at her, and then her expression cleared. "Oh, I see what you mean. You think the guys are doing all this?" She looked down at the bandanas in her hands. "That's one version of events, I suppose."

"Who else could it be?"

Roz met her eyes. "We heard someone else, remember? The first day. And I thought I heard something yesterday, too. That wasn't the guys the first day, and I'm pretty sure it wasn't them yesterday, either."

"Who, then? A stranger?"

Roz nodded. "I mean, there's no way to know, but it would explain a lot."

"How so?"

Roz stared into the woods before responding. "The guys were scared, too. That afternoon, and that first night, when we saw the marks in the trees. They were really spooked. And now this." She held up the bandanas. "Almost like…" She shook her head.

"So you think they didn't just leave us yesterday?"

Roz shrugged. "I don't know. You're right—it could be them. In fact, that's more likely, given that no one else has been back here in these woods for a long time. They know this place almost as well as I do. I'm the one that trained them."

"But if it isn't them…"

Roz nodded. "Exactly. If it isn't them, then they've been, I don't know, abducted or something. Maybe hurt." She held up the bandanas. "And someone took these from them."

"But the horses! Where are the horses?"

Roz shook her head. "I don't have all the answers, Fiona. I'm in the dark here, just like you. But like I said, you're right. They could be doing all of this." She sighed. "I don't want to think of them like that. They're my friends as much as my colleagues. I just can't imagine them doing something like this—like any of this." She paused, rubbing her mouth once more. Her lips were getting swollen from the repeated gesture, but it was clearly unconscious on her end—a tic, maybe, that came with stress.

What bothered Fiona was the fact that there were only two bandanas. Counting Fred, who'd left the first night, there should be four, total, one for each of the guys. Roz was upset, obviously closer to breaking than she'd been when they first made it to camp yesterday. Still, the idea of the two missing bandanas niggled anxiously at the edge of Fiona's consciousness as the two of them stood there. She'd have to think about it more and wait to talk to Roz about it later.

"Should we look around?" Fiona asked. "See if there's something nearby? A footprint or something?"

Roz gestured helplessly at the woods around them. "Where would we even start? This is the peak of the growth season. See all that brush? We wouldn't be able to see anything even if we tried—not unless they'd been incredibly careless." She frowned. "And so far, that's exactly what they're not. I haven't seen a single sign of another person. The traps and the marks in the trees, yes, but nothing else."

"So what do you want to do?"

Roz shook her head. "I really don't know. It's not safe here for anyone right now. Leaving someone, anyone, behind, would be stupid. But what else can we do? Carol will never make it back to the road on that ankle."

Fiona touched her arm again, this time meaning to offer some comfort. Roz didn't flinch or react in any way, so she left her hand there, squeezing lightly.

"There's nothing closer than the road? Nothing at all? Somewhere we could all go?"

Roz started to shake her head and then paused, confusion clouding her expression. "Actually, now that you mention it…"

"What?"

Roz looked as if she were trying to remember something, her brows knit and the corners of her mouth creased. Finally, she shook her head. "I can't be sure, but there might be something nearby. I need to see the map again to check."

They made their way together toward camp, careful, but one step slower than a jog. Roz still held the bandanas loosely together in one hand, almost as if she'd forgotten them. Once or twice they had to walk single file to fit on the trail, but they naturally fell in step next to each other the moment they could. Fiona felt something like hope blossom in her chest. With Roz seeming more like herself, things were better, and some of that crystalized fear was pushed down and away.

Sarah and Jill leapt up from their makeshift seats when they saw them. Carol blanched at the sight of the bandanas. There was no mistaking that color.

"Oh, God," Jill said, almost whispering.

Roz glanced down at the bandanas before handing them to Fiona. "Wait here," she said, and rushed across the camp to her tent.

"What is she doing?" Carol asked.

"She's going to check the map," Fiona answered, staring at the bandanas. Both were stiff in her hands, as if still encrusted with sweat. She made her way to one of the logs and sat down, setting the bandanas down on the ground near her feet. She didn't want to touch them anymore. She rubbed her hand on her dirty pants, the sensation of the gritty, green cloth still haunting her palm.

"You guys have to leave me here," Carol suddenly said.

Everyone stared at her, and Sarah laughed. "Don't be silly. No one's leaving anyone."

Carol shook her head. "It's not safe here. We can all see that." She peered up at her wife. "Don't you see? You have to get out of here. I'll slow you down." She pointed at the bandanas. "Two people are already dead, maybe more. I can't…" Her voice wobbled. "I can't let anyone hurt you, too."

Sarah knelt next to her and pulled her into a rough hug. Carol started sobbing into her shoulder, the two of them shaking quietly as she cried.

Jill gestured for Fiona to follow her, and they walked a few yards away.

"Did you and Roz think of something?" Jill asked.

"Roz wasn't sure, but she thinks there might be something closer—somewhere we could all go." She glanced at the two crying women. "We can't leave them. No one should stay here, especially alone."

Roz approached them then, making a wide path around Carol and Sarah. She gestured for Jill and Fiona to join her a few feet away, where the leafy branch of an aspen had fallen to the ground.

The branch was obviously new, the leaves still green and hardly wilting. It created a kind of surface, however, and Roz was able to lay her map down on it for all three of them to see.

"Here's us," she pointed, "and here's where we started. Here's Old Roach, the ghost town, and here," she indicated a closer spot, "is the old Powell homestead. It's outside of this forest to the east."

"What's there?" Jill asked.

"Not a lot. Some stonework left from an old cabin, and a few old plows and things like that."

"So why would be go there?"

"Because…" Roz traced a finger along a thin red line, "there's a trail here. A well-used trail this time of year." The other end of it met a road to the northeast.

"So what would that get us?"

"A phone, maybe."

Fiona frowned. "Would a phone even work out here? I mean, even if we find someone with one?"

Roz shrugged. "Maybe. My phone works sometimes when I have it, but I've definitely seen a lot that don't. It depends on the carrier."

"What if we don't find anyone?" Jill asked. "You say it's well-used, but that doesn't mean we're guaranteed to find anyone there. Especially on a weekday. We won't get there 'til what, Wednesday morning? Tuesday night, if we're lucky? It's going to take a long time with Carol."

"It's just another option," Roz said. Rather than angry, she sounded disappointed, whether in herself or in the fact that she'd been shot down, Fiona couldn't know. Judging from this entire morning, Roz was perhaps one or two steps from giving up, and she seemed to be grasping at straws.

"What are you guys talking about over there?" Carol called.

"I'll go fill them in," Jill said, walking away.

Fiona stayed with Roz, the two standing close enough that she could feel the heat from her arm. She squeezed her hand.

"It was a good idea," she said, trying to break the awkward silence.

Roz squeezed back and then sighed. "No. Not really. Jill's right. It might not work, and we can't risk it right now. We need certainty. Any more mistakes and we could end up worse than we are now."

"What are the distances again?"

"About forty to Old Roach, about twenty to the Powell homestead, and about thirty back to where we started with the trucks."

"How long is the trail to the homestead from the road? If we didn't see anyone at the homestead, I mean, and we had to hike all the way to the road."

Roz bent down, examining the map. "I've walked the whole thing in one morning before. Can't be more than six or seven miles one way."

"So it might still be the fastest route to a road."

"If it is, it would be only a three- or four-mile difference, maybe less, between that way and going back to where we started. If I get some paper, I can do the math, but I think that's about right. Twenty-six, twenty-seven miles to the road through the homestead. And I wouldn't be as sure of the route there, so it might take us longer, anyway."

"Which one has the better trail? I mean in terms of elevation and hills and things like that?"

Roz examined the map again and shook her head. "The one to Powell might be a little flatter on today's stretch, but tomorrow would be worse, for sure—uphill most of the way. You sort of walk down into that valley to the homestead from the road, if I remember right."

"So that's your answer," Fiona said, lifting her hands. "Shaving off three or four miles isn't enough to risk it. We can't be sure we'll see someone when at the homestead, so we have to assume we won't, which means walking the whole way to the road."

Roz's expression cleared a little, and she nodded, obviously relieved. "You're right. Thanks. I'm glad we thought it through. I wanted to make sure we weren't leaving an option unexplored."

"I get it. I really do. Let's tell the others."

She turned to leave, but Roz grabbed her hand, drawing her back around. Her expression was still strained, but some of that weariness seemed to have left her eyes.

"Thanks, Fiona. I mean it. I feel like…" She shook her head and laughed, weakly. "Like I'm losing my mind. I'm glad there's a voice of reason around here."

Surprised and pleased, it took Fiona a while to respond.

"You're welcome."

Chapter Ten

It was late morning by the time they were ready to leave. First, it had taken considerable time to get their gear organized. They needed to pack lightly, but still be safe enough to travel through the woods for three or possibly four days. The initial idea was that two people would carry their essential gear in two backpacks, while the others helped with Carol, switching roles throughout the day. Everything else would be left at camp to be retrieved later. They'd left most of the food hanging in the bear canisters, but everything else would be exposed to the elements and wildlife, so they needed to decide what was essential and what wasn't.

As for Carol, they'd discussed a number of ways to carry her through the woods. Jill suggested constructing crutches or a walking stick, but no one knew how to do that effectively or well, especially as their tools were limited to two Swiss Army knives and Roz's Leatherman. A litter, they decided, would be too hard to carry between two people, meaning those carrying the backpacks would be overburdened.

They finally settled on a travois, which was constructed using a large tarp secured to two wooden poles with bungee cords. Carol could sit in the little depression made by the tarp, almost like a seat. They used a fleece blanket as a kind of shoulder rest for the person dragging it. Only one person could drag it at a time, but, with practice and help, the others could switch with some ease. They all took turns trying to move her around in the travois in the safety of the campsite, and everyone but Fiona managed to move somewhat gracefully in a small circle without jarring her too badly. Fiona, however, couldn't do it. While she could move the travois, in jerks and stops, any fair-sized branch or rock stopped her entirely. She simply wasn't strong enough.

No one seemed upset with her, but it put more of burden on everyone else, as it meant she couldn't take her turn later today. While the others made up a schedule for the rest of the morning and early afternoon, she excused herself, telling them she was going to check their gear one more time. She was doing that, but she also wanted to hide her shame, feeling as if she would burst into tears if anyone so much as looked at her. A lot of her feelings resulted from fatigue and stress, and the last thing she needed was for someone to call attention to that state, even if they were trying to make her feel better.

"Bet you wished you spent more time in the gym this spring," Jill said, making Fiona jump. She'd snuck up behind and grinned when Fiona spun around.

Fiona frowned at her. "You think this is funny? Cause I don't."

Jill sighed. "Jeez, lady. I was only trying to make you feel better."

"Well, it didn't work. I feel like shit. Everyone else can do their part, and all I can do is watch."

"There's a lot of guilt floating around right now, Fiona. I'm guilty, Carol's guilty, and now you feel guilty, too. I know this sounds like I'm just trying to make you feel better, but you have to let it go for now. We'll have time for guilty later. Right now we need to get moving." Jill touched her arm. "And you're doing more than watching, Fiona. You'll be carrying one of the backpacks. That's something." She smiled. "After yesterday, the last thing I want to do is carry that goddamn thing all day again. At least I'll have breaks."

Fiona turned around as quickly as she could, trying to hide the tears that sprang to her eyes. Jill's pity was almost worse than the shame she already felt.

"Hey," Jill said behind her. When Fiona didn't respond, she wrapped her arms around Fiona from behind and gave her a gentle squeeze, resting her chin on Fiona's shoulder. "I'm sorry. I know you want to help. No one blames you. You're smaller than the rest of us—that's all."

Fiona's arms were stiff at her side, but she nodded. "I know. And I'm sorry for getting upset. I know you're trying to help. I feel useless. I'm…tired, and scared, and I want this to be over."

Jill released her and then walked around to face her before digging her fingers into her shoulders. She stared into Fiona's eyes for a long time before speaking.

"You listen to me now, Fiona. Are you listening?"

After a brief hesitation, she nodded.

"Good, because I want you to hear this. We are getting out of here. No one is going to die. We're going to be okay."

Tears were sliding down Fiona's face, and the lump in her throat made it hard to speak. "How can you know? Any of us could—"

Jill dug her fingers in again, harder, almost painfully. "Because I won't let it happen. From here on out, I've got our backs, okay? I won't let anything happen to you or anyone else. I'm not going to fuck up again."

For a moment, Fiona believed her. Despite Jill's disheveled appearance, with her dirty face and clothing and her wild, unkempt hair, a clear determination burned in her eyes. She meant what she said and believed it wholly, and it was almost enough to go along with her, as usual. But Fiona also knew that she couldn't always be trusted. Even when she believed things entirely, Jill wasn't always right. If yesterday didn't prove that, nothing did. Still, Fiona saw no point in challenging her now. Jill had said all of that at least as much for herself as for Fiona, possibly more.

She managed a weak smile. "Okay, Jill. I'll keep that in mind."

Jill nodded and let go of her shoulders. She started to lean down to grab one of the packs and then stopped, grinning at her with a little mischief in her eyes. "Oh, hey, I forgot to tell you something."

"What?"

"Next year, I want you to plan our vacation. I think it's time you had a turn to screw things up."

Fiona couldn't help but laugh, and they shared a quick hug. Despite everything, Jill was still her best friend. While her grandiose statements had to be accepted with some skepticism, her intentions were almost always good. Maybe believing her would make things better. She already felt better than before.

"Okay. I'll remember you said that."

By the time they rejoined the others, Carol was being lowered back into her travois. While the comfort level wasn't great, she claimed that she wasn't in pain as long as she could extend her injured ankle a little and rest it on something soft. What this meant in practice was that she had to be lowered backward into the divot that formed with the weight of her body, sitting down into the tarp, and then her injured ankle placed on top of a pile of fleece jackets they'd tied together into a kind of pillow that hung suspended between the two poles with rope. Fiona could see the strain on Carol's face as she fought against the pain, but, once she was settled, some of it eased and she relaxed slightly, closing her eyes. Her face was sickly gray, her lips pulled inward against her teeth, but her hands were no longer clenched at her side. Finally, she leaned back a little, breathing heavily. They'd rested the poles of the travois against a tree to save the first carrier's strength. Everyone waited, like Fiona, clearly recognizing that she was in considerable pain. Finally, she opened her eyes and smiled at them, tears sparkling in the sunshine.

"Better," she said. "It hurt going down, like it did earlier, but it's not so bad once I'm here. The pillow helps."

"If it's too much, hon, we can stay here while the others—" Sarah said.

"No. We're getting out of here right now. I can't stand another hour in this hellhole."

Sarah nodded, clearly upset but not willing to argue with her in her condition. "Okay. But you tell us the second you need a break. The second. Can you do that for me?"

Carol nodded. She seemed small, shrunken somehow, that strong, muscular goddess from the brewery all those months ago diminished by her pain. Most of this was an illusion brought on by Carol's uncharacteristic vulnerability, but it gave Fiona a sick, cold, sinking sensation in the pit of her stomach. If a woman like this could be brought so low, what did it mean for the rest of them?

"I wish we could elevate that leg more," Roz said, shaking her head. "I don't like that it's below the rest of you like that."

No one responded. A litter would allow her leg to be higher than the rest of her, but that simply wasn't possible until they made some miles. Maybe on the last stretch of the trail, when they could leave some more of their things, like the tents and sleeping bags, they could switch to a litter. For now, this was the only option.

"We'll take lots of breaks," Roz finally said, as if trying to talk herself into this plan.

"How long do you think it will take to get back?" Jill asked.

"There's no way to know right now. I can estimate when we stop for the day, based on how far we make it. I'm hoping for at least ten miles today. If we can do more, then we might make it by tomorrow evening if we start early enough in the morning. But that's the best-case scenario. If I had to guess, we'll do maybe eight to ten today, fifteen at most tomorrow, which would leave the rest for Wednesday morning."

Again, no one replied. Some part of her knew it would take longer than the best-case scenario, and she was pretty sure the others did, too. They'd practiced with the travois here in camp, where the ground was flat and relatively clear of debris, but the trail wasn't like that. It would be hard going most of the way. No one had even mentioned the rock scramble. Already, the sun was nearly overhead—close to noon, if Fiona was reading it correctly.

They'd be lucky to make much distance at all before they'd have to stop.

Roz insisted on the first shift with the travois, and the three of them helped lower it onto her shoulders. She grimaced as the weight of it hit her, and initially she had to plant her feet wide apart to hold it. Fiona helped move the fleece blanket around on her shoulders until the folds were smoothed out, and Roz finally let out a little breath of relief.

"It's okay now. Let's get going. I'll have to lead, whether I'm doing this or carrying a backpack."

They waited as Roz started forward, back the way they'd come. Sarah fell in line behind her, then Jill, with Fiona taking the rear. She was certain she'd spend the whole day back here, regardless of who was carrying the travois. She couldn't offer anything beyond carrying the heavier pack.

Things fell apart almost at once. The pace was excruciatingly slow. Even with Sarah, Jill, and Fiona helping Roz navigate over some of the larger stones and branches, either pushing or pulling parts of the travois to help, they couldn't move more quickly. The density of the forest slowed every step. Now and then, they would hit a surprisingly clear, wide passage, only to be blocked by two or more trees that grew too closely together. This meant backing up a few feet and then looking for a clearer way around. Fiona spent most of this time simply watching the others struggle, frustration with herself and the situation growing into something like anger as more time passed.

"I need a break," Roz finally said. This was after a tortuously slow maneuver around a grove of aspens. On their path around, they had encountered mud and boulders and thick, twisted bushes. Ten or fifteen minutes had passed, and they'd made it perhaps that many feet.

Sarah and Jill immediately leapt forward, lifting the travois off Roz's shoulders and swinging it to lean against a tree. Roz was breathing heavily, sweat streaming down her scarlet face. Fiona glanced behind them and was certain she could see something metal gleaming in the woods—something they'd left behind in the camp. It had been nearly an hour, and she could probably walk back in less than five minutes.

"This isn't going to work," Carol said from the travois. "It's taking too long."

Jill and Sarah immediately started to reassure her, but Fiona noticed that Roz didn't comment. She'd been the one doing the work, and her silence was telling. Fiona had been thinking the same thing. Roz made eye contact with her, and Fiona nodded slightly. She got it.

"Carol's right," Roz said, loud enough that the others stopped speaking.

"What the hell is that supposed to mean?" Sarah demanded.

Roz took a deep breath, sighing. "It means exactly that. This is not the way to do this. It seemed like a good idea, but it isn't working. Better to stop now than waste any more time."

"How can you say that? We've barely started."

Roz shook her head. "I'm telling you—it's not working."

"So what are we supposed to do now?" Jill asked.

"What you should have done to begin with," Carol said. "Leave me here and go get help."

"That's not going to happen," Sarah said, her voice so low and dark she was barely audible. "No one is staying here. Especially you."

Carol stared up at her wife. Leaned against the tree this way, her seat was hardly off the ground. She still looked small, vulnerable, and yet, Fiona saw, her expression was relaxed, determined, as if she no longer doubted something. Her fear had gone.

Carol's face hardened with determination. "Could you guys give me and my wife a few minutes? We need to talk."

"We're not leaving you here," Jill said.

"Jill, please." Carol spoke without pleading, without any inflection at all. She expected Jill to listen.

"Come on," Fiona said, grabbing Jill's hand. She glanced at Roz, and the three of them walked back toward last night's camp, stopping when they could no longer hear the others, some fifty yards away. Neither Sarah nor Carol had raised her voice yet. They seemed calm, but Fiona expected an argument was on the way.

Fiona slipped the heavy pack off her back and leaned it upright against a tree next to Jill's. Jill was staring back at the others, her arms clenched across her chest, clearly upset. Fiona approached, making Jill spin around, her face a mask of pure rage.

"How can you go along with this?" Jill asked.

"With what?"

"With whatever cocked-up idea this woman has for us?"

"This woman," Fiona said, pointing at Roz, "is the only reason we're alive right now."

Jill made a face. "How on earth do you believe that?"

"Gee, let me think," Fiona said, becoming angry now despite herself. She started counting off on her fingers. "For one thing, the guys are gone—probably abducted or worse. When did that happen? When she wasn't there to protect them. Two, she knew what to do with Carol—"

"Oh, don't give me that shit. She was ready to leave her behind before, and now she has an excuse."

"Three," Fiona said, as if she hadn't been cut off, "she's the only fucking person with any ideas here and the only person who knows how to get us out of here. You tell me, Jill. Do you honestly think we're getting anywhere today with Carol in that thing? Maybe we'll make it what, two, three miles before dark? How can that make any sense? We'll starve to death before we get anywhere."

"Why are you siding with her?" Jill was almost screaming now, her face inches away. "Just because you have a thing for her—"

Fiona pushed her, hard, and Jill reeled back, barely catching herself from a fall. When she'd caught her balance, she looked shocked, her eyes brimming with tears.

Roz had stayed silent throughout this exchange, standing a few feet away. She moved forward now, between them.

"Stop this right now, both of you," she said. Her voice was even, calm, but with a hint of dark anger. "Fighting each other won't do anything. You're wasting time. All we did yesterday was fight, and see where it got us."

Jill still had that startled, hurt expression, but she'd dropped her hands to her side. Her cheeks were red and splotchy with emotion. She seemed frightened now, rather than angry, but Fiona didn't feel in the least bit bad for what she'd done. Still, she kept her mouth closed rather than goad her.

"Jill—face the facts," Roz said. "There is no fucking way we're getting Carol home in that thing. I'm the strongest person here, and I know my limits. It's not going to happen. We have to go back to the original plan. Two of us will go for help, and the others will wait here."

Jill stood up straighter, her face hardening again. "Well, I don't give a shit what you think. I'm not leaving my friend out here, no matter what."

Fiona didn't understand why this had become so important to Jill. A couple of hours ago, before she'd found the bandanas, Jill had been keen to leave everyone else behind, including Carol. Fiona wanted to believe that this was some newly discovered altruism on her part, some new determination to help her friend at all costs, but that wasn't Jill. Fiona didn't think her attitude had much to do with self-sacrifice at all, regardless of what she'd said earlier. No—Jill was being stubborn. She'd gotten something into her head, and she wouldn't back down.

"Jill, come on," Fiona said.

Jill held up a hand. "I don't want to talk to you right now, so shut the hell up. You just pushed me. You have no say in anything of this, as far as I'm concerned." She shook her head. "How could you be so selfish?"

"Me?"

Jill shook her head again and stormed off, back toward Carol and Sarah. Fiona took a step forward to follow her, but Roz stopped her with a light hand on her arm. She shook her head.

"I wouldn't."

Fiona sighed and nodded. "Yeah—I know. But she's being a complete dick. I'm sorry about what she said earlier. And I meant what I said. You're the only one here that has any good ideas."

"Seems like Carol knows that, too."

"But how do we convince the others?"

"Maybe *she* will. Obviously, I don't think she should stay here on her own, but I can't imagine anyone except her going along with that possibility, anyway. Sarah will stay with her. She was right earlier, too. Another person needs to be here with them in case I don't come back."

Fiona sighed. "That means me, I guess."

Roz shook her head. "I don't think so. Not with Jill feeling like she does now. And I know it's not fair, I know she feels bad about everything yesterday, but I don't trust her to have my back, not after what's happened. We need to get everyone back to camp, and then you and I will leave. We'll use the daypacks and move quickly. We won't make it back to the road tonight, not unless we hike in the dark, but we could make it by tomorrow afternoon."

Fiona was pleasantly surprised. She'd convinced herself she was staying behind and was more than pleased that she wasn't. She knew she shouldn't feel this way, that she was, at best, being selfish, at worst cowardly, but she couldn't help it.

Trying to hide her shameful joy, she said, "Okay. Let's go talk to them." She turned to do that, but Roz grabbed her hand again, holding it this time rather than letting go.

"Before we do, I wanted to say thanks."

"For what?"

"For standing up for me like that. For saying all those things about me to Jill. I almost believed you myself."

"I meant it. I think Jill knows it, too. She's just being stubborn."

"Well, thanks anyway. I've been doubting myself a lot the last twenty-four hours. I'm glad to know at least one person has some confidence in me."

Despite everything, Fiona's face heated with embarrassed happiness. Their hands were still locked, and Roz's eyes were set on hers, so she must have seen her reaction, but she didn't say anything about the blush.

"I do," Fiona said. "Have confidence in you, I mean. I trust you."

Roz nodded, her expression serious. "Good. You should. I'm not going to let anything happen to you."

Unlike when Jill had said something like this, Fiona believed her, and her relief was so overwhelming, she felt as if she might cry. Before she could say anything in response, Roz had let go of her hand and started walking toward the others. Fiona ran forward to catch up.

Chapter Eleven

As far as Fiona could tell, it was early afternoon. She sat with her feet in the stream, the alpine water so frigid they'd long gone numb. Here in this cove, the water was diverted into two streams around a large boulder, roiling, nearly river-strength on the far side, calm and pooling here in a small eddy, almost peaceful. The water was crystalline, enough current keeping the mud and debris from gathering in this little pool. She could see minnows darting around, magnified with the refracted water.

They'd made it back to camp perhaps an hour ago. Getting back had been a little faster than going the other way. The travois had made tracks in some parts of the trail that made it easier to drag back. Everyone remembered the parts they needed to avoid, so that saved them even more time. What had taken perhaps an hour in one direction was reduced to maybe half of that. Fifty feet from camp, they'd abandoned the travois, and Sarah and Jill had simply carried Carol back to her old seat on a log in the center of camp. Tense, no one spoke, probably all afraid they'd start fighting again. As Jill and Sarah set up the tents again, unpacking what had taken an hour to pack, Roz excused herself to plan for their journey.

To get away from them all, Fiona decided she would fetch some water to leave for the others and top off the bladders she and Roz would carry in their daypacks. She'd filtered water into the Nalgene bottles and bladders and then managed a quick, cold shower-like bath by kneeling in the little pool here and splashing water onto the back of her neck and arms. She was careful to keep it off the cut on her face. The last thing she needed was giardia on top of everything else.

Now she sat, almost cold despite the heat, still slightly damp. She didn't know exactly how long she'd been gone, but the others knew where she was, and no one had come looking for her yet. Carrying the empty and near-empty water bottles and bladders had been easy enough, but she could never bring them all back to camp on her own, not in one trip anyway. She didn't know if she wanted help or if she was just lonely. She felt sick about Jill, her words and the push, but she wasn't exactly sorry, either. She regretted that it had come to that, necessary as it had been. She also didn't expect an apology, and she wouldn't offer one herself, but she didn't want things to end like this between them before she and Roz left. Letting this fight hang between them might mean the end of their friendship altogether.

Part of her, a dark part, wondered if perhaps that wasn't a good thing. Jill was a bully—everyone knew that, even Roz, who'd just met her. Some of Fiona's other friends had long ago made it clear they wouldn't see her if Jill was going to be there. Fiona nearly disappeared in the shadow of Jill's personality. She was more herself when Jill wasn't around. What made her so reluctant to drop her? Right now, it was hard to remember anything good about their friendship.

She heard footsteps long before someone spoke.

"That looks nice," Sarah said.

Fiona turned to her, smiling. "It is. You should try it."

"Maybe later. I need to get back. I came to see if you need any help."

Fiona sighed and nodded. "Yes, thanks. They'll fit in the backpack, but it would be too heavy to carry them all at once."

Sarah started stuffing the water bottles into the backpack as Fiona dried her feet and put her boots back on. It would be foolish to start hiking until her skin was completely dry—that was a recipe for blisters. Still, she didn't regret the little dip in the water. She felt better, more awake now. Some of her anxious jitters had dissolved during this long, solitary break, replaced by something like certainty, reassurance. She had a clear task to accomplish, and all she could do was try to finish it.

"I can carry this much," Sarah said, hoisting the backpack. "Can you bring the rest by hand?"

"Sure. Thanks again."

"Don't stay here too long. Roz was almost ready to leave when I headed this way."

"All right. I'll come back with you."

If Sarah heard Fiona's reluctance, she didn't say anything about it. Fiona was grateful for her tact. Clearly the fight was between her and Jill, no one else. Everyone but Jill seemed to have accepted the situation, but even that wouldn't convince Jill that she'd been wrong. Jill rarely came to a decision through any influence beyond her own.

They'd forged a new trail to the stream yesterday to avoid the traps, but their progress was still slow as they fought their way through the undergrowth here. It took almost ten minutes to reach camp again, and by the time they got there, Fiona's dip in the water was long forgotten. She was sweating heavily, and her damp feet were chafing inside her boots.

Jill was conspicuously absent. Whether she was hiding in her tent or somewhere else, Fiona tried not to care. They would either hash this out now, or it would fester between them until they were safe again, if not forever. If Jill was too much of a coward to address this situation now, Fiona was almost convinced that she was better off without her.

She sat down on one of the logs near Carol and took off her boots again, letting her feet air-dry. They were still soft and wrinkled from their time in the water, and she needed them as near to normal as possible before she started hiking again. She blotted at them with a little camp towel, the pink skin supersensitive.

Roz was leaning over the map, her back to them, two little daypacks on the ground near her feet. Finally, as if satisfied with something, she turned around, smiling at Fiona.

"You're back," she said, walking closer. She set the daypacks down on the ground, leaning one on Fiona's makeshift seat.

"Yep."

"You ready?"

Fiona peered down at her feet. "Give me five more minutes."

"That's fine. I want to talk to the others first, anyway."

Sarah, nearby, walked closer, putting her hand on her wife's shoulder. "What's up?"

Roz peered around the camp, frowning. "Where's Jill?" When no one responded, Roz cursed under her breath and stormed off, calling Jill's name. She returned a minute or two later, shaking her head.

"I saw her sitting on that log near the clearing where we found the bandanas. She didn't respond when I called her name."

Fiona and her friends shared a look. They knew this version of Jill—the childish, sulky one. No one could do anything about it until she decided she wasn't upset anymore.

"It's okay," Carol said. "Just tell us. We'll fill her in when she stops having a tantrum."

Roz seemed as if she wanted to argue, but after a quick glance at the sky, she nodded. "Fine. We've wasted enough time as it is. First, I wanted to give you this." She handed over a folded map. "You have a compass, right, Carol?"

"Yes."

"Good, okay—that means I can keep mine. I put little notes in the map with landmarks to watch for. I'm also going to tie some flags as Fiona and I go. I've only got the one roll of flagging, so they'll be pretty far apart, but I've also tried to draw the trail on there as well as I can. Carol, I know you said you're pretty good with a compass, so if you have to leave camp, you should be able to help the others follow it if you go slowly enough."

How that would physically work with Carol's injury was apparently not something anyone wanted to talk about, so no one brought it up.

"Is this the only map?" Sarah asked.

Roz nodded and sighed. "We had five of them. The guys had the others. I was planning to give all of you a copy, but I didn't get a chance before…everything happened."

"But what will the two of you use?" Carol asked.

"I think we'll be okay. We're going back over old ground. The trail here was fine."

"But what if it isn't?" Sarah asked. "What if something's changed? Or what if you see something and need to avoid it?"

Roz blew a curl of sweaty hair off her face. "We'll have to cross that bridge if we come to it. We can always follow the water if we need to. And I know these woods well enough to navigate off-trail. Regardless, I'm not leaving you guys here without a map. I know I could find my way out eventually, no matter what, but you guys would be high and dry without some guidance."

Again, no one brought up the obvious: how could they possibly even try to make it back with Carol in her present condition? The question hung in awkward silence in the air for several long seconds.

"When do you think you two'll get back to the road?" Carol finally asked.

Roz shook her head. "No way to know. If we're lucky, tomorrow afternoon, maybe late tomorrow morning. Again, if we're incredibly lucky and nothing goes wrong. The sun sets late and rises early this time of year, and we'll use all the daylight we have today. If we don't see any cars on the road, there's an emergency callbox maybe two miles back toward Highway 14. Search and Rescue might be able to bring a helicopter back here by tomorrow evening. That clearing over there is plenty big enough for one, or least big enough for them to lower a litter. I can tell them how to find you."

They were quiet for a while. Carol, after glancing back at Sarah, finally spoke. "Okay. I guess my next question is this: how long should we wait for you to come back?"

Roz didn't respond. She stared down at the ground, biting her lip. Of course Carol would be the one to ask this question. While everyone else was pretending everything was fine, Carol was the one living in real pain and danger. She was also the only person among them that hadn't lost her calm. Despite everything, she was as level-headed as always—realistic, pragmatic.

"I want to know," Carol added.

Roz looked up at the sky and down at the ground again, rubbing her mouth. After glancing at Sarah, she sighed and finally made eye contact with Carol. "Okay. Let's see—it's Monday now. The longest, and I mean the very longest, it would take us to reach the road is tomorrow evening. Say we're too exhausted to keep going, and camp at the first campsite tomorrow, or even at the parking lot, that's Wednesday morning for first contact with Search and Rescue, so they would be here in the helicopter either Wednesday afternoon or evening sometime. If they don't approve a helicopter—I can't imagine why, but let's say they don't—that would get them here on foot Thursday, at the earliest, or maybe Friday morning."

From this answer, it was clear she had thought out several scenarios. Fiona was certain there were other possibilities she hadn't mentioned, but her answer was detailed enough that she must have thought most of them through.

Carol stared down at her injured leg. Again, no one wanted to talk about what would happen next, but it was clearly weighing on her. After glancing at Fiona and Sarah, Roz walked over to the bear canisters a few feet away and touched the top of one, drawing everyone's attention.

"With the two of us gone, the three of you have about two weeks' worth of food—more if you ration it a little while you're here in camp. Cut out a snack or two, have one light meal a day, and you could last more like eighteen days without much effort.

You have two water filters with replacements, fuel for the stoves, and shelter. You're in good shape."

Everyone was quiet, anticipating the next question.

When she spoke, Carol's voice was barely audible. "You still haven't answered me. How long should we wait?"

Roz closed her eyes. The fatigue was clear on her face. She clearly didn't want to be the person to make what could be a life-or-death decision.

"If it was me—"

"It's not you," Carol said. "It's me. Tell me how long we should wait." Her confidence was back. She sounded like herself again.

Roz's expression was deadly serious. "Sunday at the very latest. Start heading back then if no one has come for you by Sunday morning. You and Jill will have to use a litter, Sarah. Aim for five miles a day, and you could get to the road in five or six days. I think you and Jill could manage that much with breaks. You're both strong, healthy. It could be done, and you'd have plenty of food to make it all the way to the road. If you wait too much longer, you might run out before you get back."

No one mentioned the obvious. If Roz and Fiona didn't find help, if they were prevented somehow, or hurt or captured by whoever had done the same to the guys, who was to say that the others would make it? And who was to say that Sarah, Carol, and Jill would be safe waiting here? This was obviously a place these people had been before. What if whoever was doing this came back before Search and Rescue got here? They would be completely vulnerable.

They had all been thinking the same thing. But talking about the *might*s was unproductive. Even the idea that she and Roz might not make it back was too much for Fiona to cope with. They had a task to accomplish and worrying about something that might or might not happen wouldn't do anyone any good.

Roz broke the tense silence. "Fiona, are you ready?"

"Yes. Just give me a second to get my boots on."

"I'm going to go tell Jill we're leaving. She might ignore me, but I feel like she should have a chance to…I don't know."

A chance to say good-bye, Fiona thought. She focused on her boots as Roz walked away, using the excuse to hide her anger. They'd been talking here for close to fifteen minutes, and Jill hadn't bothered to check in. If anything, Fiona was glad she wasn't here.

Roz was gone long enough that Fiona took the opportunity to check her daypack. It was much smaller and lighter than the one she'd carried here and earlier today, and when she peeked inside, she could see why. She saw several emergency ration bars and almost groaned. She'd eaten these before at an outdoor-supply trade show and hadn't been able to choke down more than a bite or two. They were dense and dry—salty, bitter, and disgustingly sweet at the same time. However, they had an extraordinary shelf life and packed a huge number of calories in a small size. They were often distributed at sites of natural disasters or famine, which was about the only time anyone would be grateful for them. The bars could be broken into four pieces, each with about 500 calories, as a meal replacement. There were five in her pack, or five days' worth of calories. Roz had also packed a toilet set—an orange trowel, TP, and hand sanitizer—as well as her fleece jacket and hat, a clean pair of socks, a plastic, folded poncho, a tiny space blanket, a headlamp, and a hammock. The idea, after all, was for the two of them to move quickly, almost unhindered. With two liters of water inside the back bladder, this was the lightest she could travel.

Roz's pack was heavier than hers and obviously fuller. Of course, Roz was bigger and taller overall, clearly stronger, so this wasn't exactly a surprise. Still, Fiona couldn't help but worry that she was unable to pull her own weight. Roz would have to work harder to have her along on this trip. Without Fiona, she could probably leave even more behind and move quicker, too.

Stop that, she told herself. Roz needed someone with her—that made her valuable on her own, regardless of the extra burden. Also, Roz was capable of making her own decisions and knowing what her own limits were. If she thought she could handle the heavier pack and basically speed walk for thirty miles with it on her back, then she could. Roz was not the kind of person to suffer for no reason. Maybe she could convince her to share some more of the load tomorrow.

Roz returned to camp then, and Fiona couldn't help the little trill of excitement that ran through her at the sight of the taller woman. Even now, after all that had happened, she was gorgeous. More than her looks, her calm efficiency and assured confidence were comforting, calming. With her, things would always work out. She'd always have a plan of action.

She gave Fiona a quick grin. "Okay. Let's get going. We have about six hours of full daylight left, maybe another half hour of twilight we can use, and I want all of it. If we push it, we might still make it to the first camp, or just shy of it. There's a spot I know about five miles closer to us that would be fine for camp, but I still want to try to go all the way."

They each grabbed a bladder of water and slipped it inside the pockets at the back of their packs. Roz was carrying the water filter with one replacement. In this heat they would have to filter more on almost every break. In several places, the stream was relatively far from the trail, so they'd have to be careful to fill up often enough not to run out.

After the last two days, the little daypack felt nearly weightless on her back. This was an illusion—she'd feel it soon enough—but she wondered now if this wasn't the best way to backpack: as light as possible.

"What did Jill say?" Carol asked.

Roz shook her head. "Nothing. I gave her the brief version of our conversation, and I know she heard me, but she kept her back to me the whole time."

Sarah shook her head, frowning. "I'll go talk to her in a little while. Sorry she's being such a shit."

The four of them hugged good-bye, Fiona and Roz kneeling for Carol. As she and Roz started walking back toward home, she threw one last glance behind her at the two of them. Sarah was standing with her hand on wife's shoulder, smiling and waving. Carol didn't wave. She looked scared, terrified even, the easy confidence gone when she thought no one was watching.

Fiona wished she hadn't seen her expression. The hope and reassurance she'd felt deflated, disappearing before she and Roz were even out of sight. Despite the heat, she felt chilled, the woods rising before her now menacing and dark.

Chapter Twelve

They'd been hiking long enough that, despite the small load Fiona was carrying, the daypack was starting to dig into her shoulders. Some of this came from the residual aches and pains caused by the heavier pack she'd carried yesterday. Still, Fiona also knew that most of her fatigue resulted from the simple fact that she'd barely slept or eaten in the last twenty-four hours. She was starting to shut down. She'd managed to shape up a little the last four months working out with Jill, but she was no superhero. Between the stress and the fatigue, she was reaching the end of her stamina.

If Roz felt anything like she did, she showed no sign of it. She'd kept the same brutal pace, some five or six yards ahead of her, rarely slowing or stopping. She walked shy of a trot, once or twice glancing back as Fiona fell a little too far behind, her stern expression enough to encourage Fiona without comment. She also caught up anytime Roz paused to tie a piece of bright-pink flagging. She placed each one at eye level on a low branch of a tree or a bush. As her supply was limited, she flagged only when the trail turned sharply to the left or right or in a place where it might not seem very logical to keep going straight. They had to hope that if the others eventually came this way, someone would be able to find the next flag if needed.

Fiona had been trying to search for signs of the trail all afternoon. Occasionally, the trees naturally parted in front of them, and the meandering nature of their path was easy to follow. Once or twice, she even saw the scuff mark of a boot or an animal on the ground, or a broken twig. Still, without Roz leading her, she'd have been lost. Hopefully, Carol could figure it out if she had to lead the others this way.

She shook her head, cursing herself. She shouldn't think like this. That specific worry assumed that something would happen to her and Roz. If things worked out, the others would never need to try to follow this trail. They'd be rescued directly from their camp. She had to hold on to that idea or give up right now. Why keep going if she believed their efforts were in vain?

Snapping out of her reverie, she realized she'd fallen farther behind in her musings. Roz had stopped, hands on her hips, to wait for her. Fiona pushed herself a little and jogged to catch up, but Roz stayed where she was until she reached her.

"What's up?" Fiona asked, almost wheezing.

"It's about dinnertime, and I'm out of water. Let's refill and take a food break. I'm pretty beat."

Fiona had to look away to hide her nearly giddy relief. She turned a little and focused her gaze toward the sound of the water. It was very close here, almost loud, and she could see the lighter area through the trees where the water cut through the woods.

"Good idea."

Roz started walking toward the sound of the water, and Fiona fell in behind her.

"It would be a good plan for me to check out our location, too," Roz added. "I might be wrong, but I think we're not as far as I hoped we'd be by now."

"I thought you didn't have a map."

Roz glanced back and nodded. "I don't. But I wrote down some of the information for myself so I could check in occasionally. It's not perfect—far from it, but it was the best I could do freehand and without a lot of time. Also, with no clock, some of my calculations are guesswork, but I'll have a better idea of where we are when I check the sun and my compass."

When they reached the stream, the water was rushing by in tumbling, bright-white rapids, the flow strong enough that, as they stood there watching, a large stone, almost a small boulder, loosened and rolled into the current with a thunderous crash. The spray here was such that it was misting the air around them, so cool and refreshing Fiona closed her eyes and lifted her chin, soaking it in.

Roz touched her shoulder and motioned for her to follow—the water too loud to talk—and the two of them followed the bank downstream for a couple of minutes until they found a little standing pool. It was shaded here, and the bank had been eroded enough to make a little beach of sorts. The ground was soft and almost sandy, and they sat down next to each other, both shrugging out of their backpacks and simply sitting there motionless for several minutes. It was quieter here than upriver, but still loud enough that when Roz pulled the water filter out of her pack, Fiona could hardly hear the zipper as she opened it. She handed her the filter, and Fiona, sighing, got up onto her hands and knees and crawled over to the water. It took her a minute or two to get the filter together and properly placed, and even longer to start pumping. Her earlier filtering heroics back in camp had stiffened the joints in her hands and wrists, and her scraped palms and the two tiny blisters on her index finger barked with pain as she pumped up and down.

When she finished, Roz had gotten their food supplies ready, such as they were. She'd broken off three of the 500 calorie sections of the emergency rations—one and a half for each of them. She gestured at Fiona's pile and started eating part of her own. Roz grimaced at the taste, and Fiona couldn't help but laugh—the sound startling them both.

Roz smiled. "They're pretty bad."

"The worst." She had to speak louder than was natural, but she wasn't shouting, either. The roiling water was far enough away that they could talk.

She moved back to the spot next to Roz and grabbed one of the beige ration sections. As she brought it close to her mouth, her lips and nose instinctively curled back and away from the smell as she remembered the taste. She shook her head, willed herself to keep going, and took a big bite. It was like chewing flavored sawdust. She had to put a hand over her mouth to stop herself from spitting it out. Finally, after nearly heaving, she managed to swallow her first bite.

Roz, who had been watching her, burst out laughing. "That good?" she asked.

Fiona closed her eyes and licked her lips. "Mmmm. Yummy. Tastes like I'm eating lemon-flavored mud."

Roz laughed harder, rolling backward. Fiona started giggling with her, and before long the two of them were squealing with merriment. They laughed long enough that Fiona's stomach muscles started to hurt, but just as one of them started to calm down, the other started again. They set each other off several times this way, until finally Roz gripped her arm with one strong hand and made a cutting motion with the other.

"Stop, stop. I can't breathe."

Fiona let out one last barking laugh and wiped her eyes. She forced herself to pick up the food section again, using gulps of the fresh, cold water to help herself choke it down. She managed one whole section before the thought of another bite made her stomach gurgle, and she carefully put the last chunk back into the little foil wrapper with the rest of the bar. The thought of eating nothing but this for the next day or two sobered her.

Roz, too, was back to her usual seriousness, her face streaked with sweat and dust. She was studying a little piece of paper, her compass on her knee. Finally, she looked up at Fiona and frowned.

"Unfortunately, it's like I thought. We haven't made it as far as I wanted."

"I'm sorry. I'm slowing you down."

Roz shook her head and touched Fiona's knee lightly. "Not at all. It was me. I guess I thought we'd be able to get farther, faster. I miscalculated. Even if you weren't with me, I wouldn't be able to go much quicker than this."

Fiona couldn't tell if she was telling the truth, but judging from Roz's expression, she meant it, either way. Fiona's guilt lessened a little, and she nodded.

"Okay. So how far have we come?"

"As near as I can tell, about eight, maybe almost nine miles. With heavier packs, we would have done about six in that same time, but I was still hoping for closer to ten or eleven by now."

Fiona glanced up at the sky. "Maybe it's earlier than you think."

Roz shook her head. "No. It's not. It's about six, maybe even six thirty now. We have almost an hour of full daylight left, and another hour of twilight, give or take. That gives us about an hour and half left before we'll need to set up some kind of camp. We're coming up on the rock scramble in about two miles, so we'll be lucky to make it to the bottom in that time."

Fiona closed her eyes. Climbing up the rock scramble had been bad enough. She'd almost suppressed the memory of how bad that had been. She could hardly imagine how slow it would be going down, especially as they weren't carrying rope.

"There's no way around it?"

Roz shrugged. "Yes, but not really. We could hike off trail to the east, away from the river, around the rocks, but that would add about ten, fifteen miles."

Fiona let out a breath of frustration and shook her head. "You're right—that's not an option. Okay, so say we make it to the bottom of the scramble before dark. Where does that put us?"

"Basically, we're going to make it about twelve miles today before we have to stop—either before or after the scramble."

This meant, essentially, that they wouldn't make it halfway or anywhere near it. At one point, Roz had suggested they might even get back to the first camp by tonight—some twenty miles, total. Now, with their updated timeline, they'd have to hike over twenty miles tomorrow to reach the road. Though her load was so much lighter than before, the very idea of another twenty-mile day made Fiona feel like turning around and going back to the others.

A warm hand slid into hers, and Fiona almost jerked away, surprised. Roz's lips were curled into a weak, thin smile. She squeezed Fiona's fingers.

"Hey. Don't give up on me, okay? We're in this together. We can do this. I promise you we can."

Fiona nodded, looking away to hide the tears of frustration that sprang into her eyes. "I know. I'm trying not to let it get to me. I'm just…scared. And tired." She made eye contact with Roz. "I've never been so tired."

Roz gave her that same weak smile. "Me, too. So how about this? I promise, once we make it back to civilization, and once Search and Rescue is on the way back here, we'll get a hotel room—"

Fiona started, and Roz laughed and rolled her eyes. "And we'll sleep for a week."

Fiona closed her eyes for a second, trying to picture it. "And take a hot shower."

Roz nodded. "And have a real meal, made with real food."

They watched the river for a while longer, still holding hands, and a tiny flicker of hope brightened Fiona's heart. After all, what they wanted didn't seem so far-fetched. It was a small wish, in the grand scheme of things—a hotel, a shower, a meal. It didn't seem like too much to ask the universe to grant it.

"We should get going," Roz said, startling her.

Roz helped her to her feet, and, after packing up their meager supplies, the two of them struggled back into their packs. Fiona was very stiff, and the backpack felt much heavier, her shoulders chafing under her shirt and throbbing with pain. Her hands hurt again, her finger with the missing nail pulsing unhappily, and the cut on her face was making her entire cheek ache. Why she hadn't thought to grab some of the ibuprofen from a first-aid kit was beyond her.

She followed Roz back toward the invisible trail, staying a few feet behind to make sure she didn't step on her heels—much harder to do when they were struggling through the brush like this.

Roz paused in the woods after a while, getting her bearings, and for a wild, heart-stopping moment, Fiona had the impression that she, too, was lost. After all, they'd walked downriver for a few minutes, away from where they'd left the trail, so there was no telling how far they were from where they'd diverted. She finally saw Roz's expression clear, certainty flooding back into her eyes. Fiona made herself take a deep, shaky breath. Stop panicking, she told herself. Roz started walking on what was presumably the trail, and Fiona let the distance between them extend a little more before starting after her.

They'd been hiking for perhaps fifteen minutes before they both heard it. Roz froze at once, holding up a hand for Fiona to do the same, but she needn't have bothered. Fiona had stopped at the first hint of the sound, holding her breath. At first, she could almost convince herself that it was, perhaps, an animal—deer or a pair of elk butting heads, maybe. But she was kidding herself. The sound was too regular, too singular, the same sound coming every few seconds. It was very distinct, even if she'd rarely heard it outside of the movies. It was the sound of someone chopping wood.

She and Roz made eye contact, not speaking, and Roz immediately started walking toward the sound. Fiona moved to follow and then hesitated. After all, if this was the same noise they'd heard the first day in the woods, when the men and horses were still with them, the sound represented all of this—the guys' disappearance, the marks on the trees, the pit and bear traps in the second camp, in essence everything that had plagued them for the last three days. Should they go toward it or run away?

Roz had already made that choice for her, and if she didn't move quickly, she'd be left behind. She had to jog to catch up, and Roz, hearing her, stopped and motioned with her hands to quiet down. Fiona slowed and minced her way forward, trying to avoid the small twigs and branches all over the ground, waiting to be snapped. Roz gestured for her to come closer, and, when she was standing a couple of feet away, she leaned closer and whispered in Fiona's ear.

"You should stay here. I want to see who they are so I can tell the police what and who to search for."

Fiona shook her head as violently as she could. No way was she being left behind. Roz seemed momentarily annoyed, but she finally nodded, gesturing for the two of them to keep moving. They crept forward through the woods, the old-growth trees so thick and tall here, they found very little undergrowth. Fiona felt incredibly exposed. Even with the trees around them to hide behind, they would be visible to anyone looking their way.

Eventually, the sound grew louder, more distinct, the reverberating echoes no longer blending into each other with distance. Each chop of the axe, if that's what it was, was so regular, so specific, that Fiona was having a tough time believing that a human being was making it. It was too regular, too rhythmic—mechanical, in a word. If she had some means of recording and timing the pause between the sound, it would surely be exactly the same length every time. That means something, she thought, but didn't know what.

Seconds before she was certain the two of them would walk into a clearing with this person or people, Roz gestured for her to stop, pointing at a clump of bushes off to their left. Roz moved very carefully in front of her, leading the way, lifting her feet almost to knee level to keep from stepping too loudly. Fiona followed suit, moving so slowly it took her a long while to catch up. Roz was crouched on the ground, and when Fiona joined her, the two of them resting on the balls of her feet, they were both breathing heavily. Again, Roz leant close to her ear, this time whispering so quietly Fiona had to strain to hear her.

"I'm going to inch through this bush until I can see what's making that sound. Stay here and keep an eye out. Touch my leg if you see something. Try not to make any noise."

Before Fiona could try to stop her, Roz had already shrugged out of her backpack and down on her stomach in the dirt, creeping into the brush. Fiona wanted to grab her leg and pull her back to safety, but it was already too late. Before she could do anything,

Roz had all but disappeared. Fiona could see the soles of her boots and nothing else. A long, terrifying wait followed, the steady sound of the ax grating on her nerves the longer she listened. Roz didn't move either, simply lay there under the bush, apparently watching something.

Sitting this way on the balls of her feet was starting to hurt, and Fiona tried to sit back onto her butt as quietly as possible. She lost her balance, slipping down hard, the jolt sending a spike of pain through her tailbone, her teeth biting the tip of her tongue. Her backpack rose and dropped, something metal inside it clanging.

The sound of the ax stopped at once, and suddenly Roz was backing up and out of the bush, scrambling upward.

"Run," she said, launching to her feet.

"What?" Fiona asked.

Roz yanked Fiona up, almost lifting her into the air on her upward swing. Her face inches from hers, Roz repeated herself, screaming now.

"Run! Now!" Whatever Roz had seen, it had clearly scared the hell of her. She was obviously terrified. Fiona never wanted to see anything that could put that kind of panic in her eyes.

Roz ran away, darting back the way they came, and Fiona, after one terrified last glance behind her, broke into a sprint, desperate to catch up.

CHAPTER THIRTEEN

The burst of adrenaline kept Fiona going for a long time. In fact, she didn't even feel tired for several minutes. She kept her attention on the back of Roz's head, several yards away and occasionally slipping away into the trees. She would push herself then, her legs a whirl of speed, and suddenly see the other woman again. They were running too hard to give her a chance to glance behind them, but she was fairly certain that if someone was chasing them, she would have heard them coming, even over her gasping breath.

They maintained this tortuous speed long past the point at which the initial scare had worn off. Fiona could feel herself starting to slow, her legs no longer willing to do what she told them. She was sure she would fall so far behind Roz she'd be lost forever. If Roz turned somewhere too quickly or sharply, she would never find her again.

Roz appeared then, suddenly, hiding partly behind an enormous tree, gesturing wildly at Fiona. Fiona made herself put the last of her energy into a final burst of speed, sailing over several fallen logs and rocks, finally catching up. Roz dragged her behind the tree and roughly pushed the straps of the backpack off Fiona's shoulders, slipping it onto her own back a moment later. She let Fiona catch her breath and then grabbed her arm, pulling her close. She was still whispering.

"We're almost to the rock scramble. It's maybe half a mile from here." She pointed forward in the direction they'd been running. "We're going to have to go down it as quickly as possible."

"Did they see you?" Fiona said, staring around the tree, back into the woods behind them.

Roz shook her hard. "I don't think so. But they definitely heard that sound you made."

"I'm sorry."

Roz lifted one shoulder. Nothing could be done about it now.

"What did you—"

"Shh!" Roz suddenly said, slapping a hand over Fiona's mouth.

Fiona struggled and then froze, hearing something coming from the woods. She and Roz stared back the way they came, waiting, but didn't see anything. They could hear, however, the sound of breaking branches. Even during the seconds that they listened, Fiona could tell that whatever it was, it was getting closer, coming from at least two different directions directly toward them.

Roz gestured for her to follow, and the two of them broke into a light trot away from the sounds. As they fled, Roz seemed a little more hesitant, pausing more often before moving forward again.

Finally, it was lighter ahead of them through the woods, and before long, Fiona could see the sky opening up beyond the edge of the trees where the rock scramble began. They paused there, staring down the long, treacherous valley of broken boulders and stones. Roz groaned and slapped the tree next to her, clearly furious.

"Damn it. I knew it."

"What?" Fiona asked.

"We're off course. I got thrown off by that little jog of ours. I thought it might happen after our last stop, but I wasn't sure."

"What's the problem? Can't we make it to the bottom here?"

"Of course we can. But there's a reason we went up this where we did yesterday. That area has the easiest ascent and descent. I've never tried going up or down anywhere near here. It's not safe."

"So should we try to go down somewhere else?"

Roz shrugged and shook her head. "I don't know how. We would have to backtrack over there. The only real option other than trying here is to go down near the waterfall." She pointed to their right. "There are some good handholds on the rocks along the edge. But I wouldn't want to do that without rope. It can be slippery."

In a word, Fiona realized, they were screwed. If they backtracked, they would probably run into whoever was chasing them. If they tried either of the other descents, they were risking their lives. Already, time was slipping away. She could tell by the long shadows on the ground that the sun was getting ready to set. An hour or more had passed since they sat by the river, having their awful meal, and they were hardly any distance nearer their goal.

Fiona stared down the length of the rock scramble in front of them. It didn't seem any better or worse than the one they'd come up yesterday, but she was no expert. Here at the edge, the initial drop-off was a little more extreme—five feet down to the first ledge. Beyond that, it was, perhaps, a little steeper down to the flat ground of the valley, and the boulders in their way seemed much larger here and there along that earlier route, but other than that, she couldn't tell why this was such a problem.

"It doesn't look—"

CRACK.

She instantly recognized the sound of the gun, and the two of them dropped to the ground. Fiona had heard people say that gunfire sounded like fireworks, but she'd known, instinctively, to get down and out of the way the very instant she heard the shot. Some part of her, perhaps, had also expected it. Ever since they'd started running, she'd known something would come for them.

CRACK.

A gun fired again, hitting a tree some five feet away, splinters of wood flying into the air. Both she and Roz were pressed into the dirt on their stomachs, as flat as they could manage. Fiona put her hands over the back of her head, Roz doing the same, their faces inches apart.

"We have to go," Roz said, gesturing toward the slanting scrabble to her right.

"How can we? We'll be like sitting ducks—"

CRACK. CRACK.

Again, a nearby tree let lose two bursts of broken, splintered wood.

"We don't have a choice," Roz said. "The angle will help, too. We'll have to try to hide behind a bigger boulder where they can't shoot at us."

"And then what?"

"We'll figure that out when we get there."

"Are you crazy?"

But Roz was already army-crawling toward the rock scramble, still nearly flat on the ground, and when she reached the edge, she glanced back at Fiona and motioned for her to follow. The earth was rough and painful under her elbows, and as Fiona dragged herself to the edge of the rocks, she expected to be shot in the back of the head.

Roz swung her legs over the edge and dropped off. Fiona followed suit, and Roz grabbed her waist, helping her down. They were already safer here over the edge, and for a second, Fiona wondered if they might not simply stay here. It would be difficult for whoever was shooting at them to see them here unless they peeked over the edge. Maybe she and Roz could throw something at them or grab their ankles.

Roz, however, had other ideas, as she immediately started moving down the scramble, leaping from stone to stone, huddling low between hops, a little like a giant frog. Fiona had to use every ounce of her will to follow, starting three times before she made her first jump. The boulder she landed on shifted a little, and she let out a little cry of fright. Roz whirled around, gesturing wildly for her to hurry, but it took her a second to move forward. Between the boulders and large stones, smaller rocks filled in the gaps, almost as if they'd been poured in there on purpose. Fiona stepped on a patch of this scree twice, nearly twisting her ankle both times.

She was so focused on her movement forward, it never occurred to her to look back, but when she glanced up to see where Roz had gone, she saw the other woman staring up and behind her, watching something.

"Get down!" Roz shouted.

Fiona started to drop without thinking and landed hard on her knees and one wrist. That pain was eclipsed in an instant when a searing punch of white agony flashed across her left shoulder. Instinctively, she jerked away, likely saving her own life. Another CRACK, and the stone she'd been on seconds before released a puff of dust as a bullet ricocheted off it.

Roz was there, suddenly, dragging her bodily forward, and Fiona, who was reeling from the pain, was dimly aware of the sound of gunfire above and behind them, exploding in little bursts of sound and dust all around them.

Finally, Roz dragged her behind the first large boulder, and the gunfire stopped as if it had been turned off. Roz propped her up with her back to the boulder, then removed the backpack before digging around inside. She cursed and shook her head.

"I forgot—this is your pack. Mine had the first-aid kit. And the compass."

Fiona tried to laugh and then hissed, her right hand instinctively going for her left shoulder. Roz caught it, shaking her head.

"Try not to touch it with your bare hand. It's not bleeding very much. Just a graze, I think."

"Feels like more than a graze."

"I bet. I thought for sure it was going to be worse. In fact, for a second, I thought…" She shook her head, eyes suddenly shining and cast downward. She took a deep, shaky breath. "Anyway, let me push back some of your sleeve here and check it. I'll wash it out a little with water, and we can tie a bandana around it for now."

"Are we safe here?"

Roz lifted her hands. "Who knows? They could head down this way any minute. But they don't know exactly where we are. It wouldn't be the smartest thing for them to try."

"Yeah, but they have guns and we don't."

Roz hefted a grapefruit-sized rock in one hand. "It would still hurt like hell to be hit with one of these. Maybe even knock a fucker out."

"Or kill him," Fiona said.

"We could hope. Anyway, I don't think they're coming down this way. I bet they'll descend somewhere else and wait for us at the bottom."

Gingerly, Roz pushed Fiona's sleeve back, and Fiona couldn't help but let out a low hiss of pain. Roz took out her Leatherman and snipped up the side of one sleeve, exposing the bloody shoulder. Fiona had to look away, suddenly woozy, and she hissed again when Roz poured some of their water over her wound.

"It seems okay," Roz finally said. "Like I thought—grazed the skin and muscle along the edge there. I'm going to fold one bandana to cover the wound and then tie it on with a second, so I'll need you to hold this folded one while I knot the other one. Think you can do that?"

Fiona mumbled an assent, still not looking, and Roz guided her hand to the wound. Fiona took a deep breath before pushing down, seeing stars for a second before her head cleared again. With the wound covered, she could risk peeking again, and Roz tied the second bandana under her armpit and around the top of her shoulder.

Roz studied it and then shook her head. "I don't know that it's going to hold very well. Maybe you should put your long-sleeved shirt on over all this to help hold in in place."

She seemed so frustrated and disappointed in her work Fiona almost laughed. Instead, she touched the side of Roz's face. Roz jumped slightly and then smiled, apologetically, before taking Fiona's hand in hers.

"Sorry."

"Don't apologize. And thanks."

"What? For this? It's sloppy as hell."

Fiona rolled her eyes. "It's fine, and not just for that." She squeezed Roz's fingers. "For saving my life. You ran through gunfire for me. Thank you."

Roz's fingers slipped through hers, and she went back to rubbing her mouth. It was dark enough that Fiona wasn't sure if she was blushing, but something told her she was. She touched Roz's arm.

"I owe you my life."

Roz shook her head, tried to talk, and then cleared her throat. "You don't owe me anything."

If her shoulder hadn't hurt so much, Fiona would have leant forward right then and kissed her. As it was, the moment passed. Roz looked away, staring down the rock scramble toward the flat ground at the bottom. It had never seemed farther away.

"So what's the plan?" Fiona finally asked.

Roz sighed and moved close to her, leaning back against the boulder Fiona was propped on.

"We'll have to wait. At least until it starts to get dark—maybe later. It's stupid to go down these boulders and rocks in the dark, and even stupider without a light, but it might be our only chance. I don't know how long they'll wait up there before leaving to head down themselves. And they could split up, too."

"How many are there?"

"At least three—that's how many I saw in the clearing back there."

"What were they like? Did you recognize anyone?"

Roz didn't respond beyond shaking her head, still staring at the ground in front of her. She'd crossed her arms over her knees.

"What?" Fiona asked after a long pause. "What is it?"

Roz made eye contact. "It's crazy. They were all wearing masks."

Fiona frowned. "Masks? Like ski masks?"

Roz shook her head. "No—like Halloween, but not quite. More like something you'd see in a movie. Like at a festival or a carnival or something."

Fiona continued to frown at her, still confused. "You mean like at a masquerade—that kind of mask? Wood or leather or something like that?"

Roz lifted her shoulders. "Sort of. They're hard to describe. It was hard enough to believe my eyes when I saw them the first time, but I don't understand why they were wearing them there by themselves in the woods. It was just them. Why cover their faces up like that when no one's around? It was creepy as hell."

It's more than creepy, Fiona thought. These people, whoever they are, were complete lunatics. Everything they'd done had been the behavior of someone completely detached from reality.

"Did you see anything else? Anything stand out?" Fiona asked.

Roz shook her head. "No—except that one of them is a woman. She was watching the big guy chop at the tree. The third one was a guard, maybe. He was standing apart from the big one and the woman, watching the woods and pacing back and forth."

Fiona couldn't help but shudder. Roz slid an arm around her waist, careful of her shoulder, and pulled her closer.

"So they were just standing there, chopping a tree down?" Fiona asked.

"They weren't cutting it down. The big guy was making those marks we've seen in the trees a few times now. He was standing on a ladder, of all things."

"Did you see anything else? Any other equipment, horses, anything like that?"

Roz shook her head. "Nothing. Only the three of them. I didn't even see their guns."

"So they must have some kind of camp or something nearby."

"Maybe."

They were quiet for a while. Fiona couldn't help but think that they were missing some crucial piece of information here. These people, whoever they were, had been one step ahead of them from the beginning. To her, this suggested a base of operations and maybe means of surveillance.

The sun had partially set, the world now dim and gray around them. Already, most of the heat of the late afternoon had drained away, and she couldn't help but shiver. The sweat all over her was now chill and unpleasant, and her shoulder was throbbing, dully but constantly.

"Let me get the hammock out," Roz said. "It could work as a blanket. You should put on your long-sleeve shirt, too."

"Okay, but you should wear my fleece."

Roz helped her pull her long-sleeved, silk undershirt over the shirt she was wearing, and the pain from her shoulder so sharp and searing she had to bite her tongue to keep from crying out. If their pursuers were still watching for them, they would no doubt have heard them long before this, but she also didn't want to make their location too obvious.

A few minutes later, both huddled under the space blanket and the hammock, Fiona felt relatively comfortable. Sitting here would eventually start to bother her—the rock was already hurting her butt and back—but for now she was content to wait here with Roz. They'd joined hands under the hammock over their backs and the crinkly space blanket over their legs, and Fiona's knees were slightly crossed over Roz's. They couldn't have sat closer unless she was in Roz's lap.

Surprisingly, despite the unforgiving rock behind and below them, Fiona felt herself jerk awake a few minutes later.

"You should keep sleeping," Roz said, almost whispering. "I'll wake you in an hour or two when it's darker."

"What about you?" Fiona asked, stifling a loud yawn.

"I'll be okay. Sleep now and get some rest. We can't move until there's no way for them to see us."

Fiona wanted to protest, but, half-awake, she let her eyelids drop closed and was fast asleep within seconds.

Chapter Fourteen

Fiona awoke with a start, almost calling out in fear. In her dream, she'd been trying to run away from something, but the branches in her way had been barbed, tearing at her skin and clothes. She'd been alone but knew someone or something was chasing her. The harder she tried, the thicker the brambles and thorns grew, so that eventually she'd been snared, web-like, caught and waiting for something from the woods behind her.

"Didn't mean to startle you," Roz whispered next to her.

It was so dark Fiona could barely see her silhouette. They were still cocooned inside the blanket and the hammock, and Roz felt warm and comforting pressed next to her. Her shoulder was stiff with pain, but the bandage didn't seem wetter than before, so at least there was that. Judging from the crick in her neck and the numbness on the right side of her face, she'd been sleeping on Roz's shoulder. She felt a little thrill of embarrassed pleasure, glad it was too dark for Roz to see her face.

"How long was I out?" She kept her voice low.

"Maybe two hours. I'm sorry to wake you, but we have to try to keep going."

"No. Thank you for getting me up. I'm sorry you had to just sit here all that time. Did anything happen?"

Roz shifted a little next to her. "I heard some noises, maybe half an hour after you dozed off—footsteps up at the top, that kind of thing, but nothing since. They didn't talk, or at least so I could hear."

"You think it's okay to move?"

"Even if they're still up there, they won't be able to see us. I can barely see you, and you're right next to me."

Fiona rubbed her eyes, peering into the dark. It was true—even squinting, she couldn't see anything clearly. But that created its own problem. How on earth were they going to navigate their way down these rocks in the dark?

"You're probably thinking the same thing I am," Roz said.

"How are we going to do it?"

"The moonlight is blocked a little here from this boulder, so it might be a little brighter a few feet from here, but we're going to have to go slowly. Once we're down and in the trees, I think we could risk a dim light if we keep it covered as much as possible. But I'm not sure it's a good idea when we're exposed like this."

Fiona tried to rotate her hurt shoulder a little, but the resulting pain made her grimace. She'd have to try to keep it still and not use her left arm.

As if sensing her discomfort, Roz asked, "How's that shoulder?"

"It's fine. I mean, it hurts like hell, but I think it stopped bleeding, anyway."

"That's good. Let me know if you need a break, okay? Don't push yourself too hard."

"I won't."

They spent the next couple of minutes getting their blanket and hammock folded and back in the little daypack. Without the covers, Fiona was instantly chilled. At this elevation, the air didn't hold any heat without sunshine, and she was immediately shivering. Roz pushed something into her hands, and she felt her fleece hat. Once she had it on, she was a little warmer, but she was going to be very cold soon.

Packing made another problem suddenly obvious. Roz had been carrying the bulk of their supplies in her backpack, including their water filter, but had left her pack in the woods during their hasty escape. As it was now, they had less than two liters of water for the two of them and no way to filter more. As Roz had mentioned, they'd also lost their compass and, as Fiona recalled the situation, half their food and the first-aid kit. Roz had likely thought of this already, so she saw no reason to bring it up, but it brought their situation even greater peril. If they didn't make it back to safety soon, they'd be in real trouble.

She heard rather than saw Roz slip the backpack on, and then she leaned closer to Fiona, the warmth from her body radiating off her like a beacon.

"Okay. Let's get this over with. I know it's hard to see, but try to follow me as carefully as you can. Keep low, just in case. It's maybe a couple hundred yards. Touch my back if you need to stop. Try not to say anything once we're exposed."

"I understand."

Roz immediately moved away, and Fiona finally made herself get up onto the balls of her feet, her shoulder sending out a flash of agony. She had to ignore that for now. Seconds later, she was scooting down a long, flat boulder, skittering to a stop when her boots hit the bottom. Roz had waited there and offered her a hand, and both stood upright for the first time in hours. The relief was almost enough to forget where they were, and she rubbed her butt to nurse the feeling back into it.

It was indeed brighter here out of the shadow of the boulder, but barely. Fiona could see the curve of Roz's cheek at she stared up at her, and the glimmer of her eyes, but everything in front of them was still a gray-black shadow. She sensed that it sloped downward here, sharply, but it was like peering into an abyss.

Roz crouched down, and Fiona did the same, and then it was as if Roz disappeared. Fiona crept forward, waving her hand waving wildly in front of her, and then Roz's fingers found hers. Roz guided her forward slightly, and by inching forward, Fiona was able to navigate down and over the next set of rocks and small boulders.

Things went on like this for what felt like hours. Roz, however, without a single word from Fiona, seemed to sense when Fiona needed a break, and the two of them would stand still for a few minutes, letting their backs relax and their anxiety lessen before moving onward again.

Fiona tripped twice, but both times it was a minor slip, as they were quite literally creeping along the ground, almost sliding down on their butts. Still, the jarring punch of the falls sent pain screaming through her skinned hands and injured shoulder, and on the second slip, she couldn't help the little sob that broke free of her clenched jaw.

"You okay?" Roz whispered, speaking for the first time since the safety of their boulder.

Fiona nodded and then, remembering, made a quick sound of assent.

"Almost down," Roz said, and started moving again.

Whether she'd meant this last as encouragement or whether she outright lied, it wasn't true. By the time they were, in fact, at the bottom, Fiona was quivering with fatigue, barely capable of putting one foot in front of the other. She'd kept going only through pure will. If they didn't clear this field by dawn, they'd likely be killed here. Still, perhaps half an hour before the last of the scramble, Fiona began to wonder if perhaps being shot wasn't such a bad thing. Anything was preferable to this endless torture.

When her feet hit solid ground, she almost didn't believe it. The difference was immediate, the feeling of actual earth, not stone, obvious beneath her boots, but she couldn't face the possibility that she was fooling herself. It took Roz pulling her into a rough embrace to realize that, once and for all, it was over.

Roz held her for a long time, Fiona silently crying into the rough texture of her shirt. She slid her hands under the backpack so they could more easily hold each other, and Roz's warmth seemed to seep into her like a hot bath. She was dimly aware of Roz kissing the top of her head and squeezing her almost as hard as she squeezed back, but neither of them said anything. They weren't safe yet. Those people, whoever they were, could be anywhere, waiting for them. Even in the woods, they would have to stay as quiet as possible.

Finally, she felt Roz relax and took a step backward, the cold returning almost at once. She suddenly felt worn, paper thin, wrung completely free of any last reserve of energy. If she didn't sit down soon, she would simply collapse. Roz, again as if sensing this predicament, grabbed her hand, and the two of them started moving again. Fiona barely managed to shuffle along, her feet leaden and clumsy.

She sensed the trees rising before them, finally spotting their tall heads as they began to block out the stars. Soon, they were in the woods again, and she felt safe for the first time in hours. Still, Roz kept them moving, the two of them stumbling over several fallen branches, boldly announcing their location to anyone listening. Finally, Roz stopped and pulled Fiona down to the ground.

The two of them collapsed next to each other, and Fiona soon heard Roz digging around in the backpack. She felt the mouth valve for her water bladder pushed into her hands, and the taste of the cool liquid was sweeter than any water had even been before. She had to stop herself from gulping it all down. She heard some more shuffling, and then a dim, red light appeared, illuminating the little spot they were seated in. Three fallen trees bracketed the space around them. They sat between the trunks, Roz leaning on one, Fiona on another facing her, their knees touching.

Roz had the headlamp cupped in her hands and lap, but even with the bare minimum of light it let out, Fiona's heart gave a great lurch of sorrow at the sight of her. Roz's eyes were sunken in her face, deep and dark, the red light making her pupils dilate so far hardly any iris remained. Her face was streaked with something dark—dirt and sweat, probably, and her hair was a tangle of matted, curly locks.

Not thinking to stop herself, Fiona leaned forward and brushed a sweaty piece of hair off her face, running her fingers down the edge of her cheek. Roz smiled and took her hand in hers, squeezing it gently.

"You're exhausted," Fiona said. It was a statement.

Roz's face hardened a little, that stubborn pride rising into her eyes. "So are you."

"Yes, but I got some sleep, at least. Why don't you close your eyes for a little while? I can keep watch."

"No. We have to keep going. We might be able to make it to the road if we hike all night."

"Not if you fall down from exhaustion. Two hours. One. Please."

She saw the temptation in Roz's eyes and leaned forward again, pulling Roz toward her with their linked hands. Roz met her eyes, and Fiona smiled, sensing victory.

"I'm not asking you, Roz, I'm telling you. You need some sleep. One hour is not going to make any difference. We'll still be knocking around in the dark whether we leave now or then."

Roz sighed and then nodded, her eyes downcast. She clearly didn't like admitting her own weakness. The two of them wrestled the hammock and blanket out of the pack again, and it took some time to arrange themselves comfortably. Eventually, Roz simply lay down, curled up with her knees almost touching her stomach, her head on Fiona's lap.

"We should turn off the light. To save the batteries," Roz said.

Fiona snapped it off, plunging them into impenetrable gloom. Roz fell asleep almost at once, the tension leaving her body and her breath slowing into an even, deep, peaceful rhythm. Fiona was afraid she might be tempted to fall asleep herself, so she moved her back slightly, pushing into an uncomfortable knot on the fallen tree behind her. Once or twice, her head started to nod, and she pushed back into it, hard, to wake herself, or lightly slapped the side of her face, the sting of the cut rocketing her awake once more.

Strange noises from the woods came to her at times. The occasional whir of what was likely a bat or woken squirrel was often followed by the squeak of something caught in a predator's claws. Far off, she could hear the tumbling water of the river, but closer, she heard movement once or twice off somewhere to her right in the woods. Even in her sleep-deprived stupor, she knew instinctively that it was an animal, but that realization didn't stop the terror that flashed through her both times as it caught her ears.

It was tiring staring into darkness, and she occasionally shut her eyes, pinching them closed to make the sensation uncomfortable rather than sleep-inducing. This didn't work well, so she was forced, for the most part, simply to stare blindly into the nothing around her.

The time passed very slowly. She tried counting at first but was distracted time and again by the noises in the woods or by Roz's slight movements, stilling herself in both cases, clenched with anxiety and worry.

At one point during her endless wait, she realized she was unconsciously running her fingers through Roz's hair. She stopped for a second only to recognize that it obviously hadn't woken her for however long she'd been doing it. Roz's hair was thick, and Fiona's fingers worked out some of the knots from their god-awful day. She smiled at herself in the dark as she continued. A couple of days ago, if someone had told her she'd be sitting in the dark with Roz, playing with her hair, she'd have told them they were crazy. Now, in their current situation, it seemed almost natural, normal. It was perhaps four hours since she'd been shot, less than twelve since they'd left the others back in the woods, and the experience had brought them together. She felt a strong, possessive tenderness welling inside her. What that meant in the long run, whether this would go anywhere once they were safe again, was impossible to say. In fact, safety was less than a pipe dream at this point, but she spent the rest of the hour imagining the two of them together, doing normal things together, somewhere clean and safe.

Finally, when she could no longer fool herself into thinking that less than an hour had passed, she gently shook Roz's shoulder. Roz sat up at once, clearly startled, and Fiona grabbed her shoulder.

"Shhhh. It's okay. It's been about an hour now."

"Mmmm," She could vaguely see Roz rubbing at her face.

Without speaking, the two of them started packing up again, both taking small sips of water and sharing a section of the bittersweet food bar.

"Okay," Fiona finally said. "What's the plan?"

"First, we need to find the trail, or at least try."

"Isn't that too obvious? Won't they know we'll follow it back?"

"Probably, but it's still the fastest route to the road. I think it's worth the risk. Even in the dark, I'm pretty sure I can follow it once we're on it."

"And if we don't find it?"

Roz sighed. "Then we follow the water. It would be faster if we could walk directly in the middle of the river, but we can't this time of year. Instead, we'll have to fight through all the vegetation and rocks along its banks. That will be much slower. That's why I want to try the trail first, but we'll have to walk back toward the scramble to make that happen. I don't think we're too far off—maybe half a mile, but it won't be easy to pick it up."

When Fiona didn't respond, she felt Roz's hand on her knee. "I'm sorry, Fiona. I know you're scared. I'm scared, too. I wish there was another way."

"S'okay. I understand. I guess there's no point putting this off anymore."

Roz turned the headlamp on long enough for them to walk back to the edge of the woods. She was still using the red lowlight, but after the complete darkness they'd been sitting it, even that seemed bright.

Despite the lack of sleep, the rest had done Fiona some good. Her senses felt sharper, and though she was almost groaning with fatigue and from her various pains, she had regained most of her coordination. Now, without a backpack, she felt strangely light, almost buoyant. Roz was moving with her usual grace, making hardly any sound as they traversed the thick undergrowth. They hit the edge of the woods suddenly, and Fiona was surprised to recognize that it was incredibly bright out here. The moon had risen much farther than before, and when Roz turned off their headlamp, it was still light enough to see.

"Keep close to the trees," Roz said. "We're going to walk along the edge of them until I see the trail. If you hear anything, get down and wait for my signal. We might have to get back in the woods if they spot us."

Because of the greater light, it was difficult to walk close enough to the tree line to stay relatively hidden. Walking even a couple of feet away, both were completely exposed to anyone watching. Roz led them a few feet into the woods to try to keep them under cover, but the route was such slow going they abandoned the idea almost at once. Once back in the clearing, Roz sped up a little, and Fiona had to hustle to keep up. For the last leg, they were both visible and none too quiet. Fiona clenched with anxiety, fearing the shot that was sure to come.

"Here it is," Roz finally said, stopping in front of her.

Fiona peered into the woods, finally spotting the telltale signs of the trail. The woods here parted somewhat naturally, and the earth was turned up a little. It made the path clear, obvious.

"How much farther is it to the road?" Fiona asked.

"A little less than twenty miles—eighteen, I think. It'll be harder in the dark, but we'll be going downhill most of the way. I think we can make it by morning."

Fiona's stomach gave a lurch of excitement. Even in her current state of exhaustion, eighteen miles sounded doable. Eighteen miles, and this would all be over. Some of this realization must have shown in her face, as Roz smiled broadly before giving her a quick hug.

"We can do this, Fiona."

"I know we can."

They started down the trail, each step moving them closer to something Fiona had almost given up on. Roz had to risk the headlamp more often than either of them was comfortable with, but just for a quick flash of light to get her bearings. In the light, even Fiona could see the trail. Had this whole experience somehow made her better at reading the signs? Two days ago, she'd felt like she was wandering, lost, except for her companions leading the way. Now, she believed that she could have done this on her own.

Roz suddenly stopped in front of her, and Fiona almost ran into her back. She caught herself inches shy of the backpack and waited, wondering why Roz didn't turn on the light.

"What—"

"Shhh!" Roz hissed.

Fiona heard it then. The sound that had haunted them for days now, the sound that represented everything that had gone wrong from the very beginning.

Somewhere from the woods came the sound of chopping wood.

CHAPTER FIFTEEN

"Get down," Roz said, dragging Fiona with her. They crouched there on the trail, still hearing that awful sound somewhere to the left of the trail. Fiona's heart was racing, and it was all she could do not to take in great mouthfuls of air. She felt like she'd been running.

"Sounds close," Roz whispered.

Fiona nodded stupidly in the dark before remembering and mumbling agreement.

Neither of them moved, still listening, and the shiver that ran through her had nothing to do with the chilly night air. Once again, she could sense a precise exactness to the sound, as if it were set to a metronome. Knowing now that this was a sound powered by hand made the effect even creepier. The fact that an actual person was doing this, not a machine, was uncanny and deeply unsettling.

"It's still pretty steady," Roz finally said, her voice very low. "I think we can keep going. Hopefully they don't have anyone watching for us on the trail."

Roz moved as if to stand up, and Fiona clutched at her, suddenly desperate.

"We can't risk it! What if someone's standing somewhere in the dark, waiting for us? We'll never see them until it's too late."

Roz grabbed her healthy shoulder, squeezing it. "Please try to stay calm, Fiona. We have no choice here."

"Let's go back, find the river, and go that way. I don't care if it's slower. We can't, we can't…" She was unable to talk, her chest tight, closing off her throat. She gulped at the air, fumbling at the button at her neck, her clothes suddenly too snug.

Roz hugged her then, despite their awkward position near the ground. Fiona fought her, thrashing away, but Roz held on firmly, making soothing sounds. Finally, Fiona's shoulder protested, snapping her back to something like normalcy, and she relaxed into the embrace. The two of them dropped onto their butts next to each other, still in one another's arms. Tears were streaming down Fiona's face, and she wiped them away with her good arm, suddenly ashamed of herself.

"I'm sorry. I lost it there for a second."

"It's okay," Roz mumbled. "I'm about half a step from losing it myself."

They sat there in the pitch-black, listening to that awful, telling sound. Fiona felt calmer than before, but her stomach was still twisting with anxiety and fright. She wanted, more than anything, to run away, even if it meant wandering these woods for the rest of her life. She'd do almost anything to never hear that sound again.

"You're right," Roz said, almost talking. "We have to go another way. They could have sentries posted on the trail, and we'd never know. Let's go over to the river and follow that back. It'll take longer, but it'll be safer."

Fiona was nearly overwhelmed with gratitude, and she had to fight back a little sob of relief. She let Roz help her to her feet, not replying, and soon they were walking back the way they'd come, back toward the clearing by the rock scramble, away from home. Still, even though they were losing ground again, this was obviously the right choice. All they had to do was find the river again, and they'd be on their way once more.

They hadn't walked more than a hundred feet when they both heard it—a shriek, somewhere in the woods. The sound was harrowing, terrifying, and repeated seconds later. For a moment,

Fiona almost convinced herself that it was an animal—an owl, perhaps, or another night bird—but on the third scream in the woods, she realized she was fooling herself. A person, a woman, was making that sound.

"Jesus Christ," Roz breathed, clearly realizing the same thing. They had clutched each other's hand in the dark, and Fiona's fingers protested in Roz's claw-like grip.

Both froze, waiting for the screaming to start again. When nothing happened for several long seconds, and the screaming seemed to have stopped, a tiny bit of hope rose in Fiona's chest. Maybe it was over.

Almost as if she'd summoned it, the shrieking scream began again, louder, far more broken than before, as if someone was struggling for air. The two of them dropped low, listening to that awful, agonized horror.

"We have to run now, Fiona," Roz finally said. "We have to run like our lives and that woman's life depend on it. If we don't get help soon…"

Fiona didn't press her to finish her thought. They were both thinking the same thing. Whoever was screaming out there in the woods was about to die. Strangely, the idea of escape, of running away, however ridiculous, sent of wave of certainty flashing through her. Tempting as it might be to take their chances and run, Fiona knew what she had to do. In fact, recognizing this now, she realized she'd always known it would come to this. The certainty calmed her racing heart, and her dull, sleep-deprived senses suddenly revived and came awake. The dark, so threatening seconds ago, seemed to retreat, and the sounds she heard likewise crystalized. Her hand, still clutched in Roz's, relaxed, slipping from her grip, and she warmed from the inside. She knew, without question, what they needed to do.

"No, Roz," she finally said, speaking normally.

"What?"

Though it was almost entirely dark, it was as if she had a sixth sense. She found Roz's lips and kissed her, pulling lightly at the back of her head. She pulled away, bussing Roz's lips once, twice, and leaned her forehead against the other woman's.

"We have to help her," she finally said.

Roz let out a puff of disbelief, and Fiona kissed her again, putting more feeling into it. Roz returned it with something like desperation, but she broke away this time, pulling Fiona into a hug. The two of them held on to each other as if in preparation, which was precisely what it was.

"If we…if we don't get out of this…" Roz said.

"Shhhh," Fiona put a finger on her lips. "We will. We have to believe we will, or there's no chance and no point in trying."

"Okay, but I want you to know that I…like you. I really like you."

"I know. I do, too. And I promise you this will work out."

Roz let out a single, bitter laugh. "How can you promise that?"

"I can. I have to believe it. We'll be back in town, sipping a beer—"

"A scotch," Roz said.

Fiona smiled. "Fine. You'll have a scotch, I'll have beer, and we'll both have some real food, and everything will be okay."

"Sounds like a fairy tale."

It did to Fiona, now, too, but that didn't matter anymore. Whoever was in the woods needed them now—not later today, not tomorrow, not the day after—she needed their help now. The screaming had stopped, but whoever it had been was still out there somewhere, and they had to do something about it.

Without saying another word, the two of them clambered to their feet again and started heading back the way they'd come, back where they knew they'd find the people from the woods.

They hit a point on the trail where, when they went a little farther, the sound of the metronomic chopping seemed to drop behind them. The sound was somewhere off to the left, somewhere in the woods. Fiona waited, trying to anticipate their next move. Once they left the trail, they were in this. Already, some of her certainty from a few minutes ago began to seem more than a little foolish. The trail forward, back toward home and safety, beckoned.

She shook her head to dismiss this tug, but it was still too dark to see anything. If she squinted, she could detect a brightening somewhere out there toward the sounds. She and Roz might be here in the dark, but the people from the woods needed light to do whatever they were doing.

"What's the next step?" Roz asked.

The question took Fiona aback. Somehow, despite having essentially decided they were going on a rescue mission, she'd assumed Roz would take the lead once they began. She had to scramble for a quick response.

"We'll be at a disadvantage since we can't risk a light."

"So we're just going to fumble our way over to them in the dark." Again, this was a statement.

"That's all we can do." She sounded helpless, unsure of herself. She was blowing this.

Roz let out a long sigh, then was quiet again. As they stood there, the crystalline clarity Fiona had felt earlier retreated even further. This was hopeless, stupid. Better to get the police and come at them from all sides. This idea gave her pause, and her thoughts scrambled toward a plan forming in the depths of her mind.

"We should try to go around them," she said, suddenly certain.

"What? Why?"

She turned toward Roz, trying to put her thoughts into words. "Look, I've thought from the beginning that they've been one step ahead of us. Those carvings were at the first campsite. Then the cravings and traps were at the second. Then they just happened to be near the trail when the two of us walked by. They anticipated where we'd be and when."

"Okay. So what does that mean?"

"What if they've been, sort of, leading us this whole time? Think about earlier when the two of us heard them in the woods and went to investigate. There they were, hacking a tree, just close enough to the trail for us to hear and find them. Don't you think that's awfully convenient?"

"I'm still not following you."

"Maybe they wanted us to go over there. Maybe they knew someone—maybe not the two of us, but someone—would have to leave camp and head that way, back toward home. With all those traps, someone was going to get hurt, someone would have to go back for help, and heading home was still closer than anywhere else."

"So you think they were kind of…herding us?"

"Exactly."

Roz seemed to mull that possibility over during a long, quiet pause. "Okay, but there's a problem. How would they know when we left camp and the others? How would they know when we'd find them there in the woods? We ended up staying overnight and most of the day yesterday, remember?"

"I think someone has been watching us."

Roz chuckled. "That seems like a stretch."

"Really? A group of masked maniacs is in the woods, and you think a watchman is a stretch?"

Again, Roz had no immediate response. Finally, she sighed. "Okay, I guess you could be right, though there's no way to know. Assuming you are right, what difference does any of this make? They could be watching us right now."

"They could, but they don't have to. All they had to do is wait for us to walk by. They knew we'd wait until dark before heading down the scramble, and beyond that, it's probably a lucky guess. Who knows? Maybe they're…doing something to make that woman scream on the hour, like an alarm clock, knowing that we'll eventually pass by. We came to investigate the last time they called for us, after all, if that's what they were doing."

"But if this is all a ruse, why bother going over there? Maybe that woman I saw in the mask earlier is the one that was screaming."

Fiona didn't need to respond. Both had heard those screams, and unless the woman in the mask was an Oscar-level actress, what they'd heard had been real terror, more probably pain.

Roz seemed to realize this, too. When she spoke again, she sounded almost chastened for suggesting otherwise. "So what's your plan?"

"I think they want us to go over there. They've been waiting for us to come to them. They're anticipating that we'll try the easiest route, the trail, and they set themselves up near enough for us to hear them again."

"But not near enough for us to see them."

"Exactly. They want us to leave the trail, right here, and come crashing and bumbling our way over there—announcing our arrival like lambs for the slaughter."

"So that means we can't go over there."

"No. It means we can't go this way. That's the thing about a plan. One unanticipated move, and it falls apart—theirs or ours. We have to try to approach their camp, or whatever it is, from another side. They'll be watching the woods this way."

"Okay, so what do we do?"

Fiona didn't immediately reply, a feeling of something like triumph rising in her chest. Her instincts were correct. Since this all began, some small part of her had been connecting these dots, and she'd finally put them together. Now came the hard part—doing something with this new information.

"I say we go back to the clearing by the scramble, follow the tree line for another half mile or so, in the direction we're hearing them now, and approach their camp from behind."

"That might work at first, but won't they hear us when we're that close?"

"I don't think so, not unless we're really careless. They won't have anyone watching on the far side."

"How can you be so sure?"

"I'm not. I'm guessing. But we have to try something they won't expect."

She could vaguely see movement in the dark, and she knew, without seeing her, that Roz was rubbing her mouth. The gesture was so habitual when she was worried about something, she didn't have to see it to know it was happening.

"It's a good idea," Roz said. "Even if all of what you said is conjecture, I think you're right in assuming that someone will be watching this side of their camp. Sneaking up behind them is the right call."

Her heart gave another lurch of victory. "Let's get going, then."

She started walking, not realizing for a long while that she was the one leading them back through the woods, back the way they'd come. If Roz minded, she didn't say anything. This was the first time in a long time someone had listened to and followed her lead.

Because of the bright moonlight, once they hit the clearing by the scramble, they were able to quicken their pace, almost jogging along the edge of the trees. Roz stopped them after ten minutes or so and pointed, wordlessly, into the woods. From here, they should be safely past the people from the woods, but that also meant they had to be as quiet as possible going forward. She didn't need to be told this, or told not to talk. She simply nodded, letting Roz take the lead again.

The moonlight helped somewhat. The trees were still thick here and blocked out most of it, but the light was so bright in the night sky, the branches acted more like blinds than curtains. Here and there the trees opened above them, and she could see in clear detail. It wasn't long before her ears picked up on the sound of the chopping wood again, dim but persistent, this time somewhere straight in front of them. They were going the right way.

After perhaps ten minutes of creeping as quietly as they could, Fiona glimpsed something in the woods ahead. At first, she thought her eyes were fooling her, but after a few more minutes, she was certain she was right. Somewhere ahead of them she could see the waving, dancing light of a campfire. Compared to the dampened moonlight, it was incredibly bright and clear, obvious from a good distance. Roz glanced back at her, the light bright enough for Fiona to see her face, and she put a finger on her lips. They'd been quiet all this time, but now they needed silence. Again, the brighter moonlight helped, and as they pussyfooted closer, the firelight finally helped as well.

They stopped some ten yards from the camp, crouching behind two trees to catch their breath. Finally, as if they'd agreed to it, they peered out from behind their trees into the camp.

There was a surprising number of tents. Fiona had noticed a few of these as they approached, but now, with the leisure to take it all in, she could count at least six, though possibly more behind the others she couldn't see. They were the large, canvas wall tents she remembered from summer camp as a kid—big enough to stand up in with large, two-flap doors. They'd been set up around an enormous bonfire being tended or watched by three standing people, all of them, based on their height and build, men. Two of them had their backs to Fiona and Roz, but one was facing their way.

Roz had described the masks before, but nothing had prepared her for the sight of them. Unlike the stylized Renaissance carnival masks she'd anticipated, the one she could see was crudely, almost childishly designed, with mismatched eye holes and a lumpy texture like bad papier-mâché—white and unadorned, some crooked, tall ears sticking up at the top like a rabbit's. It was horrifying and somehow so wrong and visually disturbing that Fiona whipped back behind the trunk of her tree, terrified that the masked man would look her way.

She glanced over at Roz, who was watching her, concerned, brows drawn. Fiona tried to shake off the creeps that had crawled all over her and made an okay with her fingers.

The screaming began then, sending a chill so deep through Fiona's soul that she almost called out in response. Some of this had to do with the screams' proximity. They were so much closer, it was as if the woman were screaming right next to them. This close to the shrieking, a stone's throw, Fiona was suddenly struck with an idea so deep and horrifying she had to bite down on her tongue again to keep from voicing it. In fact, she wondered then why she hadn't thought of this before. If these people had abducted the men and horses from camp the first night, who on earth had they taken now? What women were in these woods but her, Roz, and her friends?

It was one of her friends.

Chapter Sixteen

There was no way to share this insight with Roz, but she gestured wildly, still hidden behind the tree. Roz lifted her hands dramatically, obviously not understanding. Fiona was desperate to convey her thoughts somehow, but unable to talk, she couldn't do much beyond mimic her horror. Roz nodded and pumped her hands up and down in a dampening motion, palms toward the ground. She glanced over at the camp and motioned for Fiona to do the same.

The three men had moved away from the fire several feet toward the far side of the camp, their backs to her and Roz. They seemed to be watching for something, all of them staring out into the woods away from them. Roz gestured for Fiona's attention and pointed to the right at one of the tents. It was Fiona's turn to shrug, confused, and she saw Roz throw her hands up before she moved, quickly, away from the tree and toward the tents. Fiona was so surprised she almost missed her chance, but she managed to follow, staying close to the ground in a kind of half-bent, spidery crawl.

She sat down, hard, next to Roz by the side of the tent, almost sliding into place, breathing harder than the short jog merited. As they sat there, catching their breath, Fiona realized something. Like last time, when they'd still been on the trail, the screaming had stopped, which, to Fiona, suggested that they were doing something to the woman to force that noise out of her. This added further proof to what she'd thought. They meant for Fiona and Roz to hear the woman and come searching for her. They couldn't make her scream all night—they had some kind of pattern.

Roz gestured to their left, to the back of the tent, and the two of them scooted around, staying low, almost walking on their hands and feet.

A square patch of light streamed from the back of the tent—a window, Fiona realized. The two of them knelt on either side of it. Roz leaned over to her, her lips brushing her ear, and whispered so low Fiona almost didn't catch what she said.

"It's this one."

Fiona was surprised. When the screaming started, she'd been hidden behind the tree, unable to think straight. Somehow Roz had been with it enough to determine the source. This tent was next to another one some five or six feet away, and the other tents had been on the other side of the fire, so she supposed that as long as you knew which side the screaming had come from, it would be easy to make an educated guess. Now here, she could see that this tent had light coming from the inside. Roz pointed up at the window and shakily got to her feet, keeping out of the line of sight. Fiona did the same, her legs weak and quaking below her, suddenly terrified.

The window was almost opaque—a thick, reinforced plastic designed to let light in as opposed to offer a view. Peering through it was like looking into a funhouse mirror, the image distorted and fish-bowled. She could see movement, however, and the longer she squinted inside, the more sense she could make of what she was seeing.

Two people stood with their backs to them, one much shorter and slighter, another quite tall and broad. She could hear the murmur of their voices and tell that they were talking to each other by the way they turned their heads toward the other person, and though she could detect that one of the voices sounded feminine and higher and the other masculine one lower, she couldn't make out their words. Whether they were speaking low enough, or the heavy canvas masked the sound, she didn't know, but they were having an intense but quiet conversation. She saw what she presumed to be the woman gesturing with both hands and the man's mumbling reply. Whatever she was gesturing at was blocked by their bodies.

Roz motioned for her attention and then pointed into the woods, away from the tent. She then pointed at her mouth and ear. She wanted to talk.

The two of them headed out that way, moving more certainly and surely with the amplified light from the fire and the window. Fiona was still watching her footsteps as carefully as she could, certain that if she stepped on something like a branch or twig, someone would hear and investigate—one of those bulky guys by the fire, perhaps. They hadn't been armed, at least not that she could see, but that didn't mean their guns weren't within easy reach.

When they'd gone perhaps fifty feet, far enough away that it was getting hard to see again, Roz pulled her behind a large, gnarled cottonwood and down into a crouch. Even if someone did look this way, they would be hidden. Still, Roz kept her voice low, barely above a whisper.

"The woman who was screaming is in that tent. The smaller person talking to the bigger one must be the woman I saw earlier. She kind of seems like the leader."

Fiona nodded, forgetting that she could respond out loud.

"What were you trying to say earlier?" Roz asked. "Back by the other trees."

"It must be one of my friends. Who else could it be?"

Roz nodded, clearly having thought the same thing. Her lips were pinched, brows furrowed, as if reluctant to agree. Maybe she'd hoped Fiona wouldn't make this connection.

"Do you think they're all here?" Roz asked.

This possibility hadn't occurred to her. For some reason, she pictured only one person. The idea that all of her friends were here, possibly in the other tents, was so awful she couldn't immediately reply.

Roz sighed and sat down on her butt, leaning her pack against the tree. Fiona sat down too, happy to get off the balls of her feet. Once again, they faced each other, near enough that their knees touched.

"What if they all are?' Fiona finally said. She hadn't wanted to ask.

"Then this is going to be a lot harder to pull off."

"Maybe not, though," Fiona said, scrambling for some other option. "Would they have had enough time to go all the way back to camp and bring all three of them here? Only one person was screaming." She was reaching here, but she needed something to hang on to. The thought that all her friends were somewhere in those other tents was too much to take in.

"But there's a lot of tents over there."

That gave Fiona pause, and she remembered something obvious they hadn't mentioned yet.

"Do you think the guys are here, too?"

"Jesus," Roz said, her surprise suggesting she'd momentarily forgotten about them.

If more of their friends were here, they could do little about it. In fact, they could do almost nothing for the woman in the tent. No way would they be able to get in there and out without someone seeing them. Not unless—

"Hey!" Fiona said, barely holding in her excitement. "Do you still have your Leatherman?"

Roz fumbled in her pockets and pulled it out.

"We can't bust her out, cowboy style and guns blazing, but we might be able to sneak her out."

"How?" Roz asked.

"Out the back." She took the Leatherman from her and unfolded the longest of its knives. She made a cutting motion, and Roz smiled in understanding.

"Genius."

"We can't get to all the tents, but we can at least go in the back of the one with the light and maybe the one next to it."

"It's a plan. We have to wait until that woman and that guy leave, though."

"They can't be in there all night, right?" Fiona asked. "What time do you think it is?"

Roz tilted her head back and forth. "About one, maybe a little later—two, two thirty tops."

"They have to go to bed sometime."

"But if they're calling to us, like you said, don't you think they'll keep doing it? In shifts, like?"

Fiona hadn't thought of this, and the little flame of hope she'd been nursing died out. After all, who were they fooling? Even if they managed to stay quiet enough for no one to notice them slicing up the back of the tent, what then? That screaming woman, whoever she was, was probably hurt. Their situation would be the same as with Carol—someone hurt and no way to take them back to safety.

Roz took the Leatherman back from her, folded the blade down, and stowed it in a pocket. Then she grabbed Fiona's hand in hers, squeezing it.

"Don't you give up on me, Fiona. We're going to do this. We only need a few minutes to get her out. We don't even have to cut the whole back—just enough to slip in and out. But we need—"

"A diversion," Fiona said.

Roz smiled again and squeezed her hand harder. "Exactly. A diversion would do it. Some people will probably stay in camp, but I'm almost positive the two people in that tent will leave and wait outside. They're not going to keep on with whatever they're doing if they might have more victims to truss up."

They were quiet again. Roz had likely realized the major flaw with this idea. What on earth could they do that would divert enough attention for these people to go investigate? It would have to be big.

"It'll have to be me," Fiona said.

Roz shook her head. "No. It's too dangerous. You're fast, but I'm faster. Whoever does it will have to run like hell, hide somewhere for a while, and then catch up to the other somewhere safe."

"But you're stronger. I might not be able to get her out of the tent on my own."

"She might be tied up. If you cut off—"

"And if she's hurt, she'd have to be dragged out of there. I can't do it, Roz. Don't you see? Even without my hurt shoulder, I'm just not strong enough."

It was bright enough that she could see Roz rubbing her mouth again, and she touched her knee. Roz stopped, putting her hand on top of hers, brushing her thumb lightly against her wrist.

"I don't like it," Roz finally said. She sounded hurt, almost angry.

"Neither do I, but we don't have any choice."

"These assholes have been forcing our hand this whole time. Now it seems like they're doing it again."

It was light enough here that Fiona could see the sparkle of Roz's eyes and the contours of her strong, square jaw. Her fingers went there almost of their own accord, and she traced the edge to her chin and down the length of her throat to her collarbone. She rested her hand there and then they moved, as one, to kiss. Something about this kiss was sweeter than earlier. No hint of sadness or desperation now, just a shared, mutual warmth.

Roz moved back a little, and they rested with their foreheads together in the dark. Then, almost as if she hadn't stopped talking, she continued.

"So what are you going to do to grab their attention?"

"Well," Fiona said, "it has to be something major, or at least major enough to make a few of them check it out. It also can't be so important that they close ranks, so to speak, and station guards in every tent. I want something that makes them curious, but not necessarily scared."

"A fire," Roz suggested.

Fiona laughed and then realized she was serious. "Really? Won't it...cause a forest fire?"

Roz shook her head. “Not likely, not with all this rain we’ve been having. You could dig a little trench around it, too, clear the branches back a couple of feet. It only needs to be a small one. It’ll be obvious out there in the dark.”

“If someone is looking that way.”

“Exactly. You’ll have to start it on the far side—in the direction they’re watching now, toward the trail.”

“All right. Then what? Won’t they see me right away?”

“Not if you do exactly as I tell you. There’s a way to delay a start with a fire—two, maybe three minutes, if you light it the right way with some of the hand sanitizer and few leaves. It can act like a sort of fuse. That would give you enough time to run over to the trail.”

“Then what?”

“Then we have to figure out somewhere to meet up. First, head toward the rock scramble. They’ll expect you to go the other way, back toward home. One or two might investigate the other direction, but if you’re fast enough, you can hide before they see you.”

“Okay. Then what?”

“I’ve got a question first. Do you think you could find that spot we stopped, after the scramble? The one where I took a nap?”

Fiona wanted to agree, but she couldn’t. “No. I mean, maybe approximately, but not for certain.”

“That’s okay. You can hide inside the tree line somewhere to the left of the trail—maybe five minutes jogging, not running. Hide there a few feet inside the trees so you can still see out. Wait until you see me, and we’ll hide together until morning. Then we’ll follow the river back to the road.”

“But won’t they figure it out right away? I mean that one of us set the fire? Won’t that make them suspicious?”

“Why does that matter?”

“If they know we set the fire, then they’ll probably figure out why we set it. They’ll start searching for you and whoever you’re with. You won’t be able to escape quickly enough if she’s hurt.”

"You have any other ideas?"

Roz didn't ask in an aggressive way, which meant that she probably agreed with her, but Fiona was still fumbling for words. All she knew was that Roz would need help. Even if she could physically carry this woman, in no way would she be able to go very far like that.

"We'll have to hide somewhere closer than that," she finally said. "Maybe back the way we came here—close to the scramble on this side of the trail. I'll set the fire, and instead of running toward the trail, I'll circle back and come here—right here. You get the woman out of the tent and bring her here, and the two of us will take her back the way we came and find somewhere to hide somewhere in the woods until morning."

Roz was rubbing her mouth again, and Fiona let her. It wasn't a great plan—all of this was ridiculous, but that didn't mean they shouldn't try. Already, too much time had passed since they'd first heard the screams. Too much time had passed since the second time. All of this needed to happen before it started getting light out, and Fiona knew that eventually she would hit a level of exhaustion where she wouldn't be able to think clearly, not to mention hike another twenty miles. They had to act now or give up this whole thing.

"Okay, okay," Roz said, clearly reluctant. "Let me tell you how to light the fire."

CHAPTER SEVENTEEN

When she saw smoke, she started running. She'd done exactly as Roz had told her to do, following the careful steps she'd described despite feeling like her tired mind was filling up with cotton wool. Using their poop trowel, she'd dug a quick, shallow circle around a dryish patch of earth, moving as much of the ground debris nearby as far away as she could. She soaked three leaves in hand sanitizer and put them under a pile of sticks and small branches stacked in a kind of cabin-shape so that it should collapse into itself instead of lighting the whole forest aflame. Then, using most of the rest of the hand sanitizer, she'd made a long line away from the wood and the leaves and partially around the circle. Finally, she put one last drop of it on a dry leaf before setting it on fire, one end touching the line of liquid. She couldn't stay and watch to make sure it would catch. It would either work this time or not at all.

Roz was going to wait until she heard them see the fire before she started slicing up the back of the tent. A lot of things could go wrong here. The fire might not start correctly, for instance, or someone might stay in the tent with the woman they were trying to rescue. Still, this was their best option.

Unless Roz was incredibly fast, it was possible that she might make it back to the tent fast enough to help Roz carry the woman—she wasn't far away. She'd set the fire a couple hundred yards away from the camp in the direction they were watching—toward the trail. It had to be far enough that they couldn't see her there in the woods, digging the pit and lighting the fire, but close enough that they would see it when the flames started. Now, after hours in the dark, and the fully risen moon helping her find her way, she sailed through the trees at an almost normal jogging pace, circling wide and out and toward the place they'd agreed to meet. She wasn't being particularly quiet at this point, as she was out of hearing range, but she also found that the last couple of hours had given her enough practice to find her next footfall easily and quietly, and she moved in a kind of hopping near-grace.

When she was close to their rendezvous, it took her a couple of minutes to find it. She had to approximate based on the location of the tents, and it wasn't as easy to locate as she'd expected. Finally, the edge of a tree caught her eye, sending a wave of relieved recognition washing through her. She slowed her steps, inching forward, hoping now that she'd find Roz already there with their damsel in distress.

Instead, their little spot was empty, so she took the opportunity to catch her breath. The run had strangely done her some good. She felt revitalized, almost fresh, her nervous anxiety now more akin to excitement. It felt good to be doing something, finally, after all these endless days of terror. It felt good to strike back.

She peered around the edge of the tree into the dark, in the direction of the camp, trying to see something, anything, but it was dark and far enough that she could make out nothing but the silhouettes of the tents. Whether something was happening in camp, or if Roz was already cutting up the canvas backing, she had no way of knowing without investigating. The plan, however, had been for her to wait right here, and she was afraid that if she did anything different, she'd end up either screwing everything up or, at the very least, startling Roz when she started heading her way. She decided to wait five minutes, or as near as she could by counting, before doing anything.

Roz had left the little backpack here, and she took a careful, long sip of water. If all went well, three of them would have to share what was likely less than a liter of water, with almost twenty miles between them and the next clean source.

Shouts came from the camp, and instinctively she ducked down, hunching her shoulders regardless of the pain. This was a different sound than the screaming they'd heard earlier. For one, she could tell that the voices were men's. The words were indistinct, but she could tell that much, at least. Something was happening.

Careful lest she give herself away, she slowly crept to the edge of the large tree again, peering toward the camp. She could see the sweeping light of several flashlights arcing through the camp—the light strange and eerie after all these hours without anything artificial. One of the lights suddenly flashed between the tents, and she saw movement between two of them. She ducked back, heart hammering, eyes pinched closed in terror. She sat there, huddled up and waiting, certain she would be discovered. A long minute passed.

Finally calming down, she opened her eyes, recognizing that some part of her had been listening for footsteps and had heard nothing. She crept back to look past the tree again. The flashlights had moved away, with an occasional arc of light flickering through the wood on the far side of the camp.

Every fiber of her soul wanted to go, now, while it was relatively safe, and try to help Roz escape. She and Roz had made a tactical error. They should have come up with a sign to each other—a call, or maybe a whistle, to let the other know she was on her way. Fiona was afraid that if she did go to help, Roz, or possibly the woman she was helping, would be startled enough to make a sound, to call out or worse. Their only advantage was silence and surprise.

Then, almost as if watching had made it happen, Fiona once again saw movement in the woods, and she was certain it was headed her way. She could hear this person or people now, a stumbling, shuffling drag through the brush, and she caught more details as she stared in that direction. Hunched over slightly and moving slowly, the figure was almost crawling. She debated for a second or two longer before moving around the edge of the tree toward what she hoped she was seeing.

Finally, a flash of moonlight revealed the figures fully. Roz was dragging someone along on her side, one of this person's arm thrown over her shoulders, Roz's arm around their torso, shuffling forward almost like she was in a three-legged race. Fiona's movement and sound made Roz pause for a second before she motioned her closer for help. Fiona sprang forward, grabbing almost blindly for the person's other arm, realizing as she did that she'd suspected all along who they would find in that tent. Some part of her, maybe, had recognized that voice from the beginning.

It was Jill.

She was unconscious and hung between them in a limp bundle of limbs and appendages, her head lolling with each shuffling step. She and Roz leaned down and grabbed one of her legs, wrenching her up and off the ground to move her more quickly. They paused to rest in their spot by the backpack, setting her down and propping her against the biggest tree. Fiona was frantic. While the moon was brighter here than in the thicker woods, she couldn't see any obvious signs of trauma. She moved her hands over her friend, feeling for wet blood or broken skin. Her clothes were damp, though that was likely from sweat. She was also underdressed for the cold night air, wearing what she'd last seen her in—shorts and a light T-shirt. Someone had removed her socks and boots, and when she touched Jill's bare feet, she moaned and twitched a little until Fiona moved them away. She stilled at once, limp once more.

"I can't tell what's wrong with her," Fiona whispered. "Whatever they were doing to her to make her scream like that, it wasn't with a knife, at least. I don't feel any open wounds. Maybe if she wakes up, she'll be able to walk on her own. It's going to be a problem without boots, though."

"I saw them back there in the tent but couldn't grab them and her at the same time. If I'd thought about it more clearly, I could have laced them together and carried them around my neck, but I was too scared someone would come back. Do you think I should go grab them now?"

The thought was too much to take. "We have to get out of here," Fiona said. "We need to make some distance. If we wait here, they'll catch us the second they think to look this way."

"She's not going to make it very far like this. Even if she's okay now, she'll end up really hurt without shoes."

This made sense, but Fiona could feel time slipping away as the seconds and minutes ticked by. Any time now, someone would come back to camp to investigate. Even now, she was certain they hadn't abandoned it. They'd probably sent two or three people to check out the fire while the rest hung back, waiting. Once the others returned, everyone in that camp would likely start checking things out. Once they saw that Jill was gone, they'd start a real search.

"I'm going back," Roz said, standing up.

"No! We have to—"

"Not a debate."

Roz moved away, and Fiona tried to grab her leg to stop her, but she was already gone. She wanted to watch her progress, but Jill moaned again, louder this time, and Fiona was forced to focus on her, rubbing one of her hands and shushing her as quietly as possible. Suddenly, as if a light had been turned on, Jill sat bolt upright, calling out, and Fiona moved forward, grabbing her from behind and slapping a hand over her mouth. She struggled with her as she thrashed. Fiona started whispering in her ear then, trying to make her hear sense, but Jill was panicking, fighting with every ounce of her strength. Her head made contact with the tree behind her and she saw stars, but she didn't lose her grip. Soon the two of them were rolling around, Jill attempting to buck her off.

"Stop it, Jill," Fiona finally said, nearly shouting despite the danger. "It's me. It's Fiona. You're okay now."

The fighting tension drained out of her at once, and she went limp again in Fiona's arms. Fiona removed her hand and rolled away. The two of them stayed there on the ground, shoulder to shoulder, panting. Then she heard Jill sob.

"Oh, honey," Fiona said, rolling toward her and reaching out blindly toward her in the pitch-dark.

Jill found her, pulling her into a painful hug.

"You came for me. I can't believe it."

"Shhhh," Fiona said. "It's okay now. You'll be okay."

"I can't believe you came," Jill said.

Her tears were hot against Fiona's neck, and she squeezed her back, her own eyes filling up. Their earlier argument flashed through her mind, and she was overwhelmed with shame. Had Jill died out here, she would never have forgiven herself.

"Of course I did," Fiona whispered. "I love you, you jerk."

Jill didn't reply, still sobbing, and Fiona's stomach gave a great lurch of terror. She wanted to ask what had happened, how Jill came to be here, how she'd been captured, what they'd done to her, what she'd seen inside the camp, but it wasn't the time for questions. Jill needed to cry it out, and time was slipping away.

Fiona became aware of a sound moving toward them. A shadow flashed across her face, and she peered up at Roz, who was staring down at them. The moonlight made her quizzical expression obvious, even from down here, and Fiona had to fight a wild urge to laugh out loud.

Jill let go, and she and Fiona sat up. Roz crouched down next to them, handing Jill her boots.

"I couldn't find your socks," she whispered, "but there's an extra pair in the pack. Can you walk?"

"Yes," Jill mumbled. She was still tear-choked, her voice thick.

"Good. We need to hurry. I think the ones that left are coming back to camp. I could hear their voices more clearly this time, and I think one of the people they left behind in camp was checking out the tents. I could hear someone in the one nearby, one or two over from where you were."

While she was talking, Fiona dug around in the pack for the socks and handed them to Jill. Then, seeing her struggle, she helped her undo the roll and held the extra as she donned the first. Jill was moving slowly, fumbling in the dark, and Fiona could barely stop herself from taking over. Their tiny window of time was slipping away. Already, perhaps ten or fifteen minutes had passed since she started the fire. Assuming that the people in camp had seen it, investigated it, and checked out the trail, that left Fiona and her friends another five minutes at the outside to escape. All it would take was one flashlight pointed their way, and they'd be caught.

Finally, after what felt like an age, Jill had her second boot laced. She and Roz helped her to her feet and then waited as Jill found her equilibrium. She swayed slightly, and Fiona surged forward to steady her. Jill stilled, a hand to her forehead, and then shook her head briskly a few times as if clearing it.

"Let's go," Jill said.

"You sure?" Fiona asked.

"Yes."

"Tell us if you need to stop," Roz said.

Roz slipped the backpack on her shoulders and started moving, leading the way with Fiona at the rear. They'd taken these positions instinctively, Fiona knowing that someone needed to watch Jill in case she started to lag or stumble. Neither she nor Roz had any idea what she'd gone through, but the memory of those screams was enough to suggest that it had been traumatic and painful. Fiona would never have hoped she would still be able to walk. She'd assumed they'd be dragging whomever they found through these woods, which would probably have gotten them caught. Their earlier plan seemed foolhardy, at best.

Now, they reached the edge of the woods by the rock scramble easily. The moon was beginning to set now, but it still gave off a good deal of light.

"That's good," Roz said. "Now we know what time it is."

"How?" Fiona asked.

"Moonset. It's about two thirty or three this time of year, so it must be just before that."

This was hard to believe. After all their activity tonight, Fiona would have thought it was much later—almost dawn.

"Why is that a good thing?" Fiona asked.

"Well, besides knowing the approximate time, we'll also have better conditions to hide. It'll be completely dark in probably half an hour or less. We'll have maybe two, three hours before it starts to get light again."

Jill spoke for the first time since they left their hiding spot. "Where are we going to hide?"

"In the woods, over by the river. We can't take the trail, and the water's the only other way to find our way back. Plus, we're going to need something to drink. We're almost out."

"We're going to drink it right from the river?" Fiona asked.

It was bright enough to see Roz shrug. "Better than falling down from dehydration. It's a chance we'll have to take. You can treat giardia."

Fiona didn't mention the fact that the people from the woods would likely anticipate this plan very quickly. After all, if she, Roz, and Jill didn't take the trail, that was the next logical choice. She didn't need to mention it, though, as all three of them were probably thinking the same thing. Even if it was almost as dangerous as the trail itself, they had no other choice.

If Jill was curious why they didn't have a filter, she didn't say. In fact, exposed here in the light, her body language told an entire story. She looked deflated, defeated, somehow smaller than before. Now Fiona could see that one of her eyes was dark around the edges, and her lip was swollen. Other than that, however, the main issue she seemed to be having was struggling against the cold. She was shivering, hard.

Roz removed the fleece jacket and handed it to her. Jill lifted her chin slightly in thanks but said nothing. This wrung-out wreck was nothing like the usual Jill. Fiona had to hope that whatever had happened to her wouldn't be permanent.

"Let's go," Roz said, starting to walk. "I want a hiding place to nap until morning. There's going to be one more tricky part before we can stop for a little while."

"What is it?"

"When we walk past the trail. They could be watching for us there."

"There's no other way?"

Roz shook her head. "Not another way with water, anyway. We're SOL."

"You also said we were going to stop for a couple of hours. Why?"

"Because we need the light. I won't know where we're going without being able to see the water, and we need to move as quickly as possible. Plus, I think we could all use a little shut-eye. We'll have to keep watch, but even an hour would help."

They continued in silence. Jill hadn't said anything since her one question earlier, but she walked along with them willingly enough, her eyes and face downcast, her posture wilted, sagging.

Fiona's anxiety and fear were back in equal measure, now doubled for the two women she was with. They had to keep going, keep trying, but she didn't think the people from the camp would let them leave now that they'd seen them and now that she and Roz had tricked them and rescued Jill. Their situation had been life or death since those first shots rang out mere hours ago, but she was certain now of something else.

They would want revenge.

Chapter Eighteen

It was still Fiona's watch. Too wired to sleep, she'd volunteered first, and as she waited, she decided to let the others keep sleeping.

The trip here had been uneventful. When they'd reached the one dangerous spot, near the entrance to the trail, Roz had suggested with hand motions that they run past it. Roz leaned down, hands nearly brushing the ground, and disappeared almost at once in a quick scurry. Jill and Fiona were forced to sprint to catch up. When they had, Roz had pushed them much harder than before, almost jogging, all the way to the edge of the river. They'd walked along about twenty feet from the water for perhaps half an hour in the direction toward home before she'd led them away some hundred yards to this makeshift campsite.

Roz was motionless and had been since she lay down. Jill, on the other hand, had been twitching and muttering on and off the last two hours. They were all huddled close together to share the poncho, hammock, and emergency blanket, and Fiona was almost hot now. Jill's head was inches from Fiona's left hand, Roz's similar on her right. Fiona's left shoulder was still trussed up and sore, but she managed to run her fingers through Jill's fine, knotted hair once or twice to calm her down again.

The dawn's light was starting to reveal the world. Once a pale, sickly glow coming from the east, the sky overall had taken on a rosy, pink glow. The stars were starting to fade, and the forest was coming to life once more. The birds had grown louder and louder until finally one whistled in the trees above them, startling Jill awake. She sat up, jerking around in terror, and Fiona held out a hand, partially in defense, partially to catch her attention. Jill's shoulders drooped, and she sighed, rubbing her face and then jerking her hands away.

"Ouch," she whispered.

Now, with the light bright enough to see her clearly, Jill's face told most of her story. One eye was completely black with a purple, ringed bruise, and the other was starting to darken, the skin a bluish-green. She had a cut on the bridge of her nose, likely the cause of the black eyes, and the edges of her nostrils were crusted with blood. Her upper lip was cut, and they were both swollen, one of her cheekbones also bruised.

"You look like shit," Fiona said.

"Gee, thanks."

They both started giggling, and Fiona had to cover her mouth to keep from braying with laughter. Roz stirred but didn't wake, and Fiona made a quieting motion with one hand. The backpack was right behind her, and she pulled it closer, extending the water line to Jill. Two hours ago, they'd all had a careful drink before Jill and Roz went to sleep, but Fiona could tell from the weight of that pack that they were almost out. Now, with her own sip, she caught a little air, a telltale sign that they'd reached the bottom of the bladder. She stopped herself, wanting Roz to have at least a mouthful when she woke up.

She dug out one of the emergency ration bars and extended a section to Jill. Jill grimaced but started nibbling it, grimacing harder. The sight made Fiona want to start laughing again, despite everything.

"They're the worst," she whispered.

Jill nodded vigorously, and the movement was enough to make Roz stir a little more. Finally, Roz stretched, her hand brushing across Fiona's knee, and then she sat up, like Jill had, clearly startled. She glanced up at the sky and then frowned at Fiona.

"You were supposed to wake me up."

Fiona shrugged. "Yeah, well. You were too cute sleeping like that. And I was too worked up to sleep."

Roz looked like she wanted to argue, but after a quick glance at Jill, her face cleared and she nodded.

"Ahh, ha!" Jill said, grinning widely. "I see."

"What?" Fiona asked.

"You two are a thing now. I was wondering how long it'd take."

Fiona couldn't help the blood rushing to her face. Roz seemed a little embarrassed, too, her eyes downcast.

"'Bout fucking time, you two. Though your timing is a little weird."

"Breakfast?" Fiona asked, trying to change the subject. Jill snickered but didn't say anything else.

Roz nodded and took a big bite out of the section Fiona handed her. She closed her eyes, murmuring, "Mmmmm. Gourmet!"

This sarcasm set Jill and Fiona to giggling again. Despite the danger and their horrible night, Fiona couldn't help it. Roz made a quieting motion at the two of them, but she was smiling, likely recognizing their relative safety. The people from the woods hadn't followed them yet, or least they hadn't come near the stretch she'd watched from here. They, like the three of them, would have to follow the river to catch them, and there hadn't been a single sign of them these last two hours. What this meant or suggested about them was problematic in another way, as they couldn't know where they were now, but for now Fiona felt almost safe for the first time in days.

Roz drank the rest of the water, and the three of them stared at each other for a moment without speaking. They all knew what this meant. The water they drank from here on out would be dangerous, possibly infectious. How quickly would they fall sick if they caught something?

"Let's get rolling," Roz said, getting to her feet. Fiona stood up much slower, her back and wounds screaming with pain. Roz, possibly seeing her face, untied the bandage, pulled her shirt aside, and examined her shoulder.

"It's okay, though a little inflamed. But like I said last night, it just grazed you. As long as someone looks at it pretty soon, I don't see it getting much worse."

"You were shot?" Jill said, pushing Roz aside to peer at the wound.

"Yes."

Jill's eyes were huge. "Wow. Talk about badass."

Fiona chuckled again, and Jill gave her a quick, one-armed hug. Jill helped Roz retie the handkerchief around her shoulder, and when Fiona gingerly rotated it, she realized that the pain had in fact decreased. Now it burned rather than shouted, was stiff rather than achy. She'd be okay.

Jill, on the other hand…

Jill, seeing her inspection, shook her head. "Later."

Fiona didn't push it. Jill was right. Story time could happen when they were all safe again. She did, however, have one question.

"Okay. But Jill—where are Sarah and Carol?"

Jill wouldn't meet their eyes, clearly embarrassed. "They're back at camp, as far as I know."

"You left them there?"

Jill's shoulders rose and she nodded. "Yes. I made a stupid mistake When the two of you left, I decided to follow. But I didn't see them with those weirdos last night, so they're probably still back there."

"Did Carol or Sarah know you were leaving?"

Jill sighed, meeting Fiona's eyes. "I put a note in my tent."

"Jesus, Jill."

"I know. I was a fucking asshole, okay? And I'm sorry."

"What are you apologizing to me for? It's the two of them you need to apologize to. Sarah's probably losing her shit."

"Yeah, but I'm sorry for you, too. For yesterday. For everything. This is all my fault." She turned to Roz. "I know it is. You tried to warn me, and you tried to help, and I fucked everything up. I'm sorry for all of it."

Roz stared at her levelly for a long pause before nodding. "It's okay, Jill, and it's not all your fault. I should have made us go home after the first camp. Let's just get through this and put the blame where it belongs."

Jill grinned, her expression dark. "Damn right. Those wackos need to be taught a lesson."

In her pathetic, beaten condition, this statement stuck Fiona as absurdly confident, but she agreed with her entirely. It was up to the three of them to bring the hammer down on this, whatever it was. These people, whoever they were, needed to be stopped.

The three of them carefully packed their makeshift blankets and gear, the remains now so pathetic the backpack was practically empty. Once again, Roz donned it.

"At least we won't have to carry any water," she said. "We can drink it as we go."

"How far is it again?" Jill asked.

Roz frowned, looking up at the sky and rubbing her mouth.

"If we were on the trail—about seventeen, eighteen miles. Here on the river, I couldn't say for sure, but probably at least a few more than that. Twenty-two or three at the very least. We were lucky last night, since it was easy to walk nearby. But in some places, it will be much harder. There's always a lot of growth near the water, and it sometimes runs through canyons we won't be able to follow directly. Walk too far away, we'll be back on the trail, but walk too close and we might leave footprints. We'll have to weigh our options every step."

"Do you think we can make it back today?"

Roz shrugged. "If we're incredibly lucky. I once did almost forty miles in a single day, dawn to sunset, about this time of year, but the trail was in the desert, and it was clear and relatively flat for a good part. Twenty, twenty-five is the max I've done in these woods. We'll have one advantage though."

"What?"

"We'll be going downhill a good part of the day."

They walked in silence, meeting the edge of the water a few minutes later. A small eddy led off from the wild churning of the river, but the water was muddy and unappealing. A few water spiders danced across the surface, and some tiny minnows swam around in the murk. Nevertheless, it was a beautiful sight. The rising sun cast rainbows in all directions across the sparkling surface.

The far side of the river consisted of sheer rock, rising some hundred feet straight up. Fiona had thought earlier of suggesting that they cross and walk along that side as a secondary means of protection, but with the rock face and the wild water, that was clearly not an option here. She knew the river diverted later, so perhaps then the idea would be worth revisiting.

Roz motioned for them to continue, the sound of the water once again too loud to speak over. This was yet another reason to walk a bit away from it, as they would need to hear whether someone was following them.

Some fifteen minutes later, they came to a small pool of water so crystalline and pure she could see the details of every stone at the bottom. It was perhaps four of five feet deep, almost perfectly round, a few purple columbines growing on the edge in the middle of some bright, almost fluorescent wild brush and vines.

All three rushed to the edge of the water, kneeling in a semicircle. Fiona scooped handful after handful into her mouth, wetting her chin and the front of her shirt in her haste. The sensation and flavor were striking, almost cloyingly sweet and painfully cold, and she realized now how dehydrated she'd been. Her body seemed to trill with pleasure and relief. Whether she got sick later or not, she'd never enjoyed drinking something half as much.

"I've always wanted to do this," Jill said, grinning again, water running down her chin and neck.

Fiona couldn't help but grin back. She too had always fantasized about drinking directly from a river. It was tempting to think about diving in and filling up. While it was still fairly chilly in the morning air, this time of year it would warm up quickly, and she craved a bath.

Away from the edge of the river, Jill was now washing her face, scrubbing off some of the crusted blood.

"Try not to get it in your eyes," Roz warned her.

Jill laughed, water dripping off her face. "We're drinking this stuff. I hardly think this could be worse. In for a penny and all that."

Roz didn't respond, likely seeing the sense in this remark, but Fiona could tell that she was more hesitant than they were, pausing before each mouthful like she was forcing herself to drink it.

"This water's so clear and clean, I guess it might make sense to try to fill up the bladder," Roz said. "There might be some stretches where we'll have to walk farther away, so we might not have access for a stretch or two."

Or we might need to hide for a while, Fiona thought.

As Roz worked on filling it up, submerging the whole thing in the pool, Fiona splashed the water over her face and the back of her neck with her uninjured hand, rubbing off some of the sweat and grime crusted all over her. She'd forgotten about the cut on her face, and it sang with pain when the water hit it. She gingerly explored it with her fingertips, realizing now, for the first time, how deep it was. She was going to have a serious scar.

Roz pulled the bladder from the pool, twisting the cap closed, and glanced over at Fiona and winked, grinning.

At least there's that, Fiona thought, returning the smile. At least she still likes me like this.

"Uh-oh," Jill said.

"What?" Fiona asked.

"You two are getting moony on me. If you don't watch it, I'll have to push you in to cool you off."

"Jill, you wouldn't dare!"

Jill started walking toward her, hands out as if to push her, and Fiona leapt to her feet, an undignified squeal escaping her lips. Roz, alarmed as well, scooted backward a little and lost her footing. Fiona lunged forward to catch her, but Roz was already pinwheeling her arms before falling backward into the river. Fiona and Jill raced to the water's edge as she came up, sputtering and shouting.

Roz finally managed to get to her feet, the water hitting above her waist, her expression murderous. Jill's eyes were huge, her face pale, and Fiona had to fight a wild urge to laugh.

"You asked for it," Roz said, climbing out far enough to grab Jill's arm to yank her into the water. Jill came up a second later, howling with laughter, and the two of them splashed back and forth at each other, drenching Fiona's legs.

"Hey!" she said, jumping back from the splash zone.

Both of them looked over at her, and the merriment suddenly died from their faces. Jill clapped a hand over her mouth and bent in half, almost as if in pain. Roz's face hardened, her eyes narrowing to angry slits.

"What?" Fiona asked.

Roz pointed behind her. Fiona turned slowly, terrified but already knowing what she'd see.

Three trees behind her had been tagged with the carved patterns that had haunted them for days now. The people from the woods had been here before them.

Chapter Nineteen

Fiona wondered how many times she'd let herself be fooled before this was over. How many times would she relax, start to feel like herself again, only to be caught out, frightened and terrified once more. In fact, having let herself relax back at the pool, the fear seemed worse now, almost like a wound she'd probed open again by accident—familiar, but sharp and startling in its intensity.

No one had spoken during the last hour. Despite the horror she knew they all felt, she and the others had been relatively calm about it all, drying off a little with the hammock, getting the water bladder safely back in the pack, and moving on without panicking. Jill examined the trees closely, and before they'd left, she'd given them both a single nod. It was as they'd all suspected: the carvings had been done recently. Whether this meant last night or in the day or days before this hardly mattered. The people from the woods knew they would come this way. They'd been here before and were probably tracking them right now. For all any of them knew, they were being watched right now.

It was hard not to hunch as they plodded along the edge of the water. Although she suspected it was all in her mind, she could almost feel the crosshairs on the back of her head. But why were these people waiting? Why not simply shoot and be done with all this? Maybe it was simply more of the same. They were being toyed with. From the beginning, they'd been herded this way and that, from campsite to campsite, from space to space, a direct line, going wherever they were told. These psychopaths had the power here, and she and her friends were simply their hapless toys.

One thing was working in their favor—they were making good time. Fiona didn't even have to ask Roz to know that. Their pace was strong and sure, fast without being reckless, careful and certain with Roz leading the way. Without a backpack, Fiona found it almost effortless to move this quickly. Despite her fatigue and her various wounds, Fiona was sure she could keep this up for hours, especially now that they had plenty of water.

They were, in fact, also headed downhill most of the way. Generally, the descent was gradual, so slight as to be imperceptible to the foot or eye, but in other spots, it was steeper, and they all fairly jogged down the longer hills. But Fiona's knees were starting to hurt a little with the impact going down. In her larger pack she kept a pair of extendable hiking poles for descents to help with exactly this, but she didn't have them with her now. The tendons on the sides and back of her knees were aching like a sore tooth. Still, the pain was manageable, a minor annoyance. When she got back home, she'd put some ice on them and sit on the couch for a few days.

The thought almost gave her pause. For a second there, she'd imagined a time after this, as if it were going to happen. It was almost as bad as imagining what might happen to them out here in the woods. She was surprised to find herself tearing up, glad she was at the back of the group. While it was true that she had to keep hope alive, had to keep going—otherwise why even try?—she couldn't let herself think very far ahead. It was too painful. Put one foot in front of the other and repeat. That's all she could do. Later could wait.

At the bottom of a particularly steep hill, perhaps two hours after they'd left the pool of water, Roz motioned them away from the river and led them over to a clustered group of sizeable, sharp boulders. Long ago, glaciers had covered this entire area, leaving these monstrous stony remnants behind like lost marbles along its path as it receded. Today it gave them perfect cover, and they all collapsed on the ground in the middle of the stone circle, leaning back to rest.

"Sorry to push you guys," Roz said. "I was waiting until I saw something like this. I hope you're not too worn out."

"I'm fine," Jill said.

"Me, too."

Roz smiled. "Good. I think we've done close to five miles already, and we have a good deal of daylight left. We keep up this pace, we should reach the road long before sunset."

Neither she nor Jill contradicted her. They'd all made the same connections and presumptions she had. They were being followed, maybe watched. They were never going to make it out of here. Still, they could keep pretending it would happen, and who knew? Maybe at least one of them would. More people meant more targets, after all. There was safety in numbers.

As if reading her thoughts, Roz grabbed her right hand and squeezed it. Fiona met her eyes and smiled, her troubles momentarily retreating. Roz's eyes were a cool, deep brown, with a slight dark amber ring around her pupils. Despite functioning on about three hours of sleep, the whites were clear, not bloodshot, the expression in them bright, fierce, and alert. Seeing her determination, Fiona warmed from within and leaned in for a quick kiss. Her lips were salty and soft. She was somewhat chaste to avoid embarrassing Jill, but when Fiona pulled away, she saw a glimmer of heat in Roz's eyes that seemed to hint at what she'd really like to do. It all seemed so far away, so removed, the fantasy of something later, something better that could only happen somewhere else, to someone else.

"What dreams may come?" Fiona murmured.

"What's that?" Roz said.

"Nothing."

The three of them took several long sips of the water. With the river nearby and still easy to follow and refill at will, they could drink their fill now and for the foreseeable future. The water had lost some of its freshness inside the plastic bladder, but it was still cool and refreshing. Roz made them eat another square of the food ration, which Fiona was able to choke down with large mouthfuls of water. A quick memory of her last dinner before this trip—fresh sushi and dumplings—made the last bite particularly hard to swallow. She promised herself that if they made it out alive, she would never eat another ration bar for as long as she lived. In fact, if she had it her way, she'd never set foot in the woods again.

Jill was still struggling with food, her mouth full of an overly large final bite, her cheeks bulging as she chewed around it. Fiona snickered, and Jill held up a finger in warning, still chewing. Fiona laughed out loud, and Jill clapped a hand over her mouth to keep the bite inside. Finally, she grimaced as she swallowed, holding a hand to her throat.

"You asshole," Jill said, throwing a stick at her. "I almost choked."

"That's what you get for being such a pig."

"A pig? You think I wanted that crap in my mouth? I was trying to finish it all at once so I wouldn't heave my guts out."

Fiona stuck her tongue out and Jill returned the gesture, the two of them smiling at each other afterward. Despite it all, Fiona was feeling much better now, a little like she had back at the pool. She shouldn't let herself be distracted, since whatever came for them next would seem the worse for it, but she couldn't help herself. It was instinctual, after all, to seek the good, to distance yourself from the bad, even in the middle of a personal hell. Perhaps that was the only way people could keep going—by fooling themselves, every so often, and allowing happiness in. Even in small doses, it was worthwhile, necessary, even.

"Before we go, I wanted to run an idea past you guys," Roz said. "It might be really stupid."

Jill wiped the crumbs from her mouth. "Let's hear it. We've got nothing but stupid to go on."

Roz looked back and forth between them, her face creased with uncertainty. Finally, she sighed. "Okay—here it is: I think we should go off-trail."

"Isn't that what we're already doing?" Jill asked.

Roz tilted a hand back and forth. "Yes and no. No, we're not on the actual trail, but yes, we're following a secondary path—the river."

"And they know we're here," Fiona added.

The others stared at her, startled, and she shrugged. "We're all thinking it. After those last markings, it's clear they knew we'd come this way."

Jill sighed. "That's true enough. I've imagined eyes on us this whole time."

After a pause, Roz nodded.

Fiona agreed. "We all have."

"So what's your plan?" Jill asked.

Roz picked up a little twig and started drawing a straight line in the dirt in front of them. "Okay, so here's the river. The trail basically follows it, usually within a quarter of a mile." She drew another straight line, representing the trail a little to the right of the river and parallel with it. "Right now, the river and the trail go almost due south. Then, in a few miles, they start to head southeast." She curved both lines to the right. "At the end, they go almost completely east right before the trail ends at the parking lot." The finished drawing resembled two parallel, hooked *L*s.

"Okay," Jill said. "Got it."

"This is the road we've been aiming for this whole time," Roz said, drawing another parallel, jagged line a few inches to the right of the two *L*s. "The 71B, which hooks up to Highway 69. But down here," she drew a line underneath the two *L*s, perpendicular to the two roads she'd drawn, "down here is Highway 14. As you know, that's a big road—much more traffic. From where we are now, it's directly south of us." She made eye contact again. "I think we should head there."

"How?" Fiona asked.

"When the river starts to curve to the east, rather than following it, we cross it and keep heading south." She drew a little dotted line past the river to the bigger highway.

"Won't we get lost?"

"Not if we're careful. We'll have to keep checking the position of the sun. Without a compass, it'll be approximate, but if we keep our wits about us, not only are we closer to Highway 14, but we're more likely to see people right away. A lot of cars drive that highway, even at night."

She and Jill were quiet, absorbing this suggestion. Fiona couldn't help but stare at that dotted line. She knew why Roz had drawn it that way—it represented something unknown. Visually, it was obviously dangerous. Logically, however, it had great advantages. If the scale was anywhere close to accurate, and knowing Roz, it probably was, it would shave several miles off their trip and offer them the protection of an unpredicted path.

"Fuck it. Let's do it," Jill said.

Roz was startled into a laugh. "Yeah? You think so? What about you, Fiona?"

She smiled. "It's a great idea."

"I knew we kept you around for a reason, Roz," Jill said, slapping her arm.

Roz laughed again. "Well okay, then. Let's get going. We might even make it by dinnertime."

Jill groaned. "Don't talk about food—I'm begging you."

The three of them were quickly on their way. Fiona had a little spring in her step now. All along, they'd been doing what the others wanted, going where they wanted them to go. This felt like the first steps they'd made on their own.

A tiny doubt niggled at the back of her mind, however. If they were being watched, it would all be for nothing—they would simply be followed once they crossed the river. She suppressed this thought at once. It was no use to dwell on it. At least now they seemed to have a better plan.

They'd been walking for about an hour, their pace steady and almost quick, when Fiona realized that the water was getting closer again. They'd kept about fifty feet from it most of the morning, but gradually, as they continued, it drew closer and closer to them on the right. Finally, they hit its bank, the water crashing and tumbling, moving small boulders with its forceful currents. The rapids here were throwing out splashes and mist, and she tilted her face up to catch the refreshing coolness. It had been growing hotter by the minute, and while she'd avoided dwelling on it, the heat had been bothering her more and more all morning.

"This is where it starts to curve east!" Roz shouted at them. Even then, Fiona could barely hear her.

She and Jill nodded. It was obviously too dangerous to cross here.

Roz started moving again, following the riverbank from a few feet away now. The three of them were completely exposed here, the trees growing some ten or more feet away, and the sun was so bright off the rocks and water, even her sunglasses gave little protection. The river continued to broil and thunder next to them as they walked for several long minutes, the panic she'd been pushing down rising again in her heart. They'd been safer in the woods. Even if those people were literally keeping them in their sights, it would be harder to shoot them in the safety of the tress.

Roz must have realized this possibility herself, as she turned around and gestured for the three of them to move away from the water again, back into the woods. It was a little quieter here, and they paused to talk.

"I guess we'll have to keep following the river for a while yet," Roz said.

"I don't remember the current being this strong when we were hiking that first couple of days," Jill said.

Fiona agreed. "I was thinking the same thing."

"That's because I have the water stops planned for the whole of the real trail," Roz said. "We always got water where I know there's a calm spot. The river divides sometimes, briefly, and in a couple of places, the division close to the trail on this side is more like a stream."

"So should we wait for one of those places?" Fiona asked.

Roz shook her head. "It would be defeating the purpose. Those water stops are pretty clear from the main trail. You might not have noticed them the first couple of days, but you'd probably spot them now, even on your own. Anyone with some woods experience can find them easily."

Meaning the people from the woods could watch for them there.

"We'll just have to wait until we see something relatively safe," Roz said. "We'll tie up together and cross as a group."

"With what?" Jill asked.

"The hammock. We can use my Leatherman and cut it up."

"That sounds like it will take a long time," Jill said.

Fiona flushed. Jill was starting her old shit again.

"You have a better idea?" Fiona demanded.

Jill flinched and had the decency to look embarrassed. "No."

"Then let's keep going," Fiona said.

The water was still booming and rumbling to their right. Long, pregnant minutes passed, minutes stretching into half an hour, then an hour, and then, finally, Fiona realized it was getting quieter. For a long while she wondered if she was imagining things. The water was very loud, even from twenty or thirty feet away, though perhaps overexposure was dampening her hearing, like after a loud concert. The trees and undergrowth were thick enough here that she could catch only glimpses of the river, so she couldn't be sure. A few minutes later, however, the sound of it had clearly lessened. It was almost quiet now.

Then Roz stopped and turned to them with a smile. "Let's check it out."

They followed her back to the water, where it was immediately clear that things had changed. The banks had widened here, the river spread into something more like a small lake. She could see that the water was moving quickly, splashing over the tops of some rocks, a branch or two sailing past and out of sight almost at once.

"What do you think?" Roz asked. "Should we try it?"

"I think so," Jill said. "If we try to cross somewhere narrower later on, the current will be too strong."

"The water's moving really fast," Fiona said.

"But it should be pretty shallow here," Roz said. "Mid-calf, maybe."

The two of them were staring at her, waiting for her to decide. She didn't want to admit how reluctant she was. Seeing those branches go whizzing by was not remotely reassuring, but on the other hand, she could see the bottom of the water from where they were standing.

"Okay," Fiona said. "But I want to get rid of these pant legs. We're going to get soaked. And let's tie together somehow in case someone slips."

Jill was already in her shorts, but Fiona and Roz unzippered the legs of their pants at mid-thigh and put them in the pack. Roz helped her remove her long-sleeved shirt and retie the bandanas around her injured shoulder. With the sun nearly exposed above them and the summer air heating up, she realized now how hot she'd been and was beginning to look forward to the cool river water.

In the end, they needed to cut the hammock in half twice. Roz braided it into a loose rope, then looped it through a couple of their belt loops. They had to stand quite close to each other to make it work, but they were also far enough apart that they wouldn't step all over each other, either. They roped in the same order they'd walked in, with Roz at the front and Fiona at the back, the idea being that should any of them slip, the others would be strong enough together to catch her.

"Easy does it," Roz said. "We'll go as slow as we need to. Try to step where I step, Jill, and the same for you, Fiona—step where she does. If it starts to get too deep, we can always turn around."

"Or swim for it!" Jill said.

Roz took her first step into the water, and Fiona was relieved to see that it barely passed the top of her foot. Her ankles were still out of the water. Jill followed, then Fiona, and within seconds, the bank of the river was behind them. About ten feet out, the water deepened. It rose over the top of her boots, the chill startling and intense despite her protective footwear. When it climbed up her calf, she couldn't help but let out a gasp of shock, and Jill glanced back at her, smiling.

"Refreshing, right?"

"It's something, anyway," Fiona said.

Once the water hit her knees, Fiona realized she was struggling to move her legs against the strength of the current.

"Guys?" she called out. "I don't know if I can do this."

"It's only this deep for another few feet," Roz called back. "I can see shallower water ahead."

Fiona glanced backward, relieved to see that they were more than halfway. She started to turn forward, but movement caught the corner of her eye, and she jerked back around. Roz and Jill must have felt the tug on their connecting line, as they stopped dragging her.

Fiona continued to watch the trees behind them, wondering if she'd imagined it. The sunlight was throwing sparkling rainbows across the faces of the trees, and they almost seemed to dance across the forest.

That's all it was, Fiona thought. Just my imagination.

Again she turned around, but both Jill and Roz were still staring behind them.

"I thought I saw—" Jill said.

"Me, too," Roz said. "Let's get the hell out of this river. Fiona, let us help you."

Roz and Jill stepped back to her, Jill grabbing her good arm and putting it over her shoulders. Roz stood right next to her and looped an arm around her waist.

"Ready?" Roz asked.

"Let's do this," Jill replied.

They carried her between them and then sloshed forward into the deeper water. Despite the fact that she was being held up, the water rose almost to her waist before receding once again. Jill almost dropped her, but Roz steadied her until Fiona felt the ground beneath her feet again. Here the water was at calf level again, and though the current was dragging at her, she nodded that she was ready to keep going.

A loud CRACK rang out and splashed the water next to them.

"Run!" Roz screamed.

CHAPTER TWENTY

The three of them splashed forward, Fiona slipping immediately. Jill and Roz dragged her upright again, and they surged together as a group, sending a small wake outward in their progress. Another CRACK rang out, sending a chute of water skyward a few feet to their left. Fiona ducked, instinctively, once again dragging the others down with her. This time Jill lost her footing, and it was all Fiona could do to help her back to her feet with her one strong arm. Roz managed to wrench her forward into much shallower water, and Jill rocketed to her feet, the three of them finally ready to run. The far riverbank was perhaps twenty feet away now, and they loped toward it, water laden and soggy and sending splashing water flying in all directions. Fiona could see the edge of solid ground, and she used all her strength to hurl herself toward it. If they could make it to the trees, they had a chance.

She saw Roz's boot hit the earth just as Jill collapsed next to her. Everything suddenly seemed to move in slow motion. Jill dropped all at once. Fiona saw the bloody water and Jill's face contorted with pain. Roz turned, slowly, back toward them, her face bleach-white. Time caught up again, and Fiona and Roz bent down to drag Jill forward. This time she heard the shot, which whizzed by her face so closely she could feel its heat and wind. Ignoring her injured shoulder, Fiona dragged Jill out of the water,

Roz tugging her other arm, and the three of them finally lurched into the woods. They hauled Jill another ten feet and behind a cluster of thick aspens and bushes. Still tied closely together, they had to crouch there near Jill, who was thrashing.

Screaming, Jill kept clutching her right calf, blood running freely between her fingers. The water had diluted it a little, so it might look worse than it was, but the blood was plentiful. Her boot and shorts were stained with it, and it dripped through her fingers.

"Cut yourself loose," Roz said, thrusting her Leatherman into Fiona's hands.

Her hands were shaking so badly she could hardly make them function. She dropped the tool once, twice, but eventually she managed to pry out the scissors and cut herself out of the hammock rope.

Roz was trying to make Jill loosen the grip on her leg so she could see underneath her fingers, but Jill was hysterical, still screaming. Fiona knelt next to Jill's head, set it in her lap, and started soothing her, making shushing sounds as she stroked her hair. She felt Jill relax slightly.

"Let go, Jill," she said. "Let Roz help you."

Jill's eyes rolled up and back toward her, tears leaking from the corners. Her mouth was pinched in pain, and she was ghostly white. She sobbed and nodded, releasing her grip on her leg. Fiona caught a quick glimpse of a bloody hole before Roz slapped a piece of the hammock over it. Roz met her eyes, her mouth set in a grim line.

"It went right into the muscle here," she said.

Jill sobbed again, wrenching upward, and Fiona pushed down on her shoulders to keep her in place. Roz had a death grip on Jill's calf, and she managed to wrestle her legs back down to the ground. She used her body weight as leverage to keep them pinned to the ground by kneeling on her feet.

Roz took another peek under the bandage. "There's no exit wound,"

"Can you get it out?" Fiona asked.

Roz grimaced again. "Yes, but I don't know if I should. I can't sterilize anything. We don't even have hand sanitizer anymore."

"Do it," Jill moaned. "It hurts! Oh God, it hurts so bad!"

Fiona and Roz made eye contact again, and Fiona nodded. She would need to keep Jill as still as possible. She scooted forward a little, situating herself over Jill and pushing down on her shoulders. Gravity would help her here, but she braced herself for a fight.

Roz opened the pliers on her Leatherman and leaned down, the position awkward because of her need to keep Jill's legs in place. Roz removed the clump of bloody hammock again and then opened the edges of Jill's wound with the fingers on one hand. Jill bucked underneath them, but they managed to hold her as Roz probed the wound with the pliers. Jill screamed as Roz pulled the bullet from her leg, tossing it aside. Jill went limp beneath her, unconscious, and Fiona dropped onto her butt, panting.

Roz had clamped the bloody rag over Jill's wound again. "Make me some more small pieces of hammock," she said, handing her the tool. "I need two or three thick squares and several strips to wrap around her legs—three, four-feet long."

She was soon sticky with blood, which had doused the tool, and her fingers occasionally stuck together. She worked quickly, handing Roz various sections of the cloth as she made them—first the squares, then the strips. By the time they were done, Jill's calf was cocooned in cloth, the strips holding the squares firmly in place. The two of them were covered in blood, and Jill was incredibly pale and still.

Fiona leaned closer to her, listening, and felt Jill's breath. She took her pulse, alarmed at how weak it felt.

Roz moved away, over to the edge of the trees, staring back over the water. She looked, pulled her head back, looked again from another tree, pulled her head back again, repeating this pattern. After several seconds of this, she rejoined her.

"I don't see anything."

"But they know we're here," Fiona said.

Roz nodded, her brows creased. "Exactly. I don't understand why they didn't follow us."

Fiona was struck with an idea that felt like a certainty. "Maybe they don't need to," she suggested.

"What do you mean?"

Fiona gestured around them. "Maybe they already have some people over here. Maybe they're on their way right now."

"Christ," Roz said, the remaining color draining from her cheeks. "I bet you anything you're right."

"So what should we do?"

Jill stirred to life. Fiona leapt forward, grabbing her shoulders again, and Roz took her feet in her hands. Jill tried to sit up, and Fiona pushed her down. Jill's eyes popped open, and she took a deep breath.

"Shhhh!" Fiona said. "Shhhh! You're okay. Try to stay quiet."

Jill's eyes filled with tears, and she sobbed again. Fiona leant down and gave her an awkward hug. Jill squeezed her back.

"I'm going to die out here, aren't I?" Jill asked.

Fiona sat up, staring down at her. "Don't even think that. You're not dying here, goddamn it. No one is."

Jill nodded, her face still crumpled and her lip quivering. "Yes, I am. Don't you understand, Fiona? You have to leave me here."

"Nope. That's not happening. Roz—tell her. Tell her that's not happening."

Roz didn't respond right away, and Fiona spun her way. Roz was rubbing her mouth, unconsciously smearing it with blood, clearly anxious. Fiona's heart dropped.

"We're not leaving her here, are we?" Fiona asked.

Roz and Jill were staring at each other now, and Fiona saw Roz give a slight, almost imperceptible nod. Fiona looked down at Jill again.

"You can't be serious!"

Jill, however, seemed calmer again, her expression almost serene. The tears had dried up and her fear was gone. She looked determined, sure. She wiped her face with her palms, streaking semi-dried blood across her cheeks. Then she gripped Fiona's hand, squeezing it, and pulled Fiona closer, their faces inches apart.

"You're hurting me—"

"Now you listen to me, Fiona," Jill said, her tone dark and angry. "Someone has to get out of here. Someone needs to make it back and find some help, make someone track these people down and end this. If you try to take me with you, all of us will die. Do you hear me? All of us. The only chance anyone has is if you and Roz get the hell out of here."

"I can't, I won't—"

"Stop arguing with me, goddamn it! You saved my life once, and you'll save it again if you go now without fighting me."

Jill let go of her hand, and Fiona collapsed backward, sitting down so hard her teeth snapped. A long silence fell as the two of them stared at each other. Jill's eyes were steely now, determined, and Fiona knew, all at once, that Jill would fight her all the way if she tried to force her to go with them. She'd seen that same resolve in her eyes a thousand times. Jill was not going to give up quietly.

Fiona burst into tears, feeling Roz encircle her with one of her strong arms soon afterward. She turned into her, sobbing into her neck, and Roz squeezed, rubbing a hand up and down her back. Finally, almost spent, Fiona let go, and Roz's gaze was full of compassion, concern. She almost started crying again, but the reality of their situation was starting to sink in. One way one or another, they needed to leave before they were attacked again.

"Okay," she finally said. "Okay. You're right. I get it. But I don't like it, Jill. I don't like it one bit."

The others visibly relaxed.

Jill smiled and squeezed her hand. "Can you guys prop me up a little, closer to a tree? I'd like to sit up, have something to lean on."

The two of them dragged her over to a tree, careful of her hurt leg, and helped her sit upright, her back against the thick trunk. Roz left them there and started gathering their supplies. She clearly understood that they needed a moment.

Fiona and Jill linked hands again, and Jill was still smiling at her. With her bruises and her wan, blood-streaked face and leg, she looked like something out of a horror movie. That determination was still there in her eyes, dark and cool now, calm with acceptance.

"Do you remember that time when we were kids, and that jackass Ryan Heart was giving me lip in P.E.?" Jill asked.

It took Fiona a second to focus on Jill's question. She cleared her throat, suddenly choking on tears. "Ryan was always giving someone lip."

"He had a nerve, that guy," Jill said, frowning. "Ugly as hell and he still bullied everyone."

"Defense mechanism," Fiona muttered.

"That day, he said something nasty to me, and you went over there and slapped his stupid face."

Fiona couldn't help but grin. She'd gotten a two-week in-house suspension for that slap. Her parents had been furious. Still, it was one of those memories the two of them returned to time and again over the years. Jill always called it—

"Your finest hour," she said.

Fiona smiled. "What about it?"

Jill met her eyes, the steely anger there again. "You stood up for me, Fiona. He was easily twice your size, and you did it anyway. The look on his face…" She grinned. "Priceless. He had no idea what to do. No one in school had taken him on before, and you weren't exactly the school hero."

Fiona was crying openly now. She knew what Jill was trying to do, but she couldn't help but feel like this was good-bye.

"You always stand up for me," Jill said. "I know it's not easy being my friend, but you've stuck by me, thick and thin. I know some of your friends don't like me—"

"That's not—"

"I know it's true. Anyway, don't let them win. That's all. I trust you. I trust you more than anyone I know. There isn't another person I would trust to come back for me. You're going to do this for me, Fiona. Not Roz—you. You're going to save us all."

"But what if I can't do it, Jill? What if I can't save you?"

Jill shrugged. "I know you'll try your hardest. That's all I need."

"I hate the idea of you being here by yourself."

"If you and Roz get back quickly, it won't be so long."

She understood this to be wishful thinking, but the possibility still gave Fiona a flicker of hope. It was true. If they could raise the alarm soon, they might make it back to her before dark. Assuming the people from the woods left her alone.

She made herself close her eyes, picturing the rescue. Her whole life, she'd done this—pictured success. She'd tried to let go of the habit as she grew older, feeling silly, like she was making wishes instead of doing something. But now, with her eyes closed and the sun's dappled light filtering through her eyelids, she could picture the scene clearly. There would be dogs, horses, men and women with gear and guns. They'd make it here as the light was starting to fade from the day, but they'd get here before Jill was left here alone in the dark. She opened her eyes.

"I'll do it. I'll save you."

"That's my girl," Jill whispered.

Roz crouched next to them, holding up various supplies. "I'm leaving some of the food with you, Jill—some matches, the space blanket, Fiona's warmer shirt, and the fleece hat and jacket. I wish we had another water container, but the river is just a few feet away. I don't think those people are over there anymore, so you should be safe going for a drink anytime you need to. I found a walking pole, and I'll lean it here so you can keep the weight off your leg some."

Fiona didn't like the idea of leaving her here with no water, but they had very little choice. If she and Roz had any chance of making it back, they would need to carry the pack. No use running through the woods just to collapse from dehydration. They let her take several long sips from their bladder, and then they were on their feet again, staring down at her.

"Get going," Jill said, making a shooing gesture. "You've already lost a serious chunk of the day."

That was true enough. Any edge had been lost in the last hour. Now, once again, they'd be racing the clock to make it to civilization before dark. Even without much navigational experience, it would be harder and harder to keep track of their location as they lost daylight. The sun would be their only guide.

She couldn't help but kneel once more and give Jill a parting hug.

"Stay alive," she whispered.

Jill barked a single laugh. "You, too." She looked up at Roz. "And keep our girl safe."

"I will. Good-bye, Jill. With any luck, it'll just be a few more hours."

"Okay. I'll be waiting. Nothing else to do."

Fiona recognized Jill's gallows humor for what it was, but she couldn't pretend to laugh. Jill was so small, so diminished, it was almost too much. She was on the verge of begging her to come with them when Jill made another shooing gesture.

"Get out of here, guys. I'll be okay."

Roz grabbed Fiona's hand, and Fiona let herself be led away, back into the woods toward home. She didn't want to turn back, knew she shouldn't let herself, in fact, but the urge was too strong. She threw one last glance behind her shoulder, but Jill was already hidden by the thick branches and leafy bushes and undergrowth, almost as if the woods had swallowed her whole.

CHAPTER TWENTY-ONE

They seemed to meander through the woods. When they'd had the river to act as a landmark it had been easy to feel confident, sure in their direction. Here nothing told Fiona they were going the right way. Instead, it seemed they were constantly shifting direction, going one way for a while, only to go another a few minutes later. If she had to draw their progress, it would have been a kind of zigzag. Sometimes the reason was obvious. They had to walk around a large pile of boulders, or a thick cluster of trees, or a natural, murky pond. Other times, however, it seemed like they shifted direction for no reason. She didn't ask Roz why they did this, trusting her instincts and sense of direction more than her own. They were moving, going somewhere, and that was enough for now.

They walked holding hands on and off most of the late morning and early afternoon. Roz let go only when they had to, for a narrow passage between trees or a steep downward incline. They were still losing elevation at a rapid clip, but she knew the last couple of miles would be relatively flat. She kept waiting for the ground to even out, to act as a sign for the last leg. Instead, they continued to hit hills, small and long, going farther and farther down the mountain. Her knees were throbbing now, her right one occasionally trying to lock in place, and she forced herself not to limp. On a particularly steep incline, she bit her lip to stop from calling out, a single tear escaping the corner of her eye. She wiped at it, furious with herself. Her friends were injured, in actual danger, and here she was, worried about her joints. She had to keep going.

Roz paused at the bottom of the hill, watching the rest of her progress down. After keeping up all morning, Fiona was starting to fall behind again, farther and farther with each hill. She made it to the bottom and bent her knee a couple of times to stretch it, rubbing it with a dirty hand.

"Knees giving you problems?" Roz asked.

She tilted a hand back and forth a couple of times and tried to smile. "Yes and no. I'm fine on the flat parts. It's just these damn hills. But I'll be okay."

Roz stared at her evenly and, Fiona could see, suspiciously.

"All right," Roz said, "but let me show you a stretch."

She demonstrated by crossing one foot over the other. She stretched her body to the other side, re-crossed her feet the other way, and bent to the other side. Fiona mimicked her, feeling the strain run through her knees on either side. It hurt, but it stretched the correct part of her knee. She didn't think it would do much good right now, but she was still grateful for the momentary pause. She did each side a couple more times and smiled.

"Thanks. That's a little better. Let's keep going."

"You sure?"

"Yes. The only thing that would help right now is sitting for the rest of my life and staring at the TV."

Roz grinned. "Not going on any more backpacking trips this summer?"

Fiona laughed. "No. Not any time soon."

They linked hands again. Fiona couldn't help but look at their entwined, dirty fingers. Both had blood under their fingernails, dirt encrusted directly in their skin. She'd been a fastidious neat freak since she was a kid and couldn't think of a single time she'd been half as filthy. Her hair and face were just as bad, and she could see, despite the dark material, that her shirt was likewise grimy, but she didn't really care. Maybe holding hands with a gorgeous woman who also didn't seem to care helped, or maybe, for once in her life, her perspective was in the right place. It didn't matter how grody she was when she found help, only that she did.

"Do you think Jill will be okay?"

Fiona regretted asking this question the moment it was out of her mouth. They hadn't said anything about her since they left her, almost as if they'd agreed not to, as if talking about her would make Fiona go back.

Roz threw her a quick smile. "Are you kidding me? If anyone's stubborn enough to live through this, it's Jill. And anyway, she's a survivor. She's tough and mean as hell."

Fiona grinned, flushing with relief. It was true, all of it. Roz had known her only a few days, but she'd described Jill as if they'd known each other a lifetime. Tears rose in her eyes again, and she blinked a few times, trying to hide them.

Roz paused again and pulled her into a quick hug. When she let go, she put her hands on Fiona's shoulders.

"We did the right thing. I know it was shitty. I don't like it either. I fucking hate it, in fact, and she's not even my friend."

"She will be, eventually. Once all this is over. You'll get to know her like I do. You two are really going to hit it off."

Roz raised a single eyebrow, and Fiona laughed.

"Okay, well, maybe."

Roz smiled and dropped her hands. "I'll give you a maybe. But Fiona, Jill's going to be okay. As long as we get help, we're all going to be okay. I won't promise you, since that would be silly with all this going on, but I can promise you this. If we make it back, Jill, Carol, and Sarah will all be okay."

They hugged again, and this time Fiona tried to convey some of her feelings through their closeness. She ran her hands along Roz's strong muscles and shoulder blades, the back of Roz's shirt damp and clinging to her skin. She smelled of pine and earth and fresh air with a hint of something else—her sweat, probably, but appealing, nevertheless. Fiona had a flash of self-consciousness, remembering that she hadn't worn deodorant in days, but Roz was holding her so closely, so warmly, she obviously didn't care. They moved as one into a long, lingering kiss, Fiona rising slightly on the balls of her feet to meet the taller woman's lips. She dropped down again when Roz released her, her stomach fluttering.

"Jill would say we're being moony," Roz said, voice thick.

Fiona grinned at her. "And she'd be right."

"Let's get moving again. We can be as moony as we like once we're in our hotel room tonight."

"I thought you said all we'd do is sleep."

Roz barked a single laugh. "Yeah, right."

They began their zigzag path again, hands clasped, moving at a clip just short of a trot. Fiona occasionally had to jog a few steps to keep up with Roz's longer legs, but for the most part, their pace was just at the top of her peak walking speed. Long, flat stretches would give her hope, only for them to start, once again, on a steep descent. It was much too early in the day to expect that they would be nearing the highway, but she couldn't help it. Every time they walked for more than ten or twenty minutes without a hill, her heart would start to speed up again, only for her hopes to fade with the next decline.

Time ran like a sieve. She knew it was passing as the day heated and the sun rose high in the sky. They'd crossed the river an hour or so before noon, and at least two hours had passed since they left Jill. To occupy the time and keep her mind off her fears, she occasionally tried to count the minutes away, but something always distracted her, and she lost track of where she'd been.

She and Roz were moving too quickly for much small talk, though one or the other would occasionally remark on the woods around them, planning their next path forward around some obstacle. Still, even if they'd been walking slower, Fiona didn't think they would talk much. Too much was happening, and discussion would only lead them back to the things she didn't want to think about—her friends, the murderous people from the woods, Jill, the lost men and horses, hot food, showers—all of it was there, threatening to overwhelm her, and Roz had to feel the same way.

Better to focus on the now, the only thing they had any control over. She had to keep pretending. If they made it back to safety, everything would be all right again.

They were trying to be careful with the water, but on their next quick break, she heard air pockets in Roz's sip.

"Damn," Roz said, dropping the mouth valve.

"That's it? That's all we had?"

Roz nodded, her eyes downcast and worried. It was remarkably hot now. Fiona couldn't remember a time she'd been so warm this high in the mountains. She could only imagine how rough it was in town. If she'd been home, she would be sitting under her swamp cooler, trying not to move, sipping a beer maybe, watching her dog play outside in the paddling pool. The image was so clear in her mind she could almost taste the hops and smell wet dog.

"We have a long way to go," Roz said. "Probably at least another two or three hours."

"We've seen some standing water a few times," Fiona suggested. "Maybe we'll run into more."

Neither of them mentioned the obvious. The water they'd seen here in this part of the woods wasn't drinkable. They'd seen perhaps three or four ponds, all muddy and skimmed with scum and algae.

Roz gestured at the pack. "I was going to suggest we eat something, but it will just make us thirstier. Let's skip it and keep going."

Their new situation seemed to drain the remaining enthusiasm from the day. Roz was still walking quickly, setting a hard but manageable pace, but she seemed dejected, downcast next to her, shoulders slightly stooped and her eyes down and introspective. Not having any water was a big problem, but it seemed to have struck Roz hard, almost as if it had broken her. She was still moving forward, still bringing them closer and closer to home, but her heart didn't seem to be in it anymore. As if she knew, suddenly, that this was a lost cause.

Fiona shook her head, dismissing her thoughts. She was projecting. Roz might just be hot, like she was, and struggling to stay hopeful in the blistering heat.

"I'm surprised we haven't had any rain this whole time," Fiona said.

Roz glanced at her and nodded. "It's definitely weird. This is the only time of year you can actually expect rain up here."

They both looked upward at the crystalline, cloudless sky. The trees were dense and thick enough in most places to give them shade, but it was still almost blindingly bright out. A drip of sweat ran down Fiona's forehead, and she blinked it painfully out of her eyes.

"Do you think—"

Roz grabbed her injured arm, yanking her backward, and Fiona let out of little yelp of pain and fright. Roz clutched her, fingers dug into her skin, her face a pallid white.

"What the—"

"Shhhh!" Roz said, and pointed.

Fiona followed the direction of her finger, and her blood froze in her veins. There, not fifty feet away, were three trees with geometric patterns cut into them. They stood in a ring together, no different from any other cluster of trees she could see except for the telltale markings. The trees were directly in front of them, exactly where they were now headed.

"I don't understand," Roz said, shaking her head. "I've been leading us around, trying to avoid one specific direction for too long. How could this happen? I figured we would lose a mile or two if we wandered a little but still make it to the road, and it would be safer. How could they know where we'd end up? How could they anticipate our next move? There's no path, no plan for them to follow and get ahead of us. How did they do it? What does it mean?"

Fiona could hear the panic in her voice, and she forced Roz's fingers off her arm, squaring herself in front of her. Roz was still talking, occasionally pausing to rub her mouth before starting again, repeating herself now and clearly trying to figure them out. Roz peered around wildly, her head jerking every few seconds to a new direction. She hadn't noticed Fiona watching her.

Fiona took a deep breath and grabbed Roz's hand, crushing her fingers to get her attention.

"Roz, look at me."

Roz shook her head, eyes still almost rolling.

"Damn it, look at me!" she shouted.

Roz flinched, and Fiona was relieved to see her face gain a little color, whether from surprise or anger, she didn't care. Her eyes were steadying again, calmer.

"Okay," Fiona said, "we assumed all morning that they were watching us. Then, when we crossed the river, we also decided a few of them were probably on this side, or the group that shot at us would have followed."

Roz nodded eagerly.

Fiona lifted her shoulders. "So how is this any different? How is this new? These bastards have been one step ahead of us all along, and they still are."

"Yes, but the whole point of crossing over here was to give them the slip."

Fiona nodded. "Yep. And it didn't work. Who cares? We're still here, right? We're still alive, aren't we?"

Roz's brows lowered with apparent confusion. "But how does that help us?"

Fiona smiled. "Except for being alive, it doesn't help at all. But we can refuse to let them rattle us, startle us. That's what they want. They want us to panic and make poor choices. I, for one, won't let them do it anymore. I say we keep going and pretend we don't see those trees. Who knows—maybe it's just one guy over here? Or maybe there's a few of them, but they're too busy with these damn trees to do anything else. Otherwise, why aren't they chasing us?"

Roz opened her mouth as if ready to argue, but it snapped shut soon after. She kept her eyes on the ground, clearly reflecting on what Fiona had said, but Fiona knew where she'd end up. She didn't know why she was so calm about all this, but she wasn't scared anymore. She'd hit the end of her terror, apparently, and rather than shut down and give up, she'd come out the other side, almost unafraid. She refused to let them control her emotions. After all, it was just a few trees, for God's sake. If those weirdos were nearby, close enough to actually see them, they'd be shooting at them.

Roz took a deep breath, closing her eyes, and then let it out in a long, shaky exhale. She did it again, steadier this time, and then once more. When she opened her eyes, she almost seemed like herself again, eyes steely, jaw clenched.

"I'm sorry, Fiona. I lost it there for a minute."

"It's okay. We've all been there at least once the last few days."

Roz shook her head, her expression dark, and Fiona suspected she was angry with herself.

Roz met her eyes. "It's not just the trees. Before we saw them, I'd almost given up already. I was thinking about how we don't have any water, worried we wouldn't make it even after all that's happened the last few days. But I wanted to be strong for you. I see now that I was fooling myself. You can take it. You can take anything."

Fiona almost laughed. "Me? I'm a little 'fraidy cat. You must mean someone else."

Roz shook her head. "No. Ever since we left camp yesterday—and before, really—you've shown me your true self, Fiona. With your friends, you showed me true courage, standing up for Jill when I wanted to club her one, helping Carol in any way you could, and basically being the only one of them to have any good ideas."

"That was all you, though—"

Roz grabbed her hand. "It wasn't. It was you. I might have gone through with a few things on my own, but you convinced me to try. You're the real hero here, Fiona. Not me. What's incredible to me is that you can't see it in yourself."

Fiona flushed with warmth. Roz was just being nice, all of what she'd said flattery of the highest kind, but she couldn't help the pride rising in her chest. She had made it this far, after all. Just last night, she'd thought they'd be dead by now.

They didn't say anything else, both turning back toward the marked trees and walking toward them, hands linked. They passed the trees without incident, Fiona barely glancing at them again. What she'd told Roz was true. The only thing they could control was how they reacted to things, as much as possible, anyway, and fear, while useful, could also be debilitating. She could be afraid and in control. She'd learned that about herself, at any rate, and it had only taken a life-and-death situation.

She heard screeching metal and a loud SNAP before Roz collapsed next to her, all at once and in a heap. Her hand was yanked from Fiona's, almost dragging her down, and Fiona reeled backward, arms spinning to catch her balance. When she finally made herself look, she almost screamed.

CHAPTER TWENTY-TWO

Roz sprawled on the ground, her leg held by the bear trap, howling in pain. The trap had snapped closed just above her boot on the top of her wool sock on the lowest part of her calf. Fiona dropped down, desperately looking for the release mechanism. She had no idea what to do.

"Roz. Roz! How do I get this thing off?"

Roz moaned again, blinked back tears, but finally leaned forward, clasping her leg just above the wound. She whimpered a few times and then smeared dirt and blood through her tears with her filthy hands. Fiona saw her clench her teeth and swallow a few times, choking back sobs.

"You have to—agggh!" Roz's eyes snapped shut on her moan.

"Have to what, damn it?"

"You have to—have to push down on both sides." She pointed and continued sobbing.

"Here?" Fiona asked.

"No! There and there."

Fiona tried, but the trap didn't move, still stuck on Roz and piercing her skin. There were, she could see now, two curved spring mechanisms on either side of the trap, both shaped like a little arc. She stood up, centering herself directly above the trap, and pushed down with all her might. The trap moved slightly, and she pushed harder, her back and shoulders protesting with the effort. It finally opened a fraction of an inch, and Fiona could almost see the end of the barbs pulling out of Roz's leg. She was afraid now that if she tried to move to a better position for more leverage, the trap would snap closed again and hurt Roz even more. She leaned forward almost in half, the top of her head sweeping the ground, pushing, pushing. A groan of effort escaped her lips, and she tried one more time, pushing toward the ground and letting gravity help her. She heard a squealing grind as the trap finally gave, opening far enough for Roz to pull free. Leg clear, Fiona let go, and the trap closed with a loud clang.

She moved over to Roz, who was hunched up, rolling around on the ground and clutching her leg and wound between her fingers. Fiona stopped her by grabbing one shoulder, finally getting Roz's attention by shouting at her. Roz whimpered again, tears spilling down her cheeks, and Fiona gave her forehead a quick, desperate kiss. She helped Roz sit upright, and the two of them directed their gaze to Roz's leg. She was still clutching her wound, and Fiona forced her fingers away to see underneath. There was surprisingly little blood. In fact, only three of the barbs had pierced the skin, only one with any depth. All six of those that had touched her skin had left huge, angry welts already coloring into a purplish blue. Fiona put Roz's hands back on the wound, dismissing the dirt and filth for now, and then pulled the backpack off her, one arm at a time.

They were down to just a few small pieces of the hammock, the rest left wrapped in pieces around Jill's leg. The legs to their pants were still in there, however, and Fiona removed the bandanas from her shoulder, wrapping the first and then the second around Roz's leg, and tied both into knots underneath the other. She fastened strips of hammock and pants over these and managed to wrap the strips around both bandana bandages three times. The result was an ugly, brutal gathering of mismatched material, and she could tell that it would need tending often as Roz moved. Besides the two remaining food bars, nothing was left in the backpack but their little trowel, and Fiona tossed the entire thing aside, extending her hands to Roz.

"Come on. We need to see how bad it is."

She helped the taller woman stand up on her one good foot, and Roz kept her injured leg dangling in the air for a moment before gingerly putting some weight on it. She hissed and jerked her foot up again.

"That bad?" Fiona asked.

Roz nodded, her lips peeled back in pain.

"I don't think anything's broken, and you're not bleeding too bad, just some bruising. Let me look around and see if I can find something for you to lean on."

She turned, scanning the woods around her, and spotted a slender, tall branch stuck under some bushes near a tree. She dashed over, managed to pull it free from the mud, and came back, holding it out as if offering a scepter.

Roz had hopped over to a tree and was leaning on it, looking pale and weary. She gave Fiona a weak smile and took the branch from her, resting it against the tree.

"What are you doing?" Fiona said. "We have to keep going. We have to—"

Roz shook her head, still smiling. "You know what has to happen now, Fiona. How many people have we left in these woods, injured just like this? I'm the third. That's all. It's that simple. We left Carol, then Jill, and now you have to leave me. These people out here really know what they're doing, hobbling us all like this. Very effective way to keep someone from running away. They obviously planned it this way. You have to go, now, before they do the same to you."

Fiona was already crying. "No, no—I won't, I can't do it, Roz. I can't do this without you."

Roz laughed, the sound bitter. "Of course you can. What did I tell you not ten minutes ago? I just said that you were the hero, Fiona. Now it's time for you to keep being the hero. Save me, save us all. You're our only hope."

Fiona sobbed, and Roz pulled her into her chest. She was leaning against the tree to keep her leg off the ground, and Fiona put her hand on the trunk to stop herself from putting too much of her weight on Roz. She wanted to just stand here crying in Roz's arms. How on earth could she keep going after all this? Roz's chin was on the top of her head, and her body was warm—tender and strong at the same time.

"We're maybe as far as eight miles from the highway, possibly less, six or seven, if you go straight there. That's maybe two, three hours."

"Don't say it. Don't say anything more. I won't leave you here, goddamn it. You can't make me leave you."

"All you have to do is keep the sun in front of you, slightly to the right. It's past the zenith now, so it should be easier and easier to navigate with, as long as it's daytime. If the sun sets—"

"Stop talking, damn it!" She shrieked, moving back and away. "I'm not listening to you!"

She'd pinched her eyes closed and turned away from Roz. Angry, hot tears coursed down her cheeks. The blood was pounding in her ears with her fury. She'd never been so angry. Roz touched her shoulder, and she spun toward her, almost ready to slap, kick, or punch her. Seeing Roz there, deflated, pale, and injured, she felt her anger evaporate as if it had never existed. She burst into tears again, grabbing Roz around the middle and burying her face in her damp shirt.

Roz started to lead them gently down to the ground together, gasping with pain, and that was enough to snap Fiona out of her sorrow for a moment to help her. Despite a stab of agony from her shoulder, she managed to get Roz into a sitting position against the tree. Peering down at her, she was reminded of Jill's wan face back there by the river, and she almost started crying again. Roz gestured for her to kneel next to her.

"Listen to me now," Roz said. "You can do this."

"What if I can't? What if you die out here?"

"I will die out here if you don't get me some help. Sure, I might be able to hobble to the highway like this if it came to it, but it doesn't need to. You can save me, Fiona, if you go quickly. Start running and don't look back. And hurry. For me, for Jill, for Sarah and Carol, for everyone else the people from the woods have hurt. Go, go as if our lives depended on it, because they do."

"I'm so tired, Roz. So, so tired."

And she was. Her eyes were scratchy with sleep, and her lips and throat were already parched from lack of water. She was trembling all over just from trying to keep herself in a crouch. She couldn't imagine trying to run for several miles like this.

"But you can run a mile, right?" Roz asked.

Fiona considered, then nodded.

Roz grinned. "Okay—do this. Run a mile, walk half, run a mile, walk half, and repeat until you reach the highway."

"But how will I know how far I've run?"

"Run until you can't. Until your lungs feel like bursting. Then walk until your heart slows down and you can breathe regularly, and then wait a minute or two more before running again."

Their hands were entwined, fingers digging into the backs of their hands. Fiona took in her face one more time. Even now, hurt and pale and dirty, Roz was one of the most beautiful women she'd ever seen. She hadn't realized that fact until right this moment, in part because she had never truly believed they would make it out of here together. Some part of her had suppressed the very idea of it, dismissing it as a fantasy brought on by stress and horror. Now, with the real possibility that she might never see this woman again, that they might never have a chance to get a beer or a meal together, that fantasy returned tenfold.

She could see them together at Jill's Labor Day party, eating barbecue and drinking too many mojitos. She could picture the two of them at her own annual Halloween party, dressed in some cheesy couples' costume and smearing makeup on each other every time they kissed. She could see herself introducing Roz to the rest of her family at Thanksgiving, her little brother making stupid jokes, and her uncle getting too drunk and saying something awkward about their sex lives. Staring into Roz's eyes, she saw their life together stretched out with crystalline clarity.

Hands still clutched together, Fiona pulled Roz toward her and kissed her, hard, almost brutally, before releasing her grip.

"Okay," she said.

Roz's eyebrows shot up. "Just like that?"

"Just like that. If I hurry, we might be in time to catch happy hour somewhere."

Roz's laugh was a real one, this time, neither weak nor bitter, her head thrown back.

"Why—do you know a good place?"

"Yes," Fiona said. "I told you—my friend and her sister run a brewery in Loveland. Even if we're a few minutes late, she'll usually give me the happy-hour discount."

"Sounds good to me. Not much of a beer drinker—"

"You'll like their stuff. I promise."

Their merriment died a few seconds later, and Roz rested her forehead against hers, fingers digging into her shoulders.

"I want you to know I'm rooting for us. I really think we have a chance."

"Even after all this?"

Roz smiled. "Even so. I knew that first time we talked, just the two of us. By the pond."

"Serenity Pond," Fiona said quietly. Instead of days ago, the memory seemed to be from another life.

Roz laughed. "Exactly. I knew even then that I liked you, that I wanted to know you better."

"I thought I was imagining it."

Roz frowned. "Why?"

Fiona shook her head. "I couldn't believe someone like you would be into me."

Roz still looked confused.

"I mean, you could have anyone. Someone prettier—"

"I want you, Fiona. And you're pretty. I see now that you don't know that about yourself, and that makes me really sad, but you're gorgeous, inside and out."

"Even like this?"

Roz laughed. "Even now. And it's not just your pretty face and cute little body, Fiona. I like *you*. Just like this. Any way you are, I'll like you."

Fiona struggled to accept the words, even in the face of what they'd gone through the last few hours. Mostly she dismissed them as flattery, as twisted altruism on Roz's end to give her hope. Part of her, however, desperately wanted to believe her.

She kissed her then, lingering in the sinking pleasure and pain it simultaneously gave her. If this was to be their last kiss, she wanted to remember it for the rest of her life. Roz pulled away first, her eyes sparkling with tears.

"Run, Fiona. Save yourself for me. Please. I can be brave if I know you're safe somewhere."

Fiona gave her another quick kiss and stood up. "I'll do more than that. I'll save you, too. And Jill, and Carol and Sarah—all of us."

"Okay. Good-bye. Good luck. I believe in you."

Fiona stared down at her for another long moment, taking her in one last time. The sight would have to last her for however long this took—it was the only thing she would have to draw strength from, the only motivation she would have to keep trying. Even in her defeated, broken state, splattered with Jill's blood, lips parched, leg swaddled in cloth, Roz was a vision.

"Good-bye, Roz. I'll save you. I promise."

Chapter Twenty-three

Fiona turned and started running. Here in this stretch of woods, despite being at a lower elevation than before, the trees were a little sparser, more open than in other parts of the forest they'd hiked the last few days. The undergrowth was also clearer, the sun too harsh to allow much growth. She could see the path before her, almost as if it were marked, stretching directly in front of her, true and sure. She only occasionally had to dodge around a cluster of trees or bushes, finding the path, imaginary or not, almost at once when she moved past each obstacle. Once, twice in her first frantic dash, a branch or a barb caught at her arm or face, but she moved on without a second glance and ignored the small pain it brought.

While the day was still overwhelmingly hot, as she sped through the woods, she found some relief from the air flowing over her face. She ran and ran, not as if being chased, which she thought she probably was, but because she had somewhere to be. She had to get to the road, not for herself, but for the others—for Jill's future, for Carol and Sarah's, for her and Roz. Even if that future she'd imagined with her *was* a fantasy, she had to try.

On her first rest period, she had to stop a moment and catch her breath. She stood there in the middle of a wide clearing, bent in half, hands on her knees, gasping. This was, she realized, a dangerous pace to set. She couldn't run so hard she'd have to stop, or she'd lose any advantage she gained while running. It took too long for her heart and breathing to slow down before she was ready to start walking.

"Take it easy," she told herself, vaguely aware she'd spoken out loud.

She walked for a while, working at the stitch in her side by swinging her arms and pausing to stretch from side to side a couple of times. Her teeth and gums felt strangely sticky, her tongue swollen. Without any water, she risked collapse if she kept going like this. That wouldn't do at all. Next time, she had to be capable of running again much sooner than this, and she had to be able to do it without passing out somewhere.

Heart rate and breathing finally back to normal, she pushed herself into a slow trot. Within twenty yards, her knees and hip joints were already aching for relief. Each step was jarring, unsettling, sending shooting pain up through her neck and the back of her head. She could feel a major headache coming on, the cause multiple: lack of sleep, exhaustion, dehydration, hunger.

"I have to keep going. Ignore it," she whispered.

She picked up her pace a little, finding it more comfortable to jog, and, as she moved through the woods, the stitch in her side finally let go. She remembered this from training—sometimes you just had to run through it.

This pace was manageable, sustainable. She remembered the plan—run a mile, walk half, but she was probably going farther and faster by doing it this way. Walking, she and Roz and Jill had been doing a mile every twenty or twenty-five minutes this morning, and she estimated she was making closer to fifteen or twenty at this pace. Occasionally she pushed herself into an actual run but would slow down to a jog again the moment her breath started hitching in her chest.

Another branch swept her cheek, sending a stream of warm blood running down her face. She wiped at it absently, not slowing, eyes trained on the next set of trees, the next group of boulders, the next thing she could focus on.

Occasionally, she would throw a glance up at the sky, worried she was getting off course, but she only had to adjust her course forward slightly once or twice. Without Roz's more specific sense of direction, she could never hope to head precisely south, but she trusted her accuracy was close enough to get there eventually, especially as the land was sloping down that way. She could also feel the direction of the sun now on the side of her face and didn't really need to keep checking where it was. If she kept it to her right, almost directly in her eyes, she would reach the road eventually.

Except for that first time gasping in the woods, when she did slow into a walk now, she didn't feel the need to fully stop anymore, nor did she need to walk for very long. Her muscles were warmed up, her adrenaline had come back. Except for the constant thirst, she felt good, comfortable keeping this up for now. How long she could go without water was anyone's guess, but for now, she felt capable of continuing for a long spell yet.

The thirst, however, was brutal. She tried to make herself think about anything else. Even picturing her friends stuck in the woods was better than thinking about her parched, dry mouth and throat. The ache for water, however, was overwhelming, all-consuming. Picturing Jill, her mind would go to the river nearby, and she found herself almost envious of her sitting there, waiting, gunshot or no.

"Stop it. Think about something else."

She couldn't. Again and again, her mind returned to the river. Why had they decided to leave it behind? It seemed foolhardy now. There was no point in taking a new path if you didn't have access to water. The river, she thought now, had been their lifeline. Licking her lips did nothing now, but she had to fight the urge to keep herself from doing it almost constantly. The skin there was peeling away already, the corners of her mouth painfully chapped. She tasted blood there in her next probe and forced herself to keep her tongue in her mouth. Nothing would help now.

Her head was pounding, almost unbearable. The sun felt like it was roasting her here in these sparser woods. The ground itself had dried up in this heat, as she began to kick up dust as she ran.

These were the Colorado woods she was used to—arid and nearly barren.

She saw the markings on the trees before her brain absorbed what they meant. She continued jogging for a few more strides before she stopped, almost at once, nearly tripping herself in her haste to slow down. As before, three trees ahead had geometric patterns carved into them. Unlike before, at both campsites, at the pond, and just before the spot where she left Roz, these markings were much lower than before. Instead of ten or fifteen feet up in the trees, they were nearly at her level. She had no idea if that meant something, or if they'd just gotten lazier and forgot a ladder, but their location was markedly different. Still, the markings meant trouble, and she scanned the ground around her, searching for traps.

She altered her path slightly away from the trees, walking east about fifty yards before heading south again, eyes still glued to the ground and walking gingerly, mincingly forward, picking up her feet very carefully. After twenty or thirty minutes of this, she realized she was getting nowhere, fast. If she didn't get moving again, it would take her too long to reach the highway. If she didn't make it there in the next couple of hours, she wasn't sure she would. She was just too deflated and dry to keep going.

Again, she forced herself into a slow trot, trying to watch the ground and the path in front of her at the same time. The effort was exhausting, stressful. Without a real path to follow, she had to look ahead to watch where she was going. Twice she almost collided with a tree before finally giving it up. If there were more traps, she had to hope they were behind her now.

Half an hour later, her headache almost blindingly painfully, she heard a loud crashing in the woods to her right. She stopped at once, leaping over to a tree and crouching next to it, training her gaze in the direction of the sound. She could see nothing moving over there, or anywhere, but she made herself wait another five minutes, counting down the seconds in her head. Finally, legs quaking, she climbed back to her feet and stared that way for another long beat. She couldn't see anything, but she seemed to detect a sound—so slight she thought she was imagining it.

"Water," she whispered, her heart rising.

Without pausing to think, almost as if she had lost her ability to make decisions about where she went or what she did, she ran, full-out, toward the sound, almost tripping in her haste and carelessness. She rounded a large boulder and saw the source of the sound some fifty feet away: a small pond with a tiny waterfall splashing into it from a little river tributary. She didn't pause, as she might have done if she was thinking clearly, instead belting toward it at top speed.

She flung herself into the pond, landing painfully on her knees, only dimly aware of the pain as she scooped and scooped water into her mouth. It was heavenly—the taste so sweet and satisfying she might have gone on drinking until she burst. She made herself slow down, afraid she might throw up, and rubbed some handfuls on the back of her neck and through her hair. It was icy cold, or at least seemed so on her hot skin.

She scrubbed at her face and hands, feeling as if she were wiping away this whole experience. Blood and dirt flaked off in the water, and she felt a rising sense of giddy relief. She leant down and scooped some more water into her mouth. Thirst finally slaked, she leaned back and down into the water. It was perhaps a foot deep, but she was able to submerge her whole body, and when she came up, sputtering and laughing in joy and relief, it took her several seconds to realize she wasn't alone. She hastily wiped the rest of the water from her eyes and stared, and her breath caught in her chest.

It was the woman, that much she could see at a single glance. She thought of her as *the* woman, not *a* woman, as she'd been the only feminine person they'd seen among those people. She couldn't, of course, know if this was the same one Roz had seen in the clearing, or the one they'd seen in the tent, but some instinct suggested that it was. She was slight and thin, maybe just above five feet tall, her exposed arms a deep tan. Like the others, she was wearing a mask, this one more catlike than the rabbits she'd seen on the men in the camp. The mask was still freakishly shaped, one ear higher than the other, the eyes slightly misaligned, the whole thing a lumpy, poorly formed and unadorned white papier-mâché. She was dressed strangely, too, her entire outfit a pale-brown linen or hemp, shapeless and baggy, her sandals likewise lumpy and misshapen, made of twine and strips of leather, perhaps. She was holding a rusty rifle across her body, pointed up and to the left, as if in military readiness. A long bayonet had been attached to the end, but it too was rusty, dull.

Fiona held her hands up in the air. "Don't shoot. Please don't shoot me. I'll do whatever you want."

The woman didn't move or react, her eyes twinkling slightly behind the mask.

"What do you want?" Fiona asked. "What do you want from us? Why are you doing this?

Again, no response.

Fiona kept her hands in the air, muscles quivering with fatigue and terror. When the woman didn't move or speak, after perhaps a full minute, Fiona let herself begin to lower her hands, waiting for a reaction. Nothing happened. The woman stood as if frozen there, the only movement an occasional flash of her eyes behind the mask.

Despite everything, Fiona was beginning to get cold. A shiver ran through her, gooseflesh rising on her arms. Sitting here like this was also uncomfortable. She'd risen out of the water to a seated position, legs stretched out in front of her, submerged, and her back and stomach muscles were starting to complain and quiver with the effort of keeping herself upright. She leant back on her hands, still watching for a reaction, but again, the woman stayed still.

"Fuck this," Fiona said and stood up, a surge of water coming with her. She stood, dripping, soaked through, and watched for a few seconds before moving toward the edge of the pond.

This time the woman did react, lowering her rifle toward Fiona. Fiona froze, hands shooting into the air again, but nothing happened. They stayed that way for perhaps a full minute.

"Can I get out of the water?" Fiona asked.

A slight nod.

Fiona moved up and onto the shore, rubbing some of the water out of her hair and dropping her hands to her sides. The woman still had her gun trained on Fiona, but she hadn't moved her fingers nearer to the trigger—the gun was simply pointed at her. Fiona watched her, waiting for anything to change, hoping she might have a crucial second or two to try to jump out of the way. Nothing happened. The longer this went on, the more Fiona wanted it to simply be over. She couldn't take it anymore. Her temper rose, frayed from fatigue and the emotional turmoil of the last few days.

"Goddamn it! Just shoot me and be done with this, already. If you're going to kill me, do it."

The woman raised the gun to her shoulder, and Fiona closed her eyes. If she ran, she'd be shot eventually, and she was suddenly unwilling to try. Let this be done and she could finally rest, sleep. At least this way it would be quick.

In the next seconds, minutes, hours, years, time lost all meaning. She relived the last few days in total, experiencing every agony and triumph. Further back, she saw her last few days at work before the vacation, impatiently finishing several useless tasks to fill up her shift and get her boss off her back. Farther still, she saw Jill and her other friends, celebrating the Fourth of July at Carter Lake, a pony of local beer and pretty girls in swimsuits dancing around a bonfire. Memories sped up then, flickering through her mind in full relief. What she experienced and saw in that strange, everlasting moment was a life misspent. A life waiting for the next thing, nursing resentments, holding grudges, a life tainted with envy and self-created pain. This couldn't be it. This couldn't be all it meant.

"No," she whispered, snapping back into the present.

"No!" She shouted the word this time. She opened her eyes, dropped low, and got ready to run.

She was alone.

She crumpled to the ground, howling with an overwhelming sense of gratitude and joy. She screamed once, an overpowering something inside her necessary to release, and then burst into laughing tears. She wrapped her arms around her body, hugging herself, and quaking all over with an exhilarating and a thankful recognition of her own continued existence.

"Alive, alive," she said, repeating the word several times.

Finally, she crawled over to the water again, trying to scoop the liquid in shaking cupped hands. She couldn't stop trembling. Her nerves were overwrought, overexcited, and it took much longer than normal to get some more water to her mouth. She sobbed a few times, pinching her eyes shut again, opening them at once to stare up at the spot where the woman had stood. She was still alone, and she caught a sob and swallowed it painfully. She had to make herself stand up. It took several tries, her legs almost giving out each time, but she finally made it, swaying slightly before moving.

She was still light-headed and detached from her body, and her first steps away from the water were uncertain, clumsy. She made herself focus on her feet, putting one in front of the other, and her balance and equilibrium finally began to come back to her a few minutes later. She tried a shuffling jog forward, almost tripped, and dropped back into a fast walk. Running could wait. She had to find her way back to herself, first.

She refused to look back, refused to see if the woman was watching her, waiting for her to forget and then shoot. No, Fiona decided. It was better to believe that she had let her go, even if she had no reason to hope, even if believing in that didn't make any sense. It was the only way to keep going.

She heard the road long before she allowed herself to recognize the sounds for what they were—cars and trucks. The highway was a significant east-west thoroughfare for weekend campers, but on a weekday, it was still busy enough for the sounds of vehicles to reach her, one on top of the other sometimes, long pauses between others. She tried to increase her speed again but only managed a loping trot. Any faster, and she started to lose her balance again, nearly tripping.

The ground had leveled off at some point, when, she couldn't remember. It might have been before the pond or since; she had no memory of the change. All she knew was that level ground meant she was close—two miles or less.

Now they would shoot her. They knew where she was, and they had to recognize that they couldn't let her go. If the woman was their leader, which Fiona had, like Roz, begun to believe, perhaps she had simply left to rally her troops. Any moment now and it would all be over.

Though perhaps, she thought, they'll let me see the road. They'll let me see it, for one last moment of hope, and then end this charade, once and for all.

Movement ahead of her—a flash of red metal—and she finally caught her final wind. It was a car, not fifty feet ahead, driving by beyond the barbed-wire fence that protected this forest. Fiona started running then, faster than she ever had, head lowered, body tilted forward, arms pumping at her sides and feet fairly flying over the ground in front of her. The fence slowed her for no more than a few seconds, as she quickly maneuvered to a nearby tree, jumping for the lowest branch, swinging her legs over, and dropping down on the other side.

She landed awkwardly, letting out a single moan of pain, then stumbled the remaining yards to the road. Something—a car, a truck—was coming toward her on the road, the light suddenly too bright to fully comprehend the shape. She waved her hands wildly once, twice, heard honking and the squealing of brakes, and then she was falling, falling, the world fading as she lost consciousness and sank to the ground.

Chapter Twenty-four

The light was too bright, and her head hurt. She closed her eyes against it and then squinted them open, her blurry vision clearing a few seconds later. Sarah was sitting nearby, reading a book, and she could see a nurse hustling by in the hallway.

"In the hospital," she whispered.

Sarah sat forward, closing her book.

"Oh, thank goodness. I thought you'd sleep forever. The doctor said it wasn't a coma, that once the medication wore off, you'd wake up, but man, you sure slept solid. I've been going back and forth between everyone's rooms, but you're always asleep. Did you wake up at all?"

Fiona shook her head. "No. I think this is the first time, or at least the first time I remember. How long was I out?" Her voice was scratchy, painful.

Sarah glanced at her watch. "Gosh—about fifty hours, give or take. They told me they picked you up Tuesday afternoon, and it's Thursday evening, now."

Fiona struggled to believe this. She could remember fainting on the road and waking up after the trucker that found her shook her awake. She'd had a hard time explaining things first to him and then to the police officers that had soon shown up. She remembered trying to sit up, being pushed back down by one or more of them, babbling her story and pointing into the woods. She'd been desperate for them to believe her, but she remembered that her hysteria made them doubt her, made them think she was raving. Finally, she convinced someone—one of the police officers?—to send a search party for Roz. She remembered thinking they'd believe Roz. After that, her memory was cloudier. She could recall an ambulance pulling up, then, vaguely, a flash of bright lights, faces bent over her, voices, but nothing more.

But here was Sarah, clean and healthy-looking, sitting here calmly by the side of her bed, none the worse for what had happened. Two days had passed, but what *had* happened?

"You want some water?" Sarah asked.

Fiona nodded, and Sarah handed her a tan water bottle with a thick, plastic straw. She took several long sips, her body thrumming with relief. How long would it be before water would seem like water again? Sarah took the bottle from her and put it back on the little wheeled table nearby. A single rose was sitting there in a little vase. From Roz, maybe?

Fiona cleared her throat. "Thanks. Earlier, you said you were going back and forth. To Roz, Jill, Carol?"

Sarah smiled. "All fine. All safe. Everyone's here, still. All the guys are fine, too, and I think some of them checked out earlier today. I was just about to go back to Carol when you woke up."

Fiona tried to sit up and flinched with pain.

"Here, let me raise the bed a little," Sarah said. She pushed the little button, and Fiona's head raised about a foot, the motion shooting pain through her back and legs. Sarah, seeing her face, stopped the bed's movement.

"You okay?"

"Yeah. It's my back. Hurts like hell."

"Probably from lying down too much. Let me move your pillows a little bit." She stood, adjusting them, then slapped her forehead. "Shit. I'm supposed to call someone in here if you wake up."

"Can you wait a sec? I need to know some things."

"You sure? They might be able to give you something for your back."

She grabbed Sarah's hand. "Tell me."

Sarah's eye's widened, and she sat back down, patting Fiona's hand. "Okay, yeah, I'm sorry. That's right. You haven't heard any of this yet."

"Please tell me. I don't know anything."

"Well, they got to Roz first. One of the police officers said you made him promise to go search for her before you'd get in the ambulance. You were fighting everyone, tooth and nail."

Fiona grinned. "Oh, yeah?"

"Yeah. I mean, I get it. Don't worry. I don't blame you for not sending them our way first. She was closest, and it was a good idea. I guess when they first found you, you were raving. You told them about Jill, and me and Carol, and the crazy people in the woods. They thought you'd lost your mind. But something must have gotten through, because that officer did call in some backup and Search and Rescue, and they got to Roz a few hours later. She backed up your story."

Fiona, realizing she was still clutching Sarah's hand, let go and leant back in her pillows.

"Thank God."

"Once they found Roz, they realized they had a major situation on their hands. They had to get more backup, and they replaced most of the Search-and-Rescue people with police since they knew there were people with guns out there."

"How long did it take them to pick up you and Carol?"

"The next morning—Wednesday, yesterday. I heard the helicopter swirling around overhead, and Carol and I managed to get over to the clearing to be picked up. I've never been so happy."

"So everyone's okay?"

Sarah patted her hand again. "Everyone's fine. Banged up, dehydrated, scared, but fine."

"Well, you look good."

Sarah primped her hair a little. "Don't I? I'm calling it a catastrophe cleanse."

They grinned at each other, and Fiona was struck with an overwhelming surge of emotion. She started crying, soon sobbing, and Sarah rubbed her hand a little more.

"There, there, honey. You're okay. You did good, Fiona. You saved all of us."

Still crying, she was only vaguely aware of someone entering the room. Soon a nurse was standing nearby, checking the monitors on the machines next to her, and Fiona waved as Sarah left the room, unable to choke out a good-bye.

"Glad to see you awake," the nurse said. "The doctor will be here soon."

"What's wrong with me?"

"Dehydration and exhaustion, mostly, a little malnutrition. You have some injuries, a couple of which are infected. Your hand, for one, and that cut on your face. Some other bumps and bruises that aren't as severe. You're getting a course of antibiotics."

Fiona's fingers went for her face, and she noticed, for the first time, the IV in the back of her right hand.

"My back hurts."

"More of the same, I'm sure. We'll see what the doctor says. She should be here any minute. You're a real celebrity around here, you know."

"I am?"

"Well, yes! You and your friends. You're all that's been on the news the last few days. You should see the press downstairs, just itching to get up here. It's a real zoo getting in here."

Fiona wanted to ask her more, but a young, gorgeous Indian woman walked in, smiling when she saw Fiona.

"Well, hello there, sleepyhead!"

"Hi."

"I'm Doctor Lata, and you've met Ms. Williams, your nurse this evening."

Fiona nodded. Dr. Lata examined the bandages on her face and hands, asking questions about each as she went.

"These are looking good. You'll probably want to talk to our plastic surgeon about this bigger cut on your face, see if he can do something about the scarring. Everything else should shape up just fine. Besides the antibiotics, you're getting some good nutrients in your IV here. I'll order dinner up here soon so you can get something solid into you. We should have you out of here tomorrow or the next day, at the latest. I want to keep an eye on those infections a little longer, build up your strength. How does that sound?"

"Sounds good, but my back hurts really bad."

"Probably stiff from lying here. I can give you some Tylenol, and you'll likely feel better once you get up and move around a little."

"Can I go see my friends?" Fiona assumed that, like her nurse, her doctor knew what had happened and was, perhaps, treating some of the others.

Dr. Lata seemed surprised, and she and the nurse shared a quick glance. Seeing her hesitate, Fiona kept talking.

"I think I'd feel better if I could see them. We…went through a lot together."

"So I've heard," Dr. Lata said, squinting at her. "If I didn't know any better, I would think you're manipulating me."

Fiona tried to make her expression as innocent as possible, and the doctor laughed. "I suppose it wouldn't be out of the question, even tonight. We can get a wheelchair in here for you, but I want to see you try to go to the bathroom first. Ms. Williams, will you help her up? In the meantime, I'll go check and see who's up for a visit."

The process was arduous, and Fiona was surprised by how weak she felt once she was on her feet. With every step, her legs tried to collapse beneath her, and her knees were literally knocking together under her flimsy gown. It took everything in her power not to simply collapse on the toilet once she'd made it there. Ms. Williams was kind enough to turn around, but it still took her a while to relieve herself, her bladder cramping with a stinging burn.

"We'll get an aide in here to give you a sponge bath later tonight, and maybe tomorrow you can try a real shower," the nurse said, helping her clean herself. It was incredibly embarrassing, and Fiona couldn't help but try to relieve the awkwardness with a joke.

"Do I smell that bad?"

Ms. Williams laughed, bending down to help her upright again. The two of them hobbled out of the bathroom together, and then Fiona froze in place. Roz was waiting for her by the bed.

She was sitting in a wheelchair next to Dr. Lata, clean and dressed in actual clothing, not a hospital gown. Her hair had been nicely styled, and, except for the bandages around her lower leg, she appeared completely normal—rested and healthy. Those lines of fatigue around her eyes and mouth were gone, as if they'd never been there. She was, once again, the woman she'd met, standing by the horses and fully in charge.

"Hey, lady," Roz said.

"Hey, yourself."

"I thought this might make more sense," Dr. Lata said, "bringing her to you, since you're still a little under the weather. I'll see about the others in a little while."

"Let me help you back into bed," Ms. Williams said.

This was, of course, easier said than done, and several minutes passed before she was sitting up in the bed, she and Roz alone again. Roz had wheeled as close as she could, and they clasped hands, staring at each other.

"Last time I was in here, you were sleeping like a baby," Roz said.

"You watched me sleep?"

"All day today, most of yesterday."

They sat there in silence, smiling at each other. Fiona was so happy she could feel tears rising in her eyes. Roz was here, the woman of her dreams, alive and well and waiting for her, of all people. It was hard to believe.

"You did it, Fiona. You saved me."

"You saved me, too."

Roz shook her head. "You did it all, Fiona."

Fiona couldn't respond right away, too happy simply looking at her.

"Why are you dressed like that?"

Roz glanced down at herself and then smiled. "Oh, yeah. I'm getting out of here. My ankle's not too bad, really. The cuts are already scabbed over. Just bruised and banged up. I ate today and went to the bathroom on my own, which I guess is the sign they wait for. They gave me crutches for the next two weeks, but I have to use this chair while I'm here."

"How will you get home?"

"Jon's picking me up."

"Oh, good. Do you live nearby? Where are we, anyway?"

Roz smiled. "Yeah. I live about a couple miles from here. We're in Fort Collins."

"Can't believe I never asked you where you live."

"We've been busy."

Fiona waved her hands. "Hold up, hold up. I need details. What happened? Where were the guys that whole time?"

"In the camp where we found Jill. They were all there, just like we thought. Fred was there before the others, tied up and blindfolded the whole time." She shivered. "They got him almost immediately, right after he left us that first night."

"Jesus. What about the others? How did that happen?"

"Jon told me they came and took them from their tents in the middle of the night. Frog-marched them out of there with the horses."

"But how is that possible? Why didn't we hear them? Did anyone call out?"

"Jon said they did. They were yelling at first, but then those people made them shut up. They punched Mark so hard he had to be carried out, and then they gagged everyone and tied their hands behind their backs."

"So why didn't we hear them? Or the horses? And they took their tents and gear!"

Roz shook her head. "I don't know, and neither does he. Maybe Carol was right after all. Maybe they drugged us."

Fiona was shaking her head. It was, they both knew, impossible. When could it have happened? And yet, as far as explanations went, it seemed to be the only one that fit.

"So what happened to them?"

"Who? The guys?"

"No. The people from the woods. Did they catch them all? Did they catch the woman?"

Roz seemed taken aback. "You mean you don't know?"

"Don't know what? I don't know anything. I just woke up, remember?"

Roz rubbed at her mouth, absently, her eyes dark and worried. "I just thought someone would tell you…"

"Tell me what? What is it?"

Roz squeezed her hand again. "They got away, Fiona. All of them."

Fiona's heart gave a great lurch of terror, and her ears started ringing. She let go of Roz's hand and leaned back into her pillows, suddenly dizzy.

"They got away?" She almost whispered this question.

"All of them. They left everything and everyone there in camp—all the guys, the horses. And they left their tents and guns. They just walked out of the woods. The sheriff's department and the police tracked them to an unmarked road, one they probably made themselves, but didn't find anything there—no cars, nothing. They disappeared." Roz was quiet, waiting for her to comment, and when she didn't, she continued. "Last I heard, they had some helicopters and search teams combing the woods, and they're checking all their stuff for fingerprints, but we haven't had any updates. They're gone, Fiona."

"How can that be, Roz? How is it possible?"

She was crying again, weakly, the tears running slowly down her cheeks. Roz wiped them away and grabbed her hand again, kissing it.

"I'm sorry, Fiona. I shouldn't have told you now. I should have waited until you felt a little stronger."

Fiona choked on a sob and wiped her face clean again. "No. I'm sorry. I…I don't know why I'm crying. Just scared, I guess."

"We're all scared."

"Who's scared?" Jill asked from the doorway. She too was in a wheelchair, but she was still wearing a hospital gown. Unlike Roz, she looked beaten down, battered. In addition to a large cast on her lower leg, she was bandaged and pale, her eyes still black and her cut lip swollen and bruised. Even in the last couple days, she appeared to have lost a lot of weight, her hair thin and lank.

Dr. Lata appeared behind her. "Ms. Delmonico? It's time. Let's get you checked out. Your ride is here."

"Can I come back here when I'm done with the paperwork?"

Dr. Lata shook her head. "No. That wouldn't be a good idea. She needs her rest, and visiting hours are almost over. I'm going to ask Jill to keep this short. But you can come back tomorrow."

Roz met Fiona's eyes and then levered herself out of her chair, kissing her, hard. She ran her fingers along Fiona's cheek and then sat back down. "I'll be here tomorrow morning. Try not to worry too much, okay? The police are here, and they and the staff are watching you. No one will hurt you."

"Okay."

"Get out of here, Roz," Jill said. "You two can canoodle tomorrow."

Roz wheeled past her, swatting her arm, and threw a quick wave back before letting herself be pushed out the door by the doctor.

"So," Jill said.

"So."

Jill grinned and wheeled herself closer. "You saved my life, lady."

"Everyone keeps saying that."

"Well, it's true."

"But they got away, Jill. And I shouldn't have made it."

"But you did."

"No—that's not what I mean. Right before I got to the road, I saw that woman."

"You did?"

"Yes. She had a gun. She had every opportunity to kill me. I even told her to shoot me and get it over with."

Jill laughed. "You did? Badass."

Fiona shook her head. "I don't know why she didn't. And now she's still out there. They're all still out there."

Jill scooted forward in her chair, wincing slightly, and grabbed Fiona's hand in both of hers. Fiona was reminded with a sweeping wave of déjà vu when she'd done this same thing, in the woods, just before she and Roz left her by the river. That same cold determination was there in her eyes.

"You listen to me now, Fiona. Are you listening?"

"Yes, but you're hurting my hand."

Jill didn't let up, still squeezing it. "Listen carefully. You can't let this ruin your life. You have to let it go. I was out there by myself all night. Every sound I heard, I was sure they were coming for me. Then, finally it was someone, well, something, whatever—a great big, goofy search dog. He let me cry on him until his handler showed up. They dragged me out of those fucking woods on a stretcher. We finally got here to the hospital, and when I heard that those assholes had escaped, I almost died."

"What do you mean?"

"I mean I literally almost died. Technically, I had a 'cardiac event,' but it means the same thing. They had to use the paddles and everything to get me going again."

"Oh, Jill."

She nodded. "Exactly. When I came out of it, I made a choice. Either I could fret on this for the rest of my life, or I could let it go. Fiona, you have to do the same. It's the only way we'll keep going."

"But how? How can we keep going, knowing those people are still around? That they could show up any minute? Our names are in the news! They'll know who we are!"

Jill shook her head. "Stop it. Stop it right now. What the hell can you do about it? Do you want to spend the rest of your life looking over your shoulder? No one can live like that forever and not lose their mind. Just let it go. Let's put this whole shitty thing behind us and never look back."

"But—"

Dr. Lata entered then, and after one glance at Fiona, her expression darkened with annoyance.

"Are you upsetting my patient, Jill?"

"No, ma'am! I promise. I was just about to leave."

"Good, because I was just about to come get you."

"Remember what I said, Fiona," Jill said. "Think about your choices here. Choose life."

Dr. Lata, perhaps more annoyed than she was showing, quickly wheeled Jill out of the room before Fiona had a chance to respond.

She lay there, thinking about what she'd said, not moving, long into the night.

Epilogue

"So how long have you been brewing beer?" Roz asked, sipping from her Solo cup.

"Gosh, it's almost fifteen years now, though a lot of that was training," Erin said. "We've had the brewery for only six of that."

"Has it been that long?" Fiona asked.

"Yeah. I know it's hard to believe. It's downtown. Bennet Sisters' Brewing. Ever been, Roz?"

"Nope. But I don't live here in town. I'll have to have Fiona bring me over. This porter's fantastic."

"Thanks. We're tapping the Watermelon Gose on Wednesday. Also, Fiona, the expansion is finally finished. I'd love to show both of you around."

"It is?" Fiona asked. "That's good to hear."

"Yes," Erin said. "We're really pleased with how it turned out. Now Darcy's trying to get me to diversify. She thinks we should start distilling vodka and gin."

"Imagine," Darcy said, spreading her hands, "homemade gin and tonics."

"Ever thought of doing whiskey?" Roz asked.

"Roz is a scotch person," Fiona explained.

"Ah," Darcy said, "a woman after my own heart."

Fiona settled back under Roz's arm, happy the three of them were hitting it off and happy to let them keep talking without her input. She closed her eyes, sleepy from the heat and day drinking, and leaned farther into her girlfriend's body. They were sitting on an outdoor loveseat together, across from Erin and Darcy. Everyone at the party was on the patio under the pergola in Jill's backyard. Usually Jill set up her badminton/volleyball net, but even with the water misters spraying liberally, it was far too hot in the sun to consider doing anything active right now. Fiona couldn't remember a Labor Day this warm.

A little over five weeks had passed since their rescue, and everyone was on the mend or past it. Jill and Carol were still in casts, but both had recently upgraded to the walking type. As she'd predicted, Roz was already fully healed, only two or three tiny pink scars on her calf to mark where the trap had pinned her. Fiona's shoulder was back to normal, the scar faint, her fingernail was growing back, and the minor plastic surgery on her face injury had gone well. She was down to a small bandage on her cheek. Everything was almost back to normal.

No, better than normal. She and Roz were basically living together, spending every night either at her place or Roz's. Though they hadn't talked about it yet, it was probably only a matter of time before they got their own place together either here in Loveland or up in Fort Collins. Her friends and family had given her a hard time at first, the usual U-Haul jokes, but even those had let up, and neither she nor Roz had really cared about the teasing. They were happy, and they needed each other, especially those first days and weeks.

The nightmares had lessened, but plenty of nights one or both would still wake up in a panic. Sometimes it had nothing to do with bad dreams. Sometimes one or the other was just terrified. A shadow would pass by a window, they'd see movement in the backyard, and one or the other would get a faraway look in her eyes. Fiona always knew what Roz was thinking about when she did that, and she imagined it was the same for her.

Still, their time together since the hospital had been the best weeks of her life. They'd been honeymooning, mostly, so, besides a few visits with family and a couple of friends, this was their first real outing as a couple in public. Lots of Fiona's friends would be here today, so she'd been a little anxious about how well Roz would fit in. Now she knew she shouldn't have worried. Everyone loved her.

"What do you think?" Roz said, shaking her slightly.

"Hmmmm?" Fiona asked, sitting up and rubbing her face.

Roz and the others laughed.

"Were you asleep?" Roz asked.

Fiona grinned at her, scooting up for a quick kiss. "Sort of."

"Ah. Well, Darcy, Erin, and I were planning a trip together."

"Oh?"

"To Scotland, to see the Highlands, tour the distilleries."

"I'm doing a long trip there next summer for an article I'm working on," Darcy explained. "Erin's already coming with. You two should join us."

"Sounds great," Fiona said. "Count me in."

She and Roz kissed again, and Erin and Darcy chuckled.

"You're really cute together," Erin said.

"Aren't we?" Fiona asked.

Everyone laughed again, and Fiona looked up at her girlfriend. Seven weeks ago, she would never have believed this would be her life now. She'd had to go through hell to get here, but she thought if she had to go through it again to be where she was now, she'd do it. Most of the time, anyway.

"Have you guys seen Jill?" Erin asked, peering around. "We've been here for half an hour, and she's MIA."

"She was out here when we got here," Fiona said, likewise scanning the crowd. "We met her new girlfriend."

"And her boyfriend," Roz added. "Well, we didn't meet him, actually, since I already knew him. He's a friend of mine. Jon."

"Oh, gosh, that's right," Erin said. "I remember now. She's dating one of our servers, right?"

"Gina, yes," Fiona replied.

"I bet you anything that's where they are," Roz said, tilting her head at the house. "Somewhere inside together."

Fiona wouldn't put it past Jill to do exactly that. Disappearing for a booty call was par for the course at Jill's parties.

"Well, I don't know about you, hon, but I could use some food," Roz said, squeezing her shoulder. "I can't drink this much on an empty stomach."

"I'm sure we'll catch you guys again later today," Erin said, "but just in case, come by the brewery later this week. Any day but Tuesday and I can show you around."

"Will do," Roz said.

She helped Fiona up, and they fought through the crowds to the food tables set up in the garage. Huge fans were set up in here, and the big door on the far side was open, so it was relatively pleasant, though quite loud. Fiona knew perhaps half of these people. Despite her abrasive personality, Jill was incredibly popular, and her Labor Day party was the final queer event of the season in their small town.

Carol and Sarah were standing near the desserts, and Fiona was surprised to see Jill there with them, especially without one of her new lovers. The three of them were laughing together, which was a relief. Two weeks after the hospital, when they'd been interviewed, yet again, by the police, Carol and Sarah had given Jill the cold shoulder at the station. Fiona was surprised they'd even come to the party. Jill, spotting them, waved them over.

"Hey, ladies!" Jill said, giving both a big hug. "You enjoying yourselves?"

"Great time," Roz said.

"Yay!" Jill said, jumping up and down despite her cast. "I'm so glad we're all here together. Bygones and all that, right?"

She was clearly a little tipsy, and the four of them nodded in agreement with her, each of them hiding a little grin.

"Well, I have some hostessing to do, but I'll try to catch y'all later. Eat up! Drink up! It's all on the house!"

The four of them watched her leave. She was hugging and kissing her way through the crowd, hardly even limping.

Roz shook her head. "Well, she's chipper."

"She's wasted," Carol said. "She came over here and gave Sarah a great big sloppy kiss."

"I was so surprised, I didn't know what to do besides lean into it," Sarah said. "She's a good kisser."

"Hey!" Carol said, swatting her.

"I'm so glad you guys came," Fiona said. "I wasn't sure I'd see you two today."

Carol and Sarah shared a quick glance, and Carol shrugged. "Yeah, well. We talked about it, and we both decided it was time to move on."

"And Jill left us about a thousand voice mails, apologizing," Sarah added. "It seemed kind of, I don't know, petty to keep being angry."

No one had to say more than this. Jill had left the two of them, hopeless and helpless and alone in the woods. Still, Jill had suffered, too. They all had. No one, it seemed, wanted to rehash all of that, however, so no one brought it up. They hadn't talked about any of it, in fact, as a group. Fiona wondered if they ever would.

"You guys look great, by the way," Carol added.

"For real," Sarah said. "Dynamite. Is that a new haircut, Fiona?"

"Yes, it is. Thanks for noticing."

Fiona smiled up at Roz, proud. They'd been honeymooning, yes, but they were also taking care of each other in other ways, too. Roz had a much better diet than Fiona, and she'd adapted to it without a struggle. Fiona, on the other hand, had a decent sense of fashion, especially when she dressed other people. Roz's closet had been filled with nothing but hiking and ski wear. While this was a standard Colorado wardrobe for a lot of people, Fiona had bought Roz her entire outfit today—red Bermuda shorts and a pineapple-patterned, blue button-up. She was seriously gorgeous in these clothes. Yesterday, Roz had taken her to her barber, and the man had done something incredible to her usual mousy blob. Roz would always outmatch her in the looks department—nothing would ever convince her otherwise—but she had to admit they weren't entirely mismatched now. She liked to think they complemented each other.

"We'd love to have you guys over for dinner soon," Carol said.

"Yes! That's right!" Sarah said. "Thanks for reminding me, honey. Carol's birthday is in a couple of weeks. Can you come by?"

"The twentieth, right?" Fiona asked.

"Yes."

"We'll be there," Roz said.

"Good," Carol said. "And don't bring anything—just your gorgeous selves."

The four of them loaded their plates. Most of the chairs were taken on the patio, so the two couples were forced to separate to hunt for places to eat. Roz led Fiona back to where they started, but Erin and Darcy had wandered off somewhere, and the two empty chairs by the little table there weren't next to each other. They sat down anyway, Roz introducing herself to the woman next to her—someone Fiona had never seen before. It was too loud out here to hear their conversation, but Fiona was amused to see the woman preening and flirting with her girlfriend. Roz was clearly oblivious or polite enough to pretend not to notice.

Fiona turned her attention to her own plate, polishing off her food quickly before realizing she'd left her drink somewhere. Roz was still listening to the other woman, bent slightly toward her, and she waved a dismissive hand at her when Fiona mimicked raising a drink to her mouth. She took her empty plate back into the garage, relieved to see that the crowds had thinned out a little in here.

Jill was there, standing by the drinks table, her back to Fiona.

"Hey, girl," Fiona said, touching her shoulder.

Jill turned, and Fiona was surprised to see that she'd been crying. She wiped her face and gave her a sickly smile.

"What's wrong?" Fiona asked.

Jill flapped one hand. "Nothing, everything. I think I drank too much. Just being maudlin."

"So maybe you should give this to me," Fiona said, taking her drink.

Jill grinned and nodded. "Maybe you're right."

Fiona took a couple of sips from it, eyeing her friend. Unlike herself and the others, Jill hadn't quite bounced back the same way they had. She was still too thin, her face pale, and she had dark circles under her eyes. Still, Jill was dating two people, so some of this, she hoped, could be the result of sleepless nights. But probably not.

"Wanna talk about it?" Fiona asked.

Jill lunged forward, grabbing her shoulders and digging her fingers into Fiona's skin. "Do you think about it?"

Fiona didn't have to ask her what she meant. "Of course I do. All the time. We all do, I'm sure."

"So how do you keep going? How do you forget about it? You and Roz, and Carol and Sarah—you all seem like you're past it, like you've moved on." Jill's lip quivered, and she put her face in her hands. "It's all I think about. All the time, every minute of the day." She dropped her hands, her eyes dark pools of terror. "It's breaking me, Fiona. It's ruining my life. I'm not even sure I can keep my job anymore."

"I thought you were doing okay, Jill. Jesus. You told me to put it behind me. That's what I've been trying to do." She paused and squeezed Jill's hand. "Are you talking to anyone about this?"

"Who would I talk to? You and Roz have been locked away the last four weeks, and this is the first time Carol and Sarah have talked to me since…everything."

"I don't mean us, Jill. I mean have you talked to someone? A therapist? A counselor of some kind?"

Jill made a dismissive gesture. "Oh, come on. How would that help? All of it is crazy. No one would believe me."

"What are you talking about? Of course they would!"

"Maybe."

Fiona pulled her into a hug. Jill's guilt was crushing, and tiny tears sprang to Fiona's eyes. Of all of them, she would never have expected Jill to take it the hardest. It made sense, though. She and Roz had each other as distractions, as sounding boards for their worries, as did Carol and Sarah. Jill had only herself these last weeks.

"Why didn't you call me?"

Jill moved back, shaking her head. "I didn't want to bother you. I know you've been busy."

They grinned at each other, knowing what she meant.

"Is she good?" Jill asked. "I bet she is. Your skin looks amazing."

"We're *not* talking about my sex life, Jill. And hey, will you call me next time, please? Any time, day or night. And let's get together soon, just you and me."

"I'd like that."

"There you are!" Roz called from the doorway. "I wondered what was taking so long. I think that woman just proposed to me. I came to ask your permission."

Jill wiped her face one more time and spun toward her, arms wide. "There she is—the woman of the hour."

They hugged, then Jill excused herself again, moving back into the crowds now spilling off her patio into the sun-bleached yard.

Roz came closer, one eyebrow raised. "You guys okay? Jill looked upset, and you seem worried."

"It's Jill. I think she's really messed up right now. I should have been there for her these last few weeks."

Roz threw an arm around her shoulder and led her back to the doorway onto the patio. The two of them watched as Jill flitted from group to group, kissing and hugging just about everyone but never pausing for more than a moment or two. Roz kissed the top of her head.

"She'll be okay. We're all going to be okay. I promise."

Fiona didn't respond. Her eyes, following Jill, had come back to a strange woman standing apart from the crowd. She didn't recognize her, exactly, but that didn't necessarily mean anything today with all these strangers around. No, something else was drawing her gaze to her, some dim recognition. She was slight, short, her dark hair lank and greasy. She didn't seem to be with anyone, as far as Fiona could see, but that didn't necessarily mean she was here by herself. Still, somehow Fiona doubted she'd come with friends. She seemed alone, separate, and stood out somehow. Fiona thought it might be partly her expression, which was dour and almost angry, or her terrible clothing, which looked like the worst kind of thrift-store bargains. How did she know her?

It came to her then, like a clap of thunder.

"Oh my God! It's her! It the woman from the woods!"

"Where?" Roz said, staring around wildly.

Fiona pointed right as a group of people blocked their view. She grabbed Roz's hand, dragging her forward and around the group, but by the time they moved past them, she was gone.

"She was right here! I swear to God, she was standing right here!"

She spun around, pushing people out of her way, Roz trailing her. People stopped talking, staring at her, several faces around her appearing frightened and surprised.

Finally, Roz pulled her into a rough hug. "It's okay, hon. You're going to be okay. Talking to Jill made you—"

"I'm not hallucinating. She was here, goddamn it."

She cried into Roz's shirt, Roz's soothing sounds coming to her vaguely over the pounding of her heart. Her eyes were pinched closed, her body tight, and she stayed that way, worried who and what she would see if she opened her eyes.

About the Author

Charlotte was born in a tiny mountain town and spent most of her childhood and young adulthood in a small city in Northern Colorado. While she is usually what one might generously call "indoorsy," early exposure to the Rocky Mountains led to a lifelong love of nature, hiking, and camping.

After a lengthy education in Denver, New Orleans, Washington, DC, and New York, she earned a doctorate in literature and women and gender studies. She currently lives with her wife, son, and their cat in a small city in Wisconsin.

Charlotte is a two-time Golden Crown Literary Society "Goldie" Winner for *Gnarled Hollow* and *Legacy* and a finalist for a Lambda Literary Award for *Gnarled Hollow*.

Books Available from Bold Strokes Books

16 Steps to Forever by Georgia Beers. Can Brooke Sullivan and Macy Carr find themselves by finding each other? (978-1-63555-762-6)

All I Want for Christmas by Georgia Beers, Maggie Cummings, Fiona Riley. The Christmas season sparks passion and love in these stories by award winning authors Georgia Beers, Maggie Cummings, and Fiona Riley. (978-1-63555-764-0)

From the Woods by Charlotte Greene. When Fiona goes backpacking in a protected wilderness, the last thing she expects is to be fighting for her life. (978-1-63555-793-0)

Heart of the Storm by Nicole Stiling. For Juliet Mitchell and Sienna Bennett a forbidden attraction definitely isn't worth upending the life they've worked so hard for. Is it? (978-1-63555-789-3)

If You Dare by Sandy Lowe. For Lauren West and Emma Prescott, following their passions is easy. Following their hearts, though? That's almost impossible. (978-1-63555-654-4)

Love Changes Everything by Jaime Maddox. For Samantha Brooks and Kirby Fielding, no matter how careful their plans, love will change everything. (978-1-63555-835-7)

Not This Time by MA Binfield. Flung back into each other's lives, can former bandmates Sophia and Madison have a second chance at romance? (978-1-63555-798-5)

The Dubious Gift of Dragon Blood by J. Marshall Freeman. One day Crispin is a lonely high school student—the next he is fighting a war in a land ruled by dragons, his otherworldly boyfriend at his side. (978-1-63555-725-1)

The Found Jar by Jaycie Morrison. Fear keeps Emily Harris trapped in her emotionally vacant life; can she find the courage to let Beck Reynolds guide her toward love? (978-1-63555-825-8)

Aurora by Emma L McGeown. After a traumatic accident, Elena Ricci is stricken with amnesia leaving her with no recollection of the last eight years, including her wife and son. (978-1-63555-824-1)

Avenging Avery by Sheri Lewis Wohl. Revenge against a vengeful vampire unites Isa Meyer and Jeni Denton, but it's love that heals them. (978-1-63555-622-3)

Bulletproof by Maggie Cummings. For Dylan Prescott and Briana Logan, the complicated NYC criminal justice system doesn't leave room for love, but where the heart is concerned, no one is bulletproof. (978-1-63555-771-8)

Her Lady to Love by Jane Walsh. A shy wallflower joins forces with the most popular woman in Regency London on a quest to catch a husband, only to discover a wild passion for each other that far eclipses their interest for the Marriage Mart. (978-1-63555-809-8)

No Regrets by Joy Argento. For Jodi and Beth, the possibility of losing their future will force them to decide what is really important. (978-1-63555-751-0)

The Holiday Treatment by Elle Spencer. Who doesn't want a gay Christmas movie? Holly Hudson asks herself that question and discovers that happy endings aren't only for the movies. (978-1-63555-660-5)

Too Good to be True by Leigh Hays. Can the promise of love survive the realities of life for Madison and Jen, or is it too good to be true? (978-1-63555-715-2)

Treacherous Seas by Radclyffe. When the choice comes down to the lives of her officers against the promise she made to her wife, Reese Conlon puts everything she cares about on the line. (978-1-63555-778-7)

Two to Tangle by Melissa Brayden. Ryan Jacks has been a player all her life, but the new chef at Tangle Valley Vineyard changes everything. If only she wasn't off the menu. (978-1-63555-747-3)

When Sparks Fly by Annie McDonald. Will the devastating incident that first brought Dr. Daniella Waveny and hockey coach Luca McCaffrey together on frozen ice now force them apart, or will their secrets and fears thaw enough for them to create sparks? (978-1-63555-782-4)

Best Practice by Carsen Taite. When attorney Grace Maldonado agrees to mentor her best friend's little sister, she's prepared to confront Perry's rebellious nature, but she isn't prepared to fall in love. Legal Affairs: one law firm, three best friends, three chances to fall in love. (978-1-63555-361-1)

Home by Kris Bryant. Natalie and Sarah discover that anything is possible when love takes the long way home. (978-1-63555-853-1)

Keeper by Sydney Quinne. With a new charge under her reluctant wing—feisty, highly intelligent math wizard Isabelle Templeton—Keeper Andy Bouchard has to prevent a murder or die trying. (978-1-63555-852-4)

One More Chance by Ali Vali. Harry Basantes planned a future with Desi Thompson until the day Desi disappeared without a word, only to walk back into her life sixteen years later. (978-1-63555-536-3)

Renegade's War by Gun Brooke. Freedom fighter Aurelia DeCallum regrets saving the woman called Blue. She fears it will jeopardize her mission, and secretly, Blue might end up breaking Aurelia's heart. (978-1-63555-484-7)

The Other Women by Erin Zak. What happens in Vegas should stay in Vegas, but what do you do when the love you find in Vegas changes your life forever? (978-1-63555-741-1)

The Sea Within by Missouri Vaun. Time is running out for Dr. Elle Graham to convince Captain Jackson Drake that the only thing that can save future Earth resides in the past, and rescue her broken heart in the process. (978-1-63555-568-4)

To Sleep With Reindeer by Justine Saracen. In Norway under Nazi occupation, Maarit, an Indigenous woman; and Kirsten, a Norwegian resister, join forces to stop the development of an atomic weapon. (978-1-63555-735-0)

Twice Shy by Aurora Rey. Having an ex with benefits isn't all it's cracked up to be. Will Amanda Russo learn that lesson in time to take a chance on love with Quinn Sullivan? (978-1-63555-737-4)

Z-Town by Eden Darry. Forced to work together to stay alive, Meg and Lane must find the centuries-old treasure before the zombies find them first. (978-1-63555-743-5)

Bet Against Me by Fiona Riley. In the high stakes luxury real estate market, everything has a price, and as rival Realtors Trina Lee and Kendall Yates find out, that means their hearts and souls, too. (978-1-63555-729-9)

Broken Reign by Sam Ledel. Together on an epic journey in search of a mysterious cure, a princess and a village outcast must overcome life-threatening challenges and their own prejudice if they want to survive. (978-1-63555-739-8)

Just One Taste by CJ Birch. For Lauren, it only took one taste to start trusting in love again. (978-1-63555-772-5)

Lady of Stone by Barbara Ann Wright. Sparks fly as a magical emergency forces a noble embarrassed by her ability to submit to a low-born teacher who resents everything about her. (978-1-63555-607-0)

Last Resort by Angie Williams. Katie and Rhys are about to find out what happens when you meet the girl of your dreams but you aren't looking for a happily ever after. (978-1-63555-774-9)

Longing for You by Jenny Frame. When Debrek housekeeper Katie Brekman is attacked amid a burgeoning vampire-witch war, Alexis Villiers must go against everything her clan believes in to save her. (978-1-63555-658-2)

Money Creek by Anne Laughlin. Clare Lehane is a troubled lawyer from Chicago who tries to make her way in a rural town full of secrets and deceptions. (978-1-63555-795-4)

Passion's Sweet Surrender by Ronica Black. Cam and Blake are unable to deny their passion for each other, but surrendering to love is a whole different matter. (978-1-63555-703-9)

The Holiday Detour by Jane Kolven. It will take everything going wrong to make Dana and Charlie see how right they are for each other. (978-1-63555-720-6)

Too Hot to Ride by Andrews & Austin. World famous cutting horse champion and industry legend Jane Barrow is knockdown sexy in the way she moves, talks, and rides, and Rae Starr is determined not to get involved with this womanizing gambler. (978-1-63555-776-3)

A Love that Leads to Home by Ronica Black. For Carla Sims and Janice Carpenter, home isn't about location, it's where your heart is. (978-1-63555-675-9)

Blades of Bluegrass by D. Jackson Leigh. A US Army occupational therapist must rehab a bitter veteran who is a ticking political time bomb the military is desperate to disarm. (978-1-63555-637-7)

Guarding Hearts by Jaycie Morrison. As treachery and temptation threaten the women of the Women's Army Corps, who will risk it all for love? (978-1-63555-806-7)

Hopeless Romantic by Georgia Beers. Can a jaded wedding planner and an optimistic divorce attorney possibly find a future together? (978-1-63555-650-6)

Hopes and Dreams by PJ Trebelhorn. Movie theater manager Riley Warren is forced to face her high school crush and tormentor, wealthy socialite Victoria Thayer, at their twentieth reunion. (978-1-63555-670-4)

In the Cards by Kimberly Cooper Griffin. Daria and Phaedra are about to discover that love finds a way, especially when powers outside their control are at play. (978-1-63555-717-6)

Moon Fever by Ileandra Young. SPEAR agent Danika Karson must clear her werewolf friend of multiple false charges while teaching her vampire girlfriend to resist the blood mania brought on by a full moon. (978-1-63555-603-2)

Quake City by St John Karp. Can Andre find his best friend Amy before the night devolves into a nightmare of broken hearts, malevolent drag queens, and spontaneous human combustion? Or has it always happened this way, every night, at Aunty Bob's Quake City Club? (978-1-63555-723-7)

Serenity by Jesse J. Thoma. For Kit Marsden, there are many things in life she cannot change. Serenity is in the acceptance. (978-1-63555-713-8)

Sylver and Gold by Michelle Larkin. Working feverishly to find a killer before he strikes again, Boston Homicide Detective Reid Sylver and rookie cop London Gold are blindsided by their chemistry and developing attraction. (978-1-63555-611-7)

Trade Secrets by Kathleen Knowles. In Silicon Valley, love and business are a volatile mix for clinical lab scientist Tony Leung and venture capitalist Sheila Graham. (978-1-63555-642-1)

CPSIA information can be obtained
at www.ICGtesting.com
Printed in the USA
LVHW032330040221
678442LV00002B/90

9 781635 557930